FEAR AND LONGING IN LOS ANGELES

A CANADIAN WEREWOLF NOVEL

MARK LESLIE

Stark Publishing

STARK
PUBLISHING

Stark Publishing
Waterloo, ON
www.markleslie.ca

Fear and Longing in Los Angeles / Mark Leslie. — 1st ed.
Hardcover ISBN: 978-1-989351-22-2
Trade Paperback ISBN: 978-1-989351-23-9
eBook ISBN: 978-1-989351-24-6
Audiobook ISBN: 978-1-989351-25-3

First paper printing February 2020

For Julie and Joe

Table of Contents

Tuesday, July 4, 2017

Prologue: I See a Full Moon Rising, I See Trouble on the Way

Michael Andrews shuddered at the words of the flight attendant on the overhead speaker, because it meant he was trapped on the plane with no way to escape.

"Please be advised that we will be delayed for another hour while we wait for ATC clearance on our revised schedule, and where we can fit into the takeoff queue. This is a reminder to remain in your seats with your seatbelts fastened. We also remind you that all of your larger electronic personal devices should be stored in the overhead bins or under the seat in front of you. Your smaller devices, which you can store in the seat pockets in front of you, should be set to airplane mode."

He shifted uncomfortably, feeling the hot beads of sweat pouring down his forehead and his shirt soaking up the clamminess of his back.

No, this wasn't possible. It couldn't be happening.

He knew he should have gotten off the plane earlier, during that first flight delay, when they were still parked at the gate and hadn't closed the doors. But the first delay was only fifteen minutes, waiting for a crew member who was late via a delayed connecting flight. The second, while they were still at the gate, waiting for Air Traffic Control clearance, was only another half hour. The third delay, which they didn't specify, was another forty minutes. But this latest delay, an additional hour, this was pushing it too far.

He glanced out the window at the sun as it was making its way slowly towards the hills in the western sky. It was still hours away from touching down. But that was sunset in Los Angeles.

This plane was traveling east. The sun would most certainly set after he was in the air. Back in New York, which was three hours ahead, it would be nightfall.

The nightfall of a full moon. Okay, not the full moon, yet, but one that would be well more than three quarters full.

And he had absolutely no control over the change. In the many years since his lycanthropic affliction, he never had control. During the cycle of the full moon, his body morphed completely from human form and into the full four-legged form of a wolf whenever the moon was at least 80% full.

He turned to his companion, looked deep into her light blue eyes. She stared back at him, placed her hand comfortingly on top of his.

"This isn't good," he whispered.

Tuesday, June 13, 2017

Chapter One: What you Need is What You Need, or What

W hat you need is to get your head out of your ass," Mack said, slamming his hands down on the mahogany desk.

I regarded the man who I equally respected, loved, and feared as he kept his hands planted on the desk and flicked his head side to side in short, back-and-forth twitch-like movements.

For an obscure moment I reflected on how often I saw his head move like that—an odd little bobble-head type of motion, except side to side rather than up and down— and wondered if that was why he had such a small pencil-thin mustache above his top lip. A thicker mustache would match those thick bushy eyebrows, but I worried if it might fly off his face with the constant rapid motion he made when expressing his instant displeasure to something. Mack regularly displayed his displeasure in that fashion. Subtlety was not in his repertoire. It always amused me how, with his dark and bushy eyebrows and black and gray square headed buzz-cut, if he had a full thick mustache it might make him look like J. Jonah Jameson from the Spider-Man comic books.

Of course, whenever he was yelling at me, I couldn't help but think of him as the angry head of the Daily Bugle, cursing and yelling across the desk at Peter Parker. Yes, even though I'm a fully grown adult and have been for several years, I still like to fantasize about being one of the heroes I've enjoyed reading about my entire life—particularly apt since, like Parker, I live in New York, and several times in the past half-dozen years, have used my special abilities to "fight the bad guys" or "fight crime" or "bring truth, justice and the American way" to the people. No, scratch that last one. I think that might be Superman, rather than Spider-Man. And I definitely don't live in Metropolis, wherever that is.

Mack Halpin—known in literary circles as "Mack the Knife"—my agent, was a hell of a tough nut, a complete hard-ass, difficult to reason with, and he often inspired most people he spoke with to want to either punch him in the face, or liberally apply a strip of duct tape across his lips. I suppose there were other reactions people could have, such as turning and walking away. But Mack didn't just express his opinion and desire; he infiltrated it into another person, got completely under the skin and could not, would not be ignored. Most folks would quickly classify Mack as an asshole; and in several ways I suppose he was. But he was also perhaps the best thing to happen to my writing career. He took me under his wing, introduced me to opportunities that most writers only dream of and fought harder for me than I ever fought for myself.

If it weren't for Mack, I wouldn't have had all the amazing opportunities I've had in the past half-dozen years. Because of Mack, I'd been a guest on *Late Night with David Letterman*, the New York Times ran a weekly series about me every Saturday for a month, and my Maxwell Bronte novels were optioned for screen and television rights. *Print of the Predator* had been made into a feature film starting Ryan Gosling, *Tome of Terror* was currently in production. For both films Mack had negotiated my involvement as a junior executive producer. It didn't mean more than extra money in my pocket and an additional credit that scrolls by at the end of the film, but it was yet another feather in my cap as a writer.

Like I said, I respected him. I loved how he looked after me the way a father would look after a rebellious teenage son; but the man also scared the bejesus out of me. He could be slightly amusing when going off on a rant; but he could also be a terrifying adversary if you crossed him.

Heck, even with my enhanced strength, speed and sensory abilities—which get progressively stronger the closer I am to the full moon phase of those monthly cycles, thanks to the lycanthropic curse running through my veins—Mack would likely be a challenging foe. Perhaps that was because he never pulled his punches and was prepared to fight dirty—whatever it takes—in order to win.

That is why I was so thankful that he was fighting for me.

Well, most of the time.

Today, as he would sometimes do, he was fighting with me. Or, rather, that stubborn part of me that my logical mind couldn't over-power.

I stared across the desk at him, waiting patiently for the back-and-forth twitching of his head to stop. At times like this, it was difficult to suppress a mirth-filled grin while waiting for that movement to cease, and I wondered if this habit of Mack's could be parlayed into a perpetual motion machine, like those novelty drinking birds that continued to bop up and down as if going back for more drinks of water.

"For the past two-and-a-half years you have been moping around here like a pathetic love-sick teenager," Mack said. "I get it that she is a sweet piece of ass, but the world is filled with plenty of other juicy little asses. And you, my friend, looking like you do and with the stink of fame upon you, have a line up of women at your feet.

"I should know, half of the panties that get mailed to you come via this office. Hell, if they ever wanted to re-open Hogs and Heifers down in the meat-packing district with a ceiling of women's underwear, all I'd have to do is forward your fan mail for about a month."

My fingers dug into the arms of the chair to hear Mack use such a derogatory term to refer to Gail, the only woman that I had ever loved. Yes, I felt like a jerk for not standing up to such a slight, but one has to be strategic in when, where and how they argue with Mack.

I suppose that, as liberated as some men like to believe we have become regarding sexism and the objectification of women, we still have plenty of faults. Acknowledgement of the issue, of course, is always the first step towards resolving it, I suppose.

And, besides, I knew the signs, even without my extra-sensory ability to gage the man's underlying mood and intents based on his scent and his elevated heartbeat. I'd known Mack long enough to recognize that he was going off on a rant. And the best thing to do when that happens, as Cousin Eddy advises Clark Griswold in *Christmas Vacation* should the dog ever start going to town on your leg, it's best to just let him finish.

"Not once in the years I have known you have you ever taken any of these women up on their blatant sexual offers. And let me tell you, son, that you're in dire need of a good fuck. I don't understand why you're such a damn prude about the whole thing.

"Man, if it were me, I'd be all over those women like a cheap suit.

"But no, you're still all moony-eyed over Gail."

Mack had been gesturing wildly as he was speaking from behind his desk. But at this point he got up and started pacing between the desk and the plate-glass window that offered a breathtaking view of the lower west side of Manhattan.

"She told you, point blank, son, exactly where you stand. Shit, she told you this more than once in the past couple of years. And yet you continue to let some idiotic romantic notion keep you from seeing what is right in front of your face."

I stopped looking at Mack and glanced down at my

shoes. I knew he was right. Hearing it made me angry. Angry at him. Angry at myself. Angry at the situation.

But never angry at Gail.

I had, ultimately, caused this.

Meeting Gail was one of the best things that had ever happened to me. We were drawn almost instinctively to one another. And in an extremely short time our lives swirled together in a wondrous ballet of physicality, sensuality, intellect, and emotion. We were perfect for one another, connecting on so many incredible levels.

I had, truly, never experienced love in the way I had with Gail.

And I knew, when our eyes first locked together, that I had found my soulmate, the one person I was destined to be with.

But I was, ultimately, the reason our relationship ended.

More specifically, it was the lycanthropy. The werewolf curse running through my veins.

Despite the intimate sharing we experienced, I had kept the fact I was a werewolf from Gail. How *does* one explain to their sexual partner that for several nights during the cycle of the moon, their normal human body morphs into that of a wolf? Or that, during that time, the human consciousness mostly disappears, being replaced entirely by the alter-ego consciousness of a canine beast?

I didn't have to check the various dating books, or websites. There was no need to consult with Mrs. Manners on the matter. I knew, quite simply, that there was no proper way to explain such a thing.

So I kept it hidden.

And, after we had been together for several weeks, when the full moon phase was about to have its effect on me, I made spun stories about why we couldn't be together that night, why I had to be elsewhere. Gail was, understandably, confused, but accepted my feeble excuses.

But then, the following month, I had to do it again.

Then again.

And again.

I mean, how could I risk turning into a wolf and harming her in any way? I couldn't. There were things, back then, that I simply didn't know about my wolfish nature—so I simply could not take that chance.

And yes, despite Gail's background as the owner of a shop that specialized in the occult and paranormal, and her open mind, I couldn't bring myself to admit this affliction to her.

Perhaps I was afraid of rejection.

But rejection was what I ultimately received.

Gail knew I had been hiding something, and since I couldn't bring myself to share that intimate part of myself, she suspected I had been stepping out in the relationship. She'd been burned badly before with infidelity and believed she had seen the signs of that again with my deception and excuses to not be with her on certain nights.

So the relationship ended.

Or, rather, Gail ended the relationship.

And I had been a wreck about it for the longest time.

But then, one day, a little over a year after she had dumped me, she came back into my life as a friend with two pieces of stunning news: She knew I was a werewolf; and she was engaged.

She had returned to my life to ask for my help in tracking down her fiancé, whom she believed someone had kidnapped. Gail had known that I possessed extra-sensory perceptions, even when in human form, and that those senses were strongest closest to the cycle of the full moon.

Gail was an adept woman, intuitively picking up these subtle clues about my nature.

Of course, prior to me and even post me, she hadn't been all that good at choosing men.

Because we had learned, in the course of my investigation into her fiancé's disappearance, that he had actually been unfaithful to her.

Given our shared interests and mutual respect for one another, Gail and I remained friends.

Although, admittedly, I had wanted more.

I had always wanted more.

Gail had recognized that. Perhaps because I could sometimes be as subtle as a midway hawker in the middle of a library.

Her insistence on not becoming close, not being more than friends continually broke my heart. But I always considered just having her in my life to be a special privilege; and reasoned that, at the very least, I could still have that.

But it hurt. Having her so close and yet so far at the

same time continued to burn at the very fiber of my soul.

And, as usual, Mack was stone cold correct. He knew that the situation was killing me and it was taking its toll on me. He knew that I most certainly wouldn't do anything about it, and that, if the situation were to be resolved, he would have to step in.

"Listen," Mack said. "She came back into your life when?"

"About two-and-a-half years ago," I mumbled, still staring at my feet.

"And you had the ill-fated conversation about the possibility of re-kindling the romance when?"

"About two years ago."

"And what did she make absolutely clear to you?"

I hated that Mack was doing this; but a part of me was already feeling the benefit of the cross-examination approach to this therapeutic talk.

He took a step forward and in a louder voice asked it again. "What did she make absolutely clear to you?"

"That she wasn't interested in a relationship."

"Ahh," he said, holding a finger in the air, and I could swear he was imagining that we were in a courtroom. He paced a deliberate path behind his desk parallel to the window and, looking out the window at the magnificent view of the city, he repeated part of that back to me, or, perhaps, to the imaginary jury who were listening in. "She wasn't interested in a relationship.

"That is rather curious, isn't it? She was in your life again, but she was not interested in a relationship. What, pray tell, was she interested in?"

"Friendship."

He nodded his head, pacing the same path back along the window again. "Friendship." He nodded his head again and repeated the word. "Friendship.

"And so, what have you been to one another for the past two years?"

"Friends."

"That's all? Not 'friends with benefits' or anything like that?" Mack paused to lean on his desk, his big bushy eyebrows lifting high on his forehead as if being pulled to their limits by invisible marionette strings.

"No."

"Not even a single time? One quick and simple moment of carnal pleasure, benefit?"

"No."

"So," Mack said, "she made it perfectly clear, quite early on in this return to your life, that she was here as a friend, and only a friend. And, as you admit, after you expressed you wanted something more, she made it perfectly clear that she simply wasn't interested. Do I have that correct?"

"You do."

"So tell me, Mister Andrews," and Mack came out from behind the desk and leaned back against it with his arms folded across his chest, "why it is that, with the facts all laid out in front of us, I can clearly see that the woman is not interested, and you still can't get your goddamn head out of your goddamn ass?"

At that point, he broke the courtroom lawyer charade and went right back into full Mack mode.

"For god's sake, man, I've been watching you mope around here like some lovesick little puppy for two full years. You're even worse than the first time she dumped you. At least back then, you'd had the pleasure of getting your rocks off before she put a complete and utter stop to that.

"And now, without even the pleasure of a fun little nightcap and a quickie or even a hand-job in the back of a cab, you're mooning after her like some pathetic little cheese-eating high school boy.

"I normally wouldn't give a rat's ass about my top client's personal life. But *this* has been affecting your work, your production. And I have a vested interest to keep your rocket moving up, my friend."

Mack unfolded his arms, walked back around behind the desk and sat down in his chair.

"What you need is to distance yourself from that hot little lady, find a distraction from the rut that you've worked yourself into, and focus on something else for a while. What you need is exactly what I have arranged for you." He reached down, opened up a drawer on the right side of his desk, plucked out an envelope and slid it across the desk at me.

I stared at the envelope.

"Go ahead," he said. "Open it."

I gingerly reached out and picked it up. The envelope wasn't sealed. I pulled out a full sheet of paper folded into thirds around an additional slip of paper. It was a package from the travel agency that Mack's office used; I immediately recognized the letterhead. It was a return-trip ticket to Los Angeles.

"What's this?" I asked. "A getaway vacation?"

"Christ, no," Mack said. "A getaway vacation wouldn't be to LA. It would be to Aruba or Punta Cana or maybe somewhere in the south of Italy.

"You're going to LA, or, more, specifically, to Hollywood, because I have negotiated a more direct hands-on role into that of script consultant. You'll be working on the set of *Tome of Terror*.

"God knows you need the distraction, you need to get away from Gail for a while, and if the gods are smiling upon us, you need to get laid so you can start thinking with that big ball of meat sitting atop your shoulders rather than the smaller sausage you keep tucked in your pants."

"But, Mack," I said, looking down at the date. They booked my flight for tomorrow, and I was still on the tail end of my monthly cycle. I started doing quick calculations in my mind, because I wasn't sure the percentage of the full moon. Through experience, I knew I only turned into a wolf on the nights where the moon was 80% or more. Fumbling my phone out of my back pocket, I toggled the screens over to the moon app so I could check. "You know I don't take well to travel. We've been through that before."

"*I don't take well to travel,*" Mack said in a high-pitched mocking tone. "Christ, Andrews, do you hear yourself? You're whining like a pre-school toddler. It's not like I'm sending you on a sixteen-hour flight to Hong Kong. It's a five-hour flight. And what the hell are you consulting on that phone? An app for Hypochondriacs? Get over your-self, you damn snowflake."

I glanced over at the ticket again as the app was load-ing up, noting the time of the flight. It was with United and left Newark at 10 AM. That gave me a bit of a sense of relief, knowing I wouldn't be in the air during a poten-tial change. I didn't, after all, want to be the inspiration for an odd new *Wolves on a Plane* horror film franchise. But I still had to worry about changing into a wolf in a city where I didn't have a routine planned out; not like I did here in Manhattan.

"What the hell are you panicking about, Andrews?" Mack said. "They'll let you take your damn teddy bear with you. You don't need to worry about that."

The app finished its boot cycle. I thumbed in Los An-geles and hit the refresh button. On June fourteenth, tomorrow, the moon would be at 76% of its cycle. I was safe. I let out an audible sigh of relief.

Mack, sitting behind his desk, stared at me.

"Are we okay now, sugar?" he said in a condescend-ing tone.

"What? Oh, yeah."

"Good. Now get the hell out of my office. I have a call coming in that I need to take. Anne will confirm the hotel booking and a few of the other details with you." Mack was referring to Anne Lee, the tiny woman who acted as his executive assistant, his personal assistant, his chauf-feur, his whatever-he-needed right-hand person. She was the Alfred to his Bruce Wayne, or maybe more like the Whalen Smithers to his Monty Burns. "She can also check to confirm they are using hypoallergenic pillows and sheets, a smoke and fragrant-free environment, a vegan, gluten-free, carb-free, sugar-free, fucking flavor free restaurant, or whatever the hell else your pansy ass little heart desires to make sure you are comfy and cozy."

I slipped my phone into my back pocket and stood up.

"Thanks, Mack,"

"Yeah, yeah," he mumbled, already flipping open a file folder on his desk and scanning through it, well on to the next task on his list. It was another frustrating thing about him I actually admired; how he could easily compartmentalize appointments, people, situations, into neat little boxes, focus intensely and 100% on them, but then move on to the next one, completely abandoning any attachment to the previous ones to focus on the new task at hand.

As I walked over to the door to leave his office, I wondered if I could do that on this brief trip he had planned for me.

I closed my eyes for a moment, picturing Gail's beautiful smile, the delightful twinkle in her eye, and then I shook my head.

"Compartmentalize," I muttered. "Turn the page."

Chapter Two: The Gentler, Kinder Perspective of a Younger, Wiser Woman

The moment I closed Mack's office door, Mack's executive assistant, Anne, greeted me with a smile and a whiff of a combination of the wonderful confidence and genuine comradery that she always exuded.

That underlying scent about her had always inspired me.

And it reminded me of something that often eluded me when I was with Mack.

My extra-sensory abilities, my extremely heightened sense of smell and hearing, a gift that came to my human self along with the curse of turning into an animal without barely a trace of my human mind, allowed me to know things about people I was interacting with, or, heck, even just passing on the street, in a way that most people could never understand.

I was, perhaps, much like a dog in that way; particularly in the way dogs can "smell fear" or read a person and react to them, even if the person's intent is not visible in their facial expressions or body language.

In regular conversations or relationships, I could usually quickly and easily use these extra senses to my advantage. I detected subtle shifts in mood or intent in a person, via their scent, breathing, or heartbeat if I concentrated enough. For example, in the quick snapshot of Anne at this moment, I could tell that Anne had eaten a chive and cream cheese bagel earlier in the morning. I sensed she was in a decidedly jovial mood (something I failed to understand how it could be possible, given the frustrating man she worked for), and based on the elevated heartbeat and the mild tweak in anxious tension, that she was about to speak to me.

Of course, most people would notice, at least on the surface, some of those clues. But I had become adept at intuiting most of the sensory stimulation I received about people I interacted with, and adapted that into situations; often able to charm those I was speaking with in remarkable ways.

But Mack was so intense, so bold in his straightforward "attack" —yes, even amid a conversation with Mack it could often feel more like an affront or an attack—that I, subconsciously, perhaps, neglected to attend to the extra-sensory stimuli that I relied on in normal, every-day situations.

Mack seemed to have the ability to distract me from that input. It was there, I could usually recall it at the end of an encounter or interaction with him. But in the moment, I was often so focused on him that those additional details that often would give me the upper hand in an interaction were muted, almost forgotten.

Interesting.

"I trust Mack explained the trip to you," Anne said with a tight-lipped smile on her face. She knew, and I knew that Mack doesn't really explain much. He just presents the facts and lets others do all the details.

"In a… nutshell," I said. That got a slight bemused reaction out of Anne, even though she never let that show on her face. She was a pro; ever the consummate professional.

"You have your ticket. The hotel reservation, address and directions are in this envelope," she said, sliding a nine by twelve manila envelope across the desk. "You'll also find an outline of the itinerary, a list of your main contacts, the contact numbers for both them and their personal assistants. Also, the contact information for the showrunner assistant who is assigned to you is highlighted in bold on its own sheet. They will pick you up at the airport.

"You'll also find a list of some nearby restaurants, sorted by food style. And, of course, a list of the local coffee shops; the ones that are rated highest via three cross-checked sources have a little asterisk beside them and are likely to be the ones you enjoy the most."

Anne offered a slight wry grin as she said that. One thing we had bonded over was locally owned little coffee houses with their own special craft produced blends. Sure, I loved my morning Starbucks like everybody else, but whenever I was in a new neighborhood, I appreciated the special and unique offering that took you slightly off the more beaten or touristy path. Anne liked those places too, and on the few times that the two of us ended up meeting to conduct some more mundane paperwork tasks that Mack had assigned to her, we enjoyed finding new and interesting coffee shops in the city where the other hadn't yet been.

She was always efficient and thorough and never failed to drop in the little extras like that which made a person feel appreciated, respected and, of course, understood.

I loved that about her.

"I'll be sure to write up a personal report of the best places from your list, along with the ones I end up discovering on my own," I said. "And if I find a particularly unique and special brew available in bean format, I will bring it back for you."

She smiled a tight little smile, which, for Anne, was as expressive as her face got, but the room filled with the warm scent of her unbridled appreciation and joy.

I took the envelope, not even having to look inside to know everything was exactly how she explained it. All the information I required and more was in the envelope. I beamed a smile back at her, flipped her a wink and blew her a kiss.

"You are a gift to this world, Anne. Still not sure how you manage to be so cheerful all the time while putting up with this guy." I hooked a thumb toward Mack's closed office door.

Anne and I understood each other. We respected each other. We appreciated each other. She was a sweetheart and one of the kindest souls I had ever met. And I was

constantly amazed at how professional and compassionate and sweet she could be, despite working for one of
the crustiest, hard-edged and uncouth businessmen in
New York.

"Aw, Michael," she said, and her thin almond-shaped
eyes twinkled so brightly that I didn't need to smell the
pride and respect she was exuding. She sincerely liked,
respected, and cared for Mack. She was loyal and would
be there for him through thick and thin. "You only attend
to his rough edges. But you know as well as I do that
Mack is a teddy bear underneath the surface. He just
never likes to let down his guard and show that. "

Anne was speaking to me about Mack the way a
mother might explain to her son that his father really did
love him; he merely had a different, more traditionally
masculine way of showing it.

Anne was a truly wonderful and admirable woman.

And, of course, in true Anne Lee fashion, she took that
admiration to the next level with her parting words to
me.

"Good luck, Michael. I know how much you love Gail,
but maybe you both need this time apart. As they say: *If
you love something, let it go. If it comes back to you, it is yours
forever. If it doesn't it never was.*"

I thought about what she said and felt myself getting
angry. I had let Gail go, or, at least, we had parted ways,
and then she *did* come back to me. Hadn't I already done
that? I was about to retort, but could sense that Anne
wasn't done speaking. She had paused because she knew
I would react that way and wanted to give me some time

to process the thought.

Smart woman.

"Gail has been through a lot. She needs some time; and she needs that time apart from you, because when you're too close, your friendship and your undying love is a crutch for her. She needs time, away from you, to process her feelings. And, you need to be away and apart from her. You can't step back and see the larger picture when she's right there focusing on her.

"I know it hurts, and you know how much I want you to be happy. But I agree with Mack—okay, not with the way he expresses it, but with the general concept. You need to get away, distract yourself, get involved in something different, be somewhere different. Be away from the 'Michael and Gail' setting, which this city itself brings to you. Be open to possibilities that don't involve Gail. And I promise things will work themselves out for the better."

I noticed that Anne hadn't said Gail and I would resolve this together, but that things would work themselves out for the better. Whatever that better might be. Open-ended. Wise words, from a wise woman.

"Thank you, Anne," I said. Talking to her was sometimes akin to the milk and cookie talks my mom used to give me whenever I returned home from a hockey game that we lost or had a falling out with one of my childhood friends. She made it all better. "Even though you're ten years younger than me, you've always been such an amazing mom figure."

She got up from behind her desk, came around it and

embraced me in a warm hug. Even though I was a foot and a half taller than her, her hug felt giant, as if she had enveloped me inside her embrace so completely, exuding the comfort, the warmth, the consoling that seemed to be a universal motherly trait.

Stepping back from the hug, Anne placed her hands on my upper arms, and looked me in the eye. "Now go, Michael. Be open to enjoying LA. Be open to embracing the possibilities."

Chapter Three: Reflections and Memories of How I Simply Can't Fight This Feeling any Longer

On my way out of the Halpin Agency office, I reflected on Anne's wise words, her perspective and the motherly concern and embrace she enwrapped me in. I still felt warm, like she had snuggled me into a warm sweater on a cold winter night.

I was starting to feel good about this trip to LA, about being involved in something other than the regular daily routine I'd gotten into here.

Sure, given the combination of my supernatural abilities and my Spider-Man style ethic of *With Great Power Comes Great Responsibility*, it hadn't all been routine. Despite trying to live a normal life, I had a way of attracting misadventures.

But apart from a few decidedly exciting adventures, the last several years had been a consistent routine with one common theme throughout it.

Me loving Gail. Me waiting for Gail. Me wanting and longing for Gail.

When I left Mack's office building, I headed west so

that I could catch the Battery Park City Esplanade walking path that ran parallel to the Hudson river and then connected with the Hudson River Greenway and, a little further north, near Chelsea, hook back in-land to the High Line, New York City's beautiful "park in the sky" — an old elevated north to south running train platform that originally opened in the 1930s and then was shut down about fifty years later and then converted to a gorgeous public landscape, allowing you to be in the middle of the city and yet walking through a unique picturesque and narrow park that afforded you diversity and a brilliant sense of the various neighborhoods that you passed through on it.

Since I'd be leaving New York in less than twenty-four hours, and it was a gorgeous June day, I wanted to do the thing that most helped me reflect and appreciate the city I had grown to love and adore.

You never get to properly appreciate a place when you are moving through it quickly, either on public transit or via a self-directed vehicle. But walking afforded you the luxury of appreciating the subtle nuances of different neighborhoods, different communities, and different little microcosms of a vast and diverse metropolis.

As I arrived at Wagner Park, just north of Battery Park, I reflected on that one morning I had woken in Battery Park after one of those black-hole memory nights of being a wolf. My body half nestled in a small copse of bushes, I woke up naked with a bullet hole in my leg. Since I never could remember more than tiny snippets of what I had been up to when I was a wolf—and, I imagine, as a wolf,

I likely had little to no recollection of being a human—I had found myself tasked with a few interesting challenges.

The first, of course, was finding some clothes.

The second was figuring out what the heck I had been up to, who had shot me, and if I had actually hurt someone the night before; because relatively early on, I heard there had been a wolf attack in the city and that a man had been killed.

I had certainly packed a full month's worth of adventures into that single day.

It wasn't enough to learn that another wolf, a werewolf, had infiltrated my city, but we had to resolve our territorial dispute in a fight to the death. That was the same day I was a guest on *Letterman*, busted up a corrupt ring of financial scammers and kidnappers, and the only woman I had ever loved had come back into my life; not to be reunited with me, but to confront me with the fact she knew I was a werewolf and to inform me she had been engaged to a man who she believed had been kidnapped. It seems she needed the help of my extra-sensory abilities in tracking down her fiancé.

Of course, we also both learned, that day, that her fiancé was not the man she had thought him to be, and that sent her into a downward spiral of trust issues. Combined with the way our relationship had ended a few years previously, she was still going through the process of healing and figuring things out.

In the same way that long term married couples fall into well-rehearsed routines that lead them into a realm where the intimacy doesn't go beyond the intimacy you have with a best friend, Gail and I had fallen into the same pattern.

Only, as much as I adored, respected, and admired Gail, I still loved her with all of my heart, and I knew that, beneath the pain, beneath the confusion, and beneath the angst she was in, she also loved me.

And, yes, as more than a friend.

She still had a deep and extremely active sexual desire for me.

I suppose if I weren't a werewolf, I might not know about these underlying feelings and thoughts. Because Gail could be a stoic and steadfast person with the absolute best poker face. She could keep her cards close to her chest and not reveal what was going on below the surface.

But she knew I could easily see through the charade.

Just like, even though I didn't have to say anything to her about it, Gail knew how intensely I loved her.

And, in these past three years, we had only properly discussed it a few times.

In fact, it had been last week that we ended up having another one of those spiraling conversations that went nowhere and merely frustrated both of us.

We had just finished sharing a basket of garlic fries and a plate of pretzel bites with a jalapeno cheese dip at *Hellcat Annie's Tap Room* in Hell's Kitchen. The spot featured 20 rotating taps of craft beers that were displayed on giant screens mounted on the wall behind the bar. I wasn't much of a beer drinker, but Gail was a lover of craft beers, and, in particular, had an affinity for bitter and hoppy IPAs. And that location, on the corner of 10th Avenue and West 45th Street, despite having been through a couple of ownership and name changes in the past few years, had been one of her favorite spots.

It was a single room bar that was about fifty feet long and under twenty feet wide. It seated perhaps fifteen people at the bar itself and then maybe another twenty to thirty at the small benches, tables and the high stools around upright wooden beer barrels that served as mini tabletops.

Despite it being a craft beer place, a location one might associate with popular hipster culture, there was a wonderful rustic and unpretentious feel to the place. That was one of the things Gail loved most about it; it was also a reason I enjoyed hanging out there, even though beer wasn't my first beverage of choice.

"You know how much your friendship, how much having you in my life means to me," I said, picking up the light wheat beer I had been slowly sipping between hearty drinks of water.

"Yes," Gail said, her green eyes, looking much darker in the dim light of the bar, flashing across the table at me. "I do know that. And you know that you mean so much to me as well. We understand one another so wonderfully, Andrews."

"We certainly do." I took another sip of the beer before placing it back down on the table. "But I'm not sure what we're doing here, Gail.

"You know, also, even though I don't say it, that I love you more than I have ever loved another person in my life."

Despite the loud music, the background rumble of the multitude of conversations of the fully packed, beer-loving crowd, I could hear Gail's heart skip a beat.

"I know," she said.

"And I haven't stopped wanting you, Gail. I love our friendship; I love what we have. But what we experienced is something I can't unknow. And I don't think you can, either."

Gail stared at me across the table. Even though she maintained a poker face gaze, I could smell the heightened sexual desire in her. I knew she had been thinking about those times, years ago, when our intimacy wasn't just emotional, wasn't just intellectual, but also included the hot and wet skin on skin sensation.

I felt myself getting hard while detecting that desire in her, and I shifted uncomfortably in the seat.

And I knew, because Gail was the most intuitive woman, hell, the most intuitive person I had even known, that she could tell her arousal aroused me. She glanced down ever so briefly at my crotch, then immediately returned her eye contact to me. Because the desire, the lust, the thirst she was exuding was musky and strong. It was the same desire, the same lust that we had felt the first time we had gotten together.

The same mutual attraction and carnal hunger that we felt every time we came together.

And, sadly, the type of heightened sexual tension that

we had felt far too many times in the past three years.

"You're feeling it now." I said.

She maintained her stoic face. "There are underlying animalistic feelings I can't avoid, Andrews. You are an attractive man. My body can't help but remember how good it always was."

"But your mind," I said, knowing where she was going.

"And my heart," she said.

"But you love me, Gail. And more than as a friend, more than like a sister loves a brother. I can feel how much you love me. And you know, as sure as you know anything, just how much I love you."

She nodded.

"So what the hell are we doing? Why are we torturing ourselves like this?"

She closed her eyes, shook her head slowly, and I could feel the overwhelming pain, anxiety, and angst in her heart. She hated herself for hurting me; but she couldn't help the way she felt. She couldn't help how unprepared she was to accept the underlying feelings she had for me.

When she opened her eyes, they were glassy, moist, and she stared at me with the facade of the poker face slowly melting away.

"I can't," she said. "I can't explain it, but I also can't keep having this conversation, Michael.

"Love isn't enough. Lust isn't enough."

"What is enough, Gail?"

"I... I don't know." And a single tear rolled down her

left cheek. More than anything, I wanted to reach across, gently wipe it away, and then hold and comfort her. I hated the fact I had brought this up again, that I had pushed her back into the self-loathing I could smell broiling in her heart.

As much as I loved and respected her, I wouldn't be able to understand the conflict she was going through. And, in the same way that she was internalizing the blame, turning the anger towards herself, I hated myself for what my insistence was doing to her; how much it was tearing her heart apart.

"I'm sorry, Gail."

"I know. And I know how much you love me and how much you are beating yourself up right now for bringing this up, for forcing me to confront this. But I'm not ready, Andrews. I'm just not ready, and I'm not sure if I will ever be."

I reached across the table, laid my hand down palm up and stared at her.

"I know," I said. "But I'm here, anyway. And I'm not going anywhere, Gail."

"I know," she said, smiling at me, and she placed her hand to overlap mine, our fingers laced together. I watched as another tear streamed down the side of her face. "And that's one of the many reasons why I can't help but to love you so dearly, Michael."

We sat like that for a few minutes, hands clasped, a few more tears running down both her face and my own, and didn't say another word to one another.

A minute later, when the bus boy came to collect the

empty plates, Gail let go of my hand, pulled out her wallet and left a pair of twenty-dollar bills on the tabletop.

She then got up.

"Goodnight, Andrews," she said.

"Goodnight, Sommers," I replied.

And we left the bar, neither of us saying another word as we walked for a couple of blocks in silence before we each parted ways; her heading to her apartment, and me heading towards Central Park. It would still be a couple of nights before I would turn into a werewolf again, but I ended up walking through the park in quiet introspection, wishing that I *could* turn into a wolf, if only to escape the pain and frustration that I knew I'd be lying awake with all night.

Then I felt guilty, knowing that, in just a few nights, I would have that luxury.

But Gail, sadly, would never have that reprieve.

I replayed that evening repeatedly in my mind like a film loop on an endlessly repeating re-roll as I walked north along the High Line park.

When I reached the end of the park, just south of the Javits Center, and a few blocks away from that last time I had seen Gail, that last conversation we'd had a couple of weeks earlier, I figured I should let her know I would be leaving town for a while.

I didn't call Gail.

I just sent her a quick text message.

Going to LA to work on the set of Tome of Terror.

Will give you a call when I get back.

After all, good friends know the other needs. Gail needed her space. I needed to find my own. Perhaps, when I got back, I'd be better able to accept the pleasure of her incredible friendship and leave it at that.

With no more longing.

Chapter Four: Cut Loose like a Deuce, a Super Powerball Bonus Daylight Savings Time in the Night

Dang it if trying to spend a few hours writing didn't result in a bit of a mishap for me.

I found myself with a surprise of plenty of hours I had not been counting on, and that led to a decidedly different evening than I had planned.

I suppose part of the blame is on my curious nature. The other part is the fact I simply can't just sit by and do nothing when I sense trouble afoot; not stepping up and helping where I know I can help (or perhaps believe I can help) seems to be against my nature.

And, yes, I blame Stan Lee for infecting my mind with the concept that drove Peter Parker to use his radioactive spider-powers for good. If he hadn't created such an interesting character I'd been drawn to as a nerdy teenager, I imagine that I wouldn't constantly be finding myself in odd situations.

It didn't take me long to pack my clothes into a small carry-on suitcase. I didn't travel often, but I had learned, early on, the benefit of taking a small carry-on bag with me when I flew. It saved a significant amount of time—not to mention the hassle, when, on connecting flights, there was always that slim possibility of the bag not making the connection and there you were, at your destination and without your luggage. So you pack light, rolling most of your clothes to keep them as wrinkle-free as possible, folding the blazers inside out and then wearing an additional button-down top and dress pants on the flight.

Even though I would be in LA for a few weeks, I knew I could use the hotel's dry cleaning and laundry service to keep me in clean clothes.

According to the moon app, tonight's moon would be at 84% which meant it would be my last night turning into a wolf. I'd spent the afternoon packing and then preparing my usual cheap throwaway clothes to wear and the bag of "morning clothes" I would need to get to in order not to have to walk back home buck naked.

I suppose someone watching the odd routine I was forced to take during the approximate ten days out of the month where my werewolf curse meant I would lose control of my human nature and completely morph into a four-legged wolf, might wonder how a person could live with such a thing.

And early on I complained about it—at least internally—I mean, it's not like I could rant on Facebook about my horrible lot in life or send off a barrage of angry tweets bemoaning the struggle I faced with lycanthropy. But, when the affliction was fresh, I had been frustrated with the idea that such a large chunk of my life, about a third of my day for ten days each month was taken up by my alter ego, of which I had no conscious memory or awareness; except, perhaps, for the occasional snippet of sensory memory that infiltrated my human mind. Like images from a partially remembered dream.

It could be a little terrifying, actually. Losing complete control not just of one's person, but of an entire human body and giving it over to some alter-ego entity that I didn't even fully understand.

It wasn't a Jekyll and Hyde situation. There was nothing sinister about my wolf form. If anything, the human part of me had more of a chance of being evil or performing acts of malice than a wolf ever would. It was more of a situation akin to Dr. Bruce Banner and The Incredible Hulk. Except for the smashing part. As a wolf, I tended to be more subtle and slip around under the radar unlike the hulking green monster that Banner turned into.

But the disconcerting feeling of losing one's conscious awareness and then "waking up" (for lack of a better term to describe the feeling) in human form, completely naked, not truly knowing where you had gone or what you had done, took a lot of introspection and getting used to.

But even though my affliction was unique, I knew there were others who had to deal with the disconcerting nature, hell, the sheer terror, of losing control of one's consciousness in such a way.

A friend of mine in high school, Robby Horowitz, suffered from a type of epilepsy called Grand Mal seizures. I remember, over long games of chess (that's how I met Robby, he was our school's grand master chess champion, and I had joined the chess club wanting to refine my own skills in the game) having extended discussions with Robby. A few times, he explained the odd aura or sensation that overcame him when he felt a seizure coming on.

The Grand Mal seizures that Robby had had are perhaps the ones most people equate with epilepsy. But I learned, from Robby, the different types of seizures (we had hours of time to talk while playing chess over the years) and the fact that some types of seizures could be experienced by a person with no one right there in front of them being aware of it. For example, some petit mal seizures, also sometimes known as absence seizures, could cause a five to fifteen second lapse of a person's consciousness and attention. If you were looking at them, you might think they were daydreaming or focusing on something really hard, because they usually had stopped attending to something going on in front of them, whether it was a conversation, a movie, or whatever. Most people might never know that person had suffered a seizure like that and merely chalked it up to them "drifting off" and being distracted.

But Robby's seizures were all consuming. They came with a few seconds warning. Enough to position himself on the ground or the floor so that, when the darkness washed over his consciousness and he slipped into the rapid convulsive and uncontrollable jerks, he didn't get hurt.

The way Robby describes it was not at all unlike the aura that overcomes me when I'm about to turn into a wolf. I usually have less than two or three minutes, once I feel the aura coming on, before I slip into the darkness and the wolf metamorphosis takes place.

Robby had controlled the seizures with medication that he had to take daily. But sometimes, if he was overly stressed or didn't get enough sleep, he might still have a seizure. So, again, I was lucky that my own changes were predictable based on the phases of the moon, and I could plan for them.

It was disconcerting, too, particularly living in a large metropolis, which isn't the ideal place for a wolf to be living.

But, fortunately, the wolf in me must have retained at least enough of a healthy respectful fear of humans and learned it could prance around large green spaces while staying hidden from people.

And I, as a human, learned enough to get myself to a safe space for a wolf to romp around; Central Park was usually a place I could get to easily from where I lived in mid-town. I also learned that, since I usually lost the clothes I had been wearing when turning into a wolf, it was smart to hide fresh clothes to find the next day. Only a handful of times in the past decade had I ended up waking up to find that I was either nowhere near where I had stored my clothes, or that someone, perhaps a homeless person, had found my stash of hidden clothes and taken them.

So, instead of having to become adept at finding ways to cover my naked body before heading back home (although I had learned plenty of creative ways to do that over the years), I became adept at pre-preparing for the nights I was going to morph into a wolf.

Part of how I had gotten over myself and the internal complaining of my "lot in life" with having to deal with the werewolf curse, was considering the millions of people who have diabetes, for example.

I had a cousin with diabetes. Wendy had to regulate her diet, regularly prick herself to do a blood sugar evaluation, and take insulin injections at least twice per day. I remember, as a child, thinking how frustrating it must be for her to have to pause in whatever task she was doing in order to perform these rituals.

But she was wonderfully matter of fact about it. It was merely something she had to do in order to live a regular and normal life. The same way that my friend Robby had to take medication twice per day as part of his daily routine.

And I, particularly when I thought of my affliction compared to the affiliation of millions like Wendy and Robby, or those who suffered from other things, had nothing to complain about.

For ten days out of every thirty I was inconvenienced by the loss of consciousness, having to get myself to a place where a wolf could enjoy some freedom to run around and howl at the moon, had to buy a few extra clothes and become adept at stashing them.

I had that to deal with, but I also had these amazing sensory abilities of abnormally heightened sense of smell, taste and hearing. Not to mention the supernatural strength I had. All elements that become more enhanced or powerful the closer I was to the phase of the full moon.

In addition, my immunity and resistance to viruses and other illnesses was powerful. I suspected that morphing between human and wolf form involved hyper-activity in my blood that killed microbes and other invading bugs. Ultimately, the back-and-forth regeneration must have had a positive effect on the healing of injuries.

So, while I had side-effects, and an affliction to deal with, I was pretty darned lucky.

After I finished packing my bag for the next morning's flight, I then packed a small plastic grocery bag with a pair of shorts, a t-shirt, then put on an old pair of jeans, a torn t-shirt and slipped on a pair of dollar-store flip flops and headed out to Central park so I could be there for the metamorphosis.

I lived at The Algonquin Hotel in mid-town Manhattan, and the doorman and concierge knew me well. So, I never needed ID or the key to my room. They would let me in; and always chalked up my odd dress to the eccentricities of being a writer.

I ended up arriving at Central Park about an hour before I knew I was due to change into a wolf. Basically, an hour before sunset. Even if the full moon was present in the daytime sky, my body never morphed until the sun vacated the western sky. Again, there's no real manual for me to read or understand why that is. I just had to learn, understand, and accept it.

I liked to walk around the park, scout out a location that I knew would be secluded and away from others. Of course, many people, especially the tourists, vacated Central Park before sun-down, so that always made it that much easier.

And that's when the first most curious thing happened to me.

I was in a spot I favored, one of the particularly heavily forested areas of the park known as The Ramble just south of Belvedere Castle. I had taken my flip flops off and tucked them into the plastic bag with my clothes and then stored the bag in one of my favored hiding spots under an outcropping of rocks. I then sat with my back against a tree and waited for the familiar aura of the change to wash over me.

As the sun continued its descent in the western sky, that familiar sensation which had been slowly growing for the previous few minutes intensified. It started like a very subtle numbness and tingling, like that sensation of when your arm or leg "goes to sleep." Only, I felt it through all of my limbs and my torso simultaneously, accompanied by a similarly subtle auditory buzzing noise that slowly grew.

As the tingling and buzzing intensified, I took a deep breath and tried to relax myself into the change. Fighting the change, struggling with it, turned the tingling and numbing feeling into outright pulses and beats of pure pain. That's what led me to believe that the memory loss usually associated with the change into wolf form were part of some sub-conscious self-inflicted side effect that helped me maintain my sanity. I can only imagine the utter pain and angst that occurs when a human body physiologically undergoes such a dramatic and traumatic metamorphosis.

I closed my eyes, preparing to give myself over to the wolf.

And waited.

And waited.

But nothing happened.

The sensation intensified, then backed off.

It pulsed in odd waves, the intensity burning. It reached an intensity that felt like sharp needles stabbing me all over my body. I gasped and let out short almost breathless shrieks.

And then, when it seemed I could bear the pain no longer, it receded.

I opened my eyes, lifting my hands up in front of my face to look at them. I was worried that I might, perhaps have shifted into some sort of odd man-wolf form, like the Wolfman of various television shows, movies and books, and I would see my mitts covered in an abnormal amount of thick dark hair.

But no, I was staring at purely human hands. My own hands. Big hands, of course. Manly man hands. Not the puny little hands of a fellow New Yorker who currently occupied the Oval Office.

I hadn't changed.

"What the hell?" I muttered.

This had only happened to me twice before. And usually on the first or the last night of the expected moon phase cycle. If I had had my cell phone on me, I would have consulted it to confirm. But I usually knew these things relatively well. The moon's full phase was supposed to be at 84% tonight. And I usually turned when the moon was 80% or more.

But not tonight.

Like I said, this had only happened a few times, so it was not something I expected.

The tingling and the buzzing continued on, but they

were fading, ever so slowly into the background. I looked up, through the tree branches and leaves above me, to the still-darkening night sky.

"Bonus time," I said, realizing that I would not be losing this night to becoming a wolf. It was like extra time I hadn't counted on. Not just the bonus hour of the fall's Daylight Savings, but more akin to a Super Powerball type of win of more than twelve hours.

Right on.

I knew exactly how I planned on using these bonus hours.

Chapter Five: Stories from Observing Strangers in the Night

When I arrived back at the Algonquin Hotel on West 44th Street, Bruce, the doorman, greeted me.

"Back from your walk so soon, Mr. Andrews?" Bruce asked, holding the door open for me and then following me inside, where I knew he would slip in behind the concierge desk to retrieve a key for me. He insisted on the formality despite the multiple times I'd requested he call me Michael.

Bruce, who often worked the afternoon and evening shift, or Paul, the main morning-shift person, were the two longest-running doormen at the hotel since I had moved in over ten years ago. They both accepted what I'm sure they saw as my eccentric writer routine. I had explained to them that I was heading out in rough, casual and cheap clothes with no accoutrements such as keys, a wallet, a mobile phone (what both Bruce and Paul referred to, fondly, as my "walking writer attire"), to wander through various neighborhoods having conversations with my characters and getting to know them inside and out—ie, with no other elements of who I was getting in the way.

That nicely explained my need to leave the hotel in the evening dressed the way I was and then return, the next morning, dressed in a similar fashion.

"Good evening, Bruce," I replied. I had been out for a little over an hour; something I don't think Bruce had ever seen before. "Yes, it was a particularly fruitful walk. I became inspired almost immediately and had to rush back to write a number of things down before they escaped back off into the ether."

"Very good, sir." He placed the room card on a little machine and then keyed in my room code without having to look it up. He had done it so often that he knew it completely from memory. "And it was certainly a lovely evening to be out for a stroll."

He handed me the programmed card. "Thank you, Bruce. You are a scholar and a gentleman."

He nodded. "It's my pleasure."

As I took the elevator to my room, I was reminded of how amazing it was to be living at The Algonquin Hotel. Originally built near the turn of the Twentieth Century, the hotel's lobby area restaurant and bar took on a more literary feel to it with. That feel stemmed from Dorothy Parker and the other members of the round table, also known as the "Vicious Circle" taking up regular residence there in the Roaring Twenties. The group became well known in literary circles and established that lounge as a spot to be or be seen by the literary elite.

I found it particularly inspiring for writing.

Once in my room, I changed into what would be more appropriate clothing for the lobby area of the Algonquin

Hotel, grabbed my laptop and then headed back downstairs.

It was a relatively quiet evening. Only a handful of tables were occupied. I grabbed a table near the back wall and sat in one of the small comfy armchairs, placed my laptop in front of me and soaked in the ambiance.

I mentioned how much I enjoy the fact that I live in such a literary locale, but I think what I have come to enjoy far more over the years is seeing how people react to the place. So, before I began writing, I just sat there and enjoyed those moments of observation of the others.

I looked at the people around me, spotting a few locals who were there prior to going to the opera or the theater; it was easy to make out the out-of-town tourists. People watching was still one of my favorite past-times.

I found inspiration in sitting in a café or a lounge or bar and watching people. Whenever I did that, a countless number of story ideas flooded through my mind.

I thought, particularly since this was an evening I hadn't expected, that I would write a simple stand-alone short story. Unlike a novel or longer project, a short story didn't require the same time and energy commitment. Maybe it was akin to a quick cold drink hastily consumed on a hot summer day as opposed to the more casual pleasure of sipping at a fine twenty-one-year-old scotch that you might nurse carefully over the course of an hour.

My eyes flitted from table to table, from person to person, and I took in as much as I could, imagining details about all of those people that I was watching.

The middle-aged man and woman sitting in the front right corner of the room were the first I focused on. He was in a fancy light brown tweed jacket complete with patches on the elbows and a European looking scarf wrapped around his neck, despite the warm New York summer weather; she was in a long and flowing elegant gown—the type that you might attend a ball in—and an intriguing hat with a beautiful feather sticking out of the side of it.

I fancied the two of them as a touristy academic couple who were in the city from out of town. Perhaps they were here for some sort of academic related conference and were out for the evening to enjoy a Broadway show.

I speculated he was an anthropologist. Also, that they'd been together for over twenty years. They were quite intent and leaned in towards one another in hushed conversation; and I did my best to not listen in on exactly what they were saying—I wanted to intuit what they were saying based merely on the body language that they were displaying.

It was challenging, I know. That's why I often brought my mobile phone and a pair of ear buds; so that I could play loud music directly into my ears which would drown out most of the background noise. Sure, if I focused in the correct manner, I could listen around the pounding music in my ears and pick out the conversation in the surrounding room. But I allowed the music to flood over that sense, and, instead *not* listen in on the actual conversation, but create my own imagined version of the discussion taking place.

So, I popped the earbuds in and I attended to them visually.

I imagined that this was their twenty-fifth wedding

anniversary. They visited New York once a year, near their anniversary because he proposed to her, back when they were both still in college, in the middle of movie theater. It had been during a repertoire movie night in which Frank Sinatra, Gene Kelly and Jules Munshin were performing *New York, New York* in the classic 1944 film *On the Town.*

Because he proposed to her with that song in the background, they always associated the city of New York and all the possibilities that it held with that moment of their lives coming together and all the amazing possibilities that existed in their brave new life together.

I speculated that, once a year, on the anniversary of their marriage, they began that pilgrimage to the metropolis of New York and it became a habit. As the years moved on, it was an important ritual they had clung to, because it was the one thing that kept them together throughout all the travesty and hardships they had faced over the years.

I speculated that they were talking about the breast cancer that she was a survivor of. She was in remission now, but they knew that their time was limited and that this could possibly be their last annual visit together to the city. Her family had a history of breast cancer and not a single person in her family—not her sister, her mother or her aunt, who had all suffered from the same wretched disease, survived more than two years after their diagnosis. She was, of course, over two-and-a-half years into her treatments, and they believed she was now living on borrowed time.

If it weren't for the cancer that she had been afflicted

with, they might have actually parted ways. I speculated that is exactly what the man was reflecting on when she had been diagnosed. He had been fully prepared to break things off and had everything planned right down to the words he had practiced for a couple of weeks, complete with the details of the affair that he had been having with the receptionist in the faculty office where he worked. He had been sitting in their living room, steeling himself up for the difficult task, when she came home with the news.

She came home with that news and it changed everything in his heart.

He realized how selfish he had been.

He realized how self-centered he had been. That he hadn't been paying any attention to her and to her needs, and that soon, she might be gone permanently. Not gone out of his life in the manner he had planned for the previous six months; but gone from his life and from this world.

That allowed him to come to the shocking realization that he loved her deeply. He loved her more than anything in the world and he recommitted himself, quietly, introspectively, to her. Giving himself to her for the rest of her life, so he could be everything that she needed, everything that she had always loved about him.

He immediately broke off the relationship with the receptionist and never turned an eye towards any other woman since then. He focused one hundred percent on his wife, the woman he had adored and cherished most of his adult life. He took up personal hobbies after realizing that, the affair had been born out of a combination of boredom and wanderlust.

And that is what he was reflecting on when she was talking about the play that they were getting ready to go see.

I reflected on that speculation about them for a moment and wondered what story I might write that expressed those details, that sudden turn of face back to duty, back to love, back to respect and honor.

Then, a moment later, I turned my attention over to another couple.

They were younger. They were in their mid twenties. And they looked like actor wannabes. They were both attractive looking people; exquisite and pleasing to the eye to gaze at. He with his chiseled solid chin and strong brow and wonderful piercing light blue eyes. He had a sort of young and roguish Kirk Douglas look to him. A wry smile on his face as he sat there in his fedora and a jacket that looked more stylish than appropriate for this warm summer evening.

She was beautiful with her long flowing blonde hair with just the right number of curls. She had high and strong cheek bones and wonderfully dark and smoldering eyes.

The two of them were not actually a couple. The two were best friends.

They were here together following a dream. They met in the theater club. Their high school theater club in Missouri, and they grew up together with a passion and a deep love for acting and for the stage.

They had always been close friends and adored and protected one another like brother and sister. They had never been involved with one another in any sexual way although they could easily recognize the appeal and sexual attraction that they each possessed. This made their friendship incredibly intense and strong.

Throughout high school they had grown together like brother and sister, in their love for acting. And they had wondered if they should continue to pursue the stage acting that they had fallen in love with during their high school tenure, pursuing Broadway and New York. Or, should they pursue the acting for television and movies, and head to Los Angeles and Hollywood?

They'd been through many things together, had been room mates in New York almost the entire time they had been in the city. They had only separated as room mates when she became engaged to an off-Broadway director.

They were apart for those nine months when she had moved in with her director fiancé. He had moved in with another actor friend that the two of them had met. And, as that relationship had grown between the young woman and the director she was with, the two friends grew apart. Instead of the daily connections and long all-night conversations they'd had for the previous decade, they grew distant.

The director she was engaged to was jealous of their relationship and suspected that there was more to the friendly, brotherly and sisterly love they had for one another. So, he drove a wedge between them; he forced her to distance herself from the young man.

And, being so enraptured in love, she let it happen.

And he, not wanting to come between her and the love of her life, let it happen and let them slip apart, even though he was miserable for the experience.

It had been almost six months since they had regularly spoken and were merely acquaintances who saw one another about town in the restaurants and cafes and the various theater spaces they ran in, when the engagement ended.

The engagement had been broken off after she realized that her director fiancé had been sleeping around with other young women who wanted, desperately, to have a part in the plays he had been producing.

The young brother-like-friend, of course, took her back into his apartment and into his life with open arms. He comforted her, sat up all night with her, ate gallons of ice cream with her and cried. They watched a handful of romantic comedies together; then cried some more and laughed.

He gave her reasons to laugh and to love and to respect herself. And he reminded her of how precious and beautiful and special she was. And that, regardless of any man or woman who came into either of their lives, they would always have one another, they would always have one another's respect and love. And that they would always have one another's back.

I speculated about writing a story about the two of them meeting in high school and what that might be like. I wondered if I might set up the tale like a romantic comedy where the reader might suspect that they would, in the end, come together as a couple. I wanted to come up with a tale that twisted in a way that, even though the reader was surprised and slightly upset that they didn't get together as a couple, they were overwhelmed with emotion at just how genuine and pure a true friendship could be.

I thought about what their names might be.

And that's when something caught my attention.

Something that disturbed me and snapped me out of writerly mode.

Chapter Six: Waltzing Matilda to the Tune of the Stray Cat Strut

It was an overpowering emotional response to threat that caught my attention.

Fear.

The overwhelming and overpowering sense of fear.

Sure, my headphones were firmly ensconced in my ears and I was enjoying the sounds of the Canadian rock band July Talk, so it was easy to block out any actual disturbing noises. But there was no blocking the scent that came through to me, striking a discord of fear so strong that I almost jumped out of my chair.

I reached up and clicked the button on my headphones that would pause the music as I surveyed the room visually while attending to the sounds.

Nothing seemed out of the ordinary—other than that intense scent of fear.

And as I smelled it, I realized I recognized the smell. It was familiar. It was fear from someone that I knew. No, not someone, or at least not a human person.

It was coming from Matilda, the Algonquin's house cat.

Matilda, or Matilda III, has been the hotel's house cat

for the past seven years here; continuing a long-standing tradition at the Algonquin Hotel that started sometime in the 1920s.

The hotel's first general manager, Frank Case, had an affinity for cats, particularly for rescuing strays. The very first cat Case took in was named Billy. And, shortly after Billy passed away, a stray cat named Rusty wandered into the hotel. The cat, who became a bit of a personality at the hotel, was renamed Hamlet, in honor of the classical actor John Barrymore, who was a resident of the hotel in the early 1930s.

The hotel has had eleven cats, six of them males named Hamlet, the others females named Matilda.

Matilda II was the resident when I first moved in, and she usually bolted from the lobby area the minute I walked into the hotel, obviously sensing my wolfish nature. But Matilda III and I certainly had an interesting relationship. She, like most other animals, could detect there was something different about me, the wolf-blood coursing through my veins. And although she reacted differently to me than she did to other humans, she also toyed with it, and played with me in a strange and fiercely competitive way.

We had a cute back-and-forth teasing that only the two of us truly picked up on and appreciated. Although a loving and personable cat who made tourists and locals alike adore her, whenever nobody else was looking or paying attention, she would arch her back at me, her hair would stand on end and she would hiss at me. Or she would attempt to sneak up upon and stalk me, knowing, full well, that, unlike other humans, I could easily detect her activities, sense what she was up to. That, you see, was the ultimate challenge for her. Because stalking other humans was boring and non-interesting. They rarely detected or even noticed when she did that. But with me, she had to be on high alert, because I was in tune with and sensitive to her every movement.

And I, of course, played along with it. I enjoyed teasing her as, over the years, we would go back and forth between playing stalker and prey.

Matilda was a cat who had been content with her life at the Algonquin Hotel. She adored Alice, an executive assistant at the hotel also known as the "chief cat officer." And she enjoyed the non-stop attention and fawning that she received from so many of the hotel guests who seemed as eager to see her as they were to be at this world-famous hotel.

But Matilda III and I also had a thing; a tight and almost secret relationship that nobody else knew about. And, as a long-time resident, I became used to the various scents and feelings she gave off. The two of us could, relatively easily, detect when there was someone who was a little "off" coming through the lobby or staying at the hotel. And we even seemed to exchange what one might consider "knowing glances" at one another whenever a suspicious person wandered through our domain.

That was when we bonded rather than play fought; over that sense of protecting our domain, our home, from less than desirable visitors.

But this intense emotion, this overpowering scent of fear that was coming from Matilda was more than just the presence of a less than desirable visitor.

This scent I picked up, that was virtually screaming at me in intensity, was of outright terror. And, perhaps, a dash of anger mixed with the slightest tinge of humility.

And the smell, which had come from the front lobby area where Matilda often sprawled out in her chase lounge, was fading.

I jumped up from my chair while snapping the laptop shut. I hadn't written a single word about either of the couples whose potential stories had intrigued me, but that was no matter now.

My feline companion, the only other resident of the hotel who possessed an animal nature, was in peril and needed my help.

I rushed over to the front desk and smiled at the concierge.

"Where's Matilda?" I asked.

"Hi Michael," she smiled, glancing over at Matilda's lounge area. "She was right here a minute ago. Laying down on her lounger."

As I stood there, I made out another scent. Male, sweaty, nervous. It still lingered in this front area of the lobby and, as I leaned closer to Matilda's spot, I pinpointed the original hot spot for it. Right here. Right where Matilda had been perhaps a minute earlier. There was also the lingering scent of burlap in the air. And I could tell that the scents had moved toward the front door.

Why hadn't I smelled the anxiousness, the nervousness of this man who had obviously been expecting doing something nefarious? Had I been that intent on the story I'd been searching for? Or was there something more?

Was I losing something? Usually, this close to the full moon, my senses and supernatural strength were extremely heightened and intense. So how could I miss out on something so obvious, something I should have easily detected? I mean, there was absolutely nothing wrong with my senses, my ability to trace what seemed to have occurred here now; but did it have anything to do with the fact that, earlier this evening, I hadn't morphed into a wolf? Was there something wrong with me?

I couldn't think about that. I had to focus on the evidence that was coming into my senses.

Someone, a male, had kidnapped Matilda. He had quickly slipped her into a burlap sack and then rushed out the door.

"I think that Matilda's in trouble," I said, handing the laptop across the counter at her. "Can you please hold on to this for me? I need to investigate."

And without waiting for a response, I hurried out the front door, following the path of the quite recent scent of the anxious man and the angry, fearful cat. The trail was still warm, and the culprit was not all that far away.

On the sidewalk outside, populated with a relatively heavy stream of pedestrians for this time of the evening, the scent revealed that the kidnapper had headed West down West 44th Street. Looking ahead as I walked in that direction, I determined that none of the folks immediately ahead of me on the crowded sidewalk were the culprit. I couldn't make out any of them as matching that nervous smell, nor that burlap sack.

When I arrived at the corner of 44th and 6th Avenue, I deduced by the scent trail that he had turned south.

Again, as a hastened down the street following the invisible path he left, I scanned ahead to see if I could figure out which person heading in the same direction might be him. But I couldn't tell. I also listened to see what I might pick up, and while I could make out voices, shuffling footsteps, heartbeats, the steady thrum and roar of traffic, the rumble of the subway below, I wasn't able to distinguish any sound that might be coming from the man I was following; except, perhaps for one of three or more footstep patterns heading south that seemed to move at a quicker than normal pace.

I hastened my pace as I followed his trail south along 6th Avenue. The scent was getting stronger, so I could tell I was getting that much closer to him. But I still couldn't pick out which of the people moving south on 6th Avenue ahead of me were my target.

One block south and the trail continued, not turning.

Then again, the same straight-line south crossing West 42nd Street. But after crossing the street, the trail deviated slightly, heading down the path and up the small, short flight of stairs into Bryant Park.

I found my quarry sitting on the ground with his back against the side of the building that was the New York Public Library's main building, with Matilda cradled in his arms, the lower half of her body still in the burlap sack.

This guy didn't look like a master kidnapper. And even though he was sitting in the typical stance of a homeless person, he didn't look like a vagrant either. Nor did he exude the long-settled stale smell of sweat and body odor I usually detected in those living on the streets.

He actually smelled a little of sawdust and drywall compound.

He looked up at me as I approached.

"Hi there," I said. His nervousness increased; what was I going to do? What was I going to say? Matilda, who was also giving off a tense nervousness, recognized me immediately, and that calmed her down a little. That seemed to calm him down a little too.

"Do you mind if I join you?" I asked.

He paused, confusion pumping out of his pores.

"Uh, yeah, sure. Go ahead."

I took a spot on his left, leaning up against the wall. Matilda let out a low meow in my direction and I reached over and stroked the top of her head.

"Hey there, girl," I said softly to her. Then, I lifted my hand in the 'let's shake' gesture to the guy. "I'm Michael."

He took my hand and gave it a quick pump.

"Hey Michael. I'm Ralph."

We sat together not looking at each other. Ralph was stroking Matilda on the top of the head.

"So, Ralph. What's the deal, here? What's your story? I can tell you mean Matilda no harm. So, what's with the catnapping?"

A sense of relief washed over him, along with a hearty dose of anticipation. There was something he was dying to talk about; that he desperately wanted to share.

"I wanted to do something. To make a difference about an issue that nobody seems to care about."

"What's that?"

"The homeless. There are so many of them in this city.

"People see them, but they don't see them. They look right through them.

"When I came to this city, I came with dreams of a city built by hard-work, the American dream; that if you put your back into it, you could make anything happen—build anything.

"But we're all looking up, we're looking at building more, we're creating these giant skyscrapers, reaching into the sky. But we're never looking down, at the people we're stepping on as we build these palaces they'll only ever get to stand or sleep outside of."

I nodded, not saying anything. I knew there was more he was eager to share.

"I'm just a construction worker. I make decent enough money. I work hard. And I'm doing my best to save. I have my real estate license, and I want to own property here; I want to earn a living not building the structures but owning them.

"I know it'll take a long time. But I'm healthy, and of sound mind. I've had a good life, come from a good family; had support all along. I came here with dreams of being something more, building something more. But I can't help but see, in the pursuit we all take to build, to achieve, we're ignoring the plight of our fellow man.

"And I've tried to see what I can do. But over the years it feels like we're just shoveling water, just moving problems around. I've gotten angrier and more frustrated that there didn't seem to be enough anyone could do. The problem just seems to be getting worse and worse."

He paused, scratched Matilda's head.

"Then I read a story in the paper about this cat. This

beautiful little cat. She enjoys comfort, and luxury ever since being adopted by the Algonquin Hotel. She went from being a homeless cat to a famous cat. There's even a book about her.

"I marveled at how people could fuss and bother so much over a cat, a single animal, pamper it, coddle it, do so much for it," Ralph said. "But then completely ignore or step over a fellow human being who was sleeping on the sidewalk and wasn't sure where their next meal was coming from.

"I remember reading an article about this group called the Guardians of Rescue that ran in the *New York Times* last winter. The group goes out and looks for the pets of homeless people. And they look after the pets, then the homeless person, in that order.

"But if they encounter a homeless person who doesn't have a pet, they ignore them.

"Hell, in my own experience, I have found myself twice as likely to give money to someone sitting on the street with a sign and a hat out if they have a pet with them. It's usually a dog. And I reason to myself that this person must be a good person, because they have a pet. And I also reason that if I give them some money, not all the money is going to go towards a bottle of cheap whisky or some other alcohol, but some of that money will be for their pet. Because how terrible for that pet to live such a life.

"But seriously. Are you kidding me? Not that I'm making light of it, because I'm sure that, like the human, the pet isn't getting full and solid meals. But animals don't have the same sense of worry that humans do—

they are much better at simply living in the moment.

"If you really think about it, a pet living with a homeless person might be far more content than the thousands of pets sitting alone in apartment buildings throughout the city.

"The pet of a homeless person has one thing pets love the most. They have the constant and day-long companionship of their owner. One who doesn't leave them alone in an empty apartment for eight to twelve hours a day—lonely, bored, and desperate to get outside and relieve themselves.

"The pet of a homeless person is with their master, outside, enjoying being out in the fresh air all day.

"It might even be, if I were to be so bold to suggest it, the ideal life for a pet. And, for many of those neglected pets of the working class, a better situation.

"But isn't it so strange that we care more for homeless people when there's a pet involved?"

As he'd been talking, he exuded a tremendous sense of compassion and conviction. He was deeply frustrated, angry, confused, and really wanted to do something. There was also a sense of relief at being able to share what he'd just shared with me. Like he had been holding all of that in for a long time.

I nodded. "It's a rather odd element of human nature. I suppose we can more easily see the vulnerability in an animal. Maybe because it doesn't have opposable thumbs. But we don't recognize the same vulnerability in other humans.

"But why did you kidnap Matilda?"

"I don't know," he said. "I had this idea, since she was

so well known, and she had been a homeless cat, that I might be able to use her to call attention to this issue. Get people to *actually* do something."

"Like what?"

"I don't know. It was a bit impulsive of me, I know. I thought maybe I could contact the newspapers; tell them I was holding the cat and would return it for a ransom."

"Ransom?"

"Yeah, but not paid in cash, to me. Paid in donations to food banks, to homeless shelters, to those services that provide hot food and fresh clothes and socks and toques and mittens to the homeless; to anything that would help.

"I just wanted to do something to help."

"I get that, Ralph. I just don't think this is the way."

"I know. But I was just so tired of doing nothing, of watching everything happening and not doing anything to help. I was tired and angry at myself. And this idea came to mind, so I thought I'd wasted enough time being actionless."

"Well, you certainly got my attention. But I'm not sure if a catnapping is a long-term answer. In fact, I don't think there's any decent short-term answer, either. This isn't an easily fixed issue. It's likely going to take a lot of work, a lot of effort, a lot of different moving parts. Like you, I have no idea what can be done. But I do know one thing."

"What's that?"

"You made a difference. You reminded me of something I normally ignore. You made me think about it. Perhaps getting people to recognize, to think about it, to reflect—maybe that's a start.

"You speak quite eloquently about it, Ralph. I'm not

sure if that's an answer. But getting people to think about it is a start."

"I suppose. And it felt good just to get all that off my chest."

"I don't have any answers. You don't have any answers. But you care deeply about an issue, and that's always a good place to begin."

Ralph nodded. "I suppose I should bring the cat back."

"That's okay," I said, taking Matilda into my arms. "I'm staying at the Algonquin. I know the staff. I'll make sure to bring her back safe and sound. Nobody needs to know about the catnapping."

"Thanks, Michael."

"Don't mention it."

We both stood up, looking at one another.

"What are you going to do now?" I asked.

He shrugged his shoulders and had been about to say something, then he looked over his left shoulder. "Huh."

"What?"

"This is the New York Public Library. I'm going to go inside and do some reading. I'm going to learn as much as I can. I likely won't have an answer, but maybe I can learn something that might eventually provide some answer to a way I can make a difference. Even if it's a small answer. At least it'll be a start."

"Yeah. At least it'll be a start. Good luck, Ralph."

He turned and started walking in the direction of the side entrance to the library.

He didn't have an answer. But his heart was in the right place and he was passionate about learning more and seeing if there might be a way to make a difference.

I was reminded that, though I was the one with enhanced powers and abilities, everyone had their own perception, talent, and strengths, that they could apply, with passion, for ways they wanted to make a difference.

We all just had to start.

Wednesday, June 14, 2017

Chapter Seven: Just the Flapjacks, Ma'am

I arrived at the airport with plenty of time to spare, despite the previous evening's adventure resulting in less sleep than I had intended on getting. While I didn't travel often, I did like to get to the airport well ahead of time.

Even before I became a werewolf, I wasn't fond of traveling. I preferred arriving as early as I could, scouting out and understanding my location, and only then settling down. But, now that I carried with me the lycanthropic element, it was that much more important for me to fully scope out, scan and understand the locations I would be in, if only to understand where I might hide, how I might escape, how I might get to either a closed and secured locked in location, or, better yet, to some sort of green space where I could comfortably roam during the night as a wolf.

I wasn't a big fan of Newark Liberty International Airport. But I knew it far better than I knew either LaGuardia or JFK airports, the other two major airports that served New York City. I had done some research about Newark because it was a major setting for one of my previous novels, *Frightening Flights of Fancy*. In that novel, Maxwell Bronte, an antiquarian bookseller with a penchant for solving crimes, gets involved in a secret ring of collectibles smuggling operated through Newark Airport via an employee at Terminal A.

I learned a lot about the airport and the terminal, that handles domestic and Canadian flights. And a flood of trivia about the airport rushed through my mind. Newark, which opened in 1928, was the first major airport in the United States of America. It covers over two thousand hectares of land and was home to the country's first commercial airline terminal.

The name of the airport, Newark International Airport was changed shortly after the tragedy of September 11, 2001. The word Liberty was inserted; partially in honor of the victims of the September 11 attacks, and partially for the landmark of the Statue of Liberty, which is less than ten miles east of the airport.

I also knew that about twenty thousand people were employed at Newark Airport and that the airport contributes more than twenty-two billion dollars in economic activities.

Research about Newark led me to research the adjacent green space of Weequahic Park, which is over 311 acres and boasts an 80 acre lake, the largest lake in Essex County.

Knowing all these facts about the airport, of course, gave me a bit of extra padding of comfort to help to understand the locale, understand where I was, and understand the potential escape route. I actually paused for a moment reflecting on that and tucked that into a corner of my mind that I preserved for writing nuggets. This was about a character whose past involves having to have a very secure escape route from every single location he or she is in. The nearby park could also provide plenty of natural hiding spots.

A writer's mind works that way. You see, perceive, hear or notice something either about your surroundings, or, like in this case, an aspect of yourself, and you tuck it into that little nook. I've often thought of them as character nuggets or setting nuggets or situational nuggets. You tuck those nuggets away and file them in some limitless sized reserve for when, one day, you are writing, and you need to draw upon that nugget. Then you have a virtual treasure trove, or perhaps a flea market or neighborhood bazaar, of a plethora of elements you can draw from to help add dimensions and depth to those people and places.

I suppose that's why, even when a writer isn't sitting in front of a notepad or a keyboard, they can still be writing.

That's how it always has been for me, at least.

Getting through security was quick and painless. All I carried with me were my laptop and my carry-on bag; and even though I didn't fly often, and rarely crossed the border, Mack had forced me to get a NEXUS card. This was an additional level of security check performed by a combination of the US Customs and Border Protection and Canada Border Services Agency to allow for expediting border crossings between the two countries. Even when flying domestically, having a card qualifies a person for getting into the TSA pre-check lines.

I remember arguing with Mack when he suggested — no, wait, let me rephrase that — when he insisted I get a NEXUS card.

"But, Mack," I started. I often began my responses to him with those two words. "I rarely ever travel; hardly ever return to Canada, and I can count on one hand the number of times I have gotten on a plane in the past ten years."

"Don't be an ass, Andrews," Mack said, sticking a cigar into his mouth and patting down his jacket to feel for where he had kept his matches or his lighter. "Time is precious and spending a single minute more standing in line for something as rudimentary as air travel with the rest of the cattle is inconceivable."

I laughed whenever Mack used that word, because the way he said the word always reminded me of Vizzini from the movie *The Princess Bride*.

But I loved how you could see Mack's blood pressure going up at the mere thought of time being wasted, even if it wasn't his own time. Sure, I flew so infrequently it made little sense. But Mack wouldn't rest until I had a valid NEXUS card.

I had, of course, been annoyed at Mack, at the time, as I often was.

But every time I saved myself a good hour or so of time standing in line for the security check at an airport, I quietly blessed Mack. Dammit if that SOB wasn't right again.

Going through this particular TSA Pre-Check line was simple. I didn't even need to take off my belt, or my jacket or remove the keys or coins or cell phone from my pocket. All I had to do was drop my carry-on bag and my laptop bag on the conveyer (without even having to remove my laptop) and waltz through the security gate. I'm not sure how these gates differ from the other ones where even the foil from a wrapped piece of gum, or some of the buttons on a pair of jeans can set off the metal detector, but I was more than happy to take advantage of the time savings for passengers who had been pre-screened for flight safety.

Because I had plenty of time to wait before my flight, I did what I always did once getting through security. I double-checked the gate on my ticket (which, of course, I already knew, having looked at it half a dozen times already before), then sought out the gate and walked straight for it.

I found the gate within a few minutes, and being comfortable at knowing where it was, I used the time to explore the terminal on foot.

Given that I would be on the flight across the country for several hours and would be stuck in a single seat, I thought it would be good to stretch my legs, move around a bit, and get a few extra steps in.

No, I wasn't one of those Fitbit fanatics who eagerly sought to register 10,000 steps every day. I merely enjoyed the mind-liberating experience of walking.

There was nothing like a good and vigorous constitutional.

Walking was a simple, yet effective manner of feeling good physically, but it also stimulated something deeper inside and regularly helped me with my writing, or, better yet, to clear my mind when I was focusing too hard on something that had frustrated me.

I recall reading Henry David Thoreau's essay "Walking" in high school; I'd had a teacher who was a big fan of Thoreau's and so he introduced us to much of the man's work. I re-read the essay when in university, and, filled with angst, I learned the joy of simply taking a walk across the campus. Every few years I picked Thoreau's essay back up and, in the manner that you might enjoy the sights on a familiar walking route, I enjoyed the familiar words of this masterful writer. But every time I returned to the essay, I was a new person, just like the same person can't step into the same river twice.

In the essay Thoreau explained the meaning of the word saunter, which was derived from people who roved about the country, in the Middle Ages under the pretense of going *à la Sainte Terre* or, to the Holy Land.

There was something, if not mystical, then perhaps spiritual in talking a walk—a long walk, a hearty walk, and I relished that.

Walking was the way I preferred to explore new towns and cities I visited.

It was the manner I initially made my way to New York.

Walking, at night, was how I had been infected by that wolf and gained these extra-sensory powers; which, of course, forever altered the course of my life.

I wondered if my obsession for walking was enhanced, somehow from the wolf blood in my veins. Even when human, was there something in me that felt that pull, that desire, to just run freely across an open field or through a thick wooded area; that sucked the marrow of the moment of moving so quickly and with abandon through whatever landscape awaited?

As I walked through the airport, I marveled at all the different people I passed along the way going about their own business.

Even if I wasn't walking in a character's shoes, there was never any shortage of nuggets of characters and moments and scenes to pick up on and store in the back of my mind when walking through a crowded place like this.

So many stories, so many unique dramas quietly, or sometimes not so quietly unfolding before me.

I thought back to that Bruce Willis movie; *Die Hard 2* — the one where he is at an airport over the holidays and, while waiting for his wife's plane, can't help but notice something strange going on.

It was a film I enjoyed. And I loved his character, John McClane, and the quick quips he relayed.

A moment from *Die Hard 2* came to me. When McClane was struggling to convince Carmine Lorenzo something more than luggage punks was going down at the airport.

"Hey, Carmine, let me ask you something. What sets off the metal detectors first? The lead in your ass or the shit in your brains?"

I laughed under my breath.

I'd have to watch that movie again.

But not before I returned from this trip. I was nervous enough about flying.

Then I remembered the opening scene of the first *Die Hard* movie with McClane on the flight coming in to Los Angeles gripping the seat rest nervously. The passenger beside him tells him to take off his shoes and socks when he got to his hotel room and then to walk around on the rug barefoot and to make fists with his toes.

I'd have to give that a try when I landed in LA.

I glanced at my watch, saw that I still had another forty minutes before my flight boarded, and acknowledged that my invigorating walk was completed. I had time to grab something to eat for breakfast. Turning around I headed over to one of the restaurants I'd walked past that had smelled particularly appealing.

I took the one vacant stool at the counter between a woman in a long red coat with long black hair on my right and a young boy on my left who seemed to be with a set of parents.

"Is this stool taken?" I asked the woman.

"No," she smiled. "Go ahead." Then she turned back to the folded newspaper she'd been reading.

I pulled myself onto the seat, and the waiter behind the bar, having noticed me, smiled, said he'd be right with me and slid a laminated single page menu in front of me on his way down the bar to refill a few coffee cups along the line.

I picked up the menu while taking in the scent of different foods that were cooking in the kitchen or had already been served.

There were a few standard yogurt parfait, egg, meat, hash brown, and toast, and eggs Benedict options. Judging from the smell of things, the variations of the egg dishes were the most popular choice here. Below those options was a term I wasn't as familiar with.

"Flapjacks?" I muttered.

The woman beside me heard my confusion, I could sense her return to awareness of the person now sitting beside her, and she leaned over. "It's another term for pancakes."

I laughed. "Oh, I know that. Thanks. I just don't see it often. But I'm always interested in how different regions use different terms for things. Where I grew up, we always just called them pancakes."

As I introduced the concept, I sensed her distinct interest in the conversation. Even had I not had the additional sensory ability, her putting down the newspaper would have been a clear indication.

"It is fascinating. I've also heard them called hotcakes, and griddlecakes. Where I'm from, Southern Carolina, we called them johnnycakes." She paused and took a long look at me. She was pretty with a small round face, wide dark eyes, rounded cheeks and a cute tiny upturned nose. She had long black hair, but on her left side her head was shaved to a brush cut just over her ears. As she similarly took me in, I could tell that she also found me attractive.

"I'm Nancy, by the way," she smiled.

"Michael."

"So, Michael, where are you from where it's always pancakes on the menu?"

"Ontario, Canada."

She laughed. It was a cute laugh; her cheeks actually warmed and reddened a slight bit when she laughed, which I found charming.

"You mean you don't just have poutine for breakfast?"

I laughed in reply. "Nope. We usually have poutine for lunch or supper."

"Supper, not dinner?" she asked.

I laughed again. "Funny you should mention that. Growing up, my Mom always called lunch dinner, and dinner was supper."

"That's another regional thing. I think in parts of England, dinner is the middle meal of the day and they use tea for the evening meal."

"It's not a thing you drink?"

"No. I'm a coffee girl myself."

I laughed. She was charming, intelligent, fun. And she liked me. I was still hurting over Gail, but it was good to know I seemed able to have a natural flowing conversation with an attractive woman.

"It's so interesting how the same language can have such variations," I said. "No wonder people get so confused."

"Well, I'm not confused about what I want to eat. I'm eager to try these flapjacks."

"You haven't ordered yet?"

She laughed. "No, I hadn't actually looked at the

menu. I ordered a coffee and then fell into this article I was reading."

"About what?"

Before she could reply, the waiter behind the bar returned, coffee pot in hand.

"Can I get you a coffee?" he asked me. "Refill?" he asked Nancy.

Nancy and I nodded in unison, and then both laughed.

"Ready to order?" he asked.

"You go first," Nancy said.

"You sure?"

"Yeah," she laughed. "If you don't mind my saying it, you look pretty peckish. But I'm also curious to see if you ask to have cheese curds and gravy added to whatever you order."

The bartender gave off a confused scent, not understanding the previous joke we'd shared about poutine.

"I think I've got to have the flapjacks," I said.

"Bacon, ham, or sausage on the side?" he asked.

"Can I have all three?"

"Sure. I'll just charge the extra two as sides. And for the toast, white or brown?"

"Brown, please."

"Excellent." He then addressed Nancy. "And for you?"

"I'll have the same," she said. "But hold the meat. No, wait, maybe give my friend my side of—"

"Bacon," I said. "And thank you, Nancy."

"My pleasure," she grinned, and again there was that

mutual sense of attraction between us. It felt good, but also made me uncomfortable. A beautiful woman was into me. I was into her. But I was still stinging from Gail and eager to rush into anything. This was just a fun chance encounter between two people who hit it off. I needed to leave it at that.

"I do have a question, though," Nancy asked the bartender. "I have a severe peanut allergy. You don't use nuts in any of ingredients for the flapjacks, do you?"

"No," the waiter assured her. "Okay, I'll go put the order in and it'll be out shortly."

"Peanut allergy?" I asked her. "That must be tough, when traveling."

"Yeah. It's pretty bad. If food has even touched something that has come into contact with peanuts, it'll send me into anaphylactic shock. I should point out, by the way, that I have an EpiPen® in the front flap pocket of my handbag, you know, just in case.

"How about you? Any allergies?"

"Just arsenic...and old lace, I said with a wry grin on my face.

"Ah, Cary Grant."

"Pardon?"

"You mentioned an old film that starred Cary Grant. I'm a bit of a movie buff. And I love Cary Grant's films."

"I've never seen it. I was just pulling out an old joke my dad used to say whenever asked about allergies. But you're a Cary Grant fan, huh?"

"Yeah, I love his films. I love so many different movies. But there was something about that black and white era of movies. Cary Grant, Rock Hudson, Burt Lancaster, Gene Kelly. Frank Sinatra, too. I know most people think of him as a singer, but he was in over sixty movies; and I just love watching him in them.

"Sinatra had this style, this presence, that really resonates with me. There was something about the way he could fill the space. Whether it was on stage, or in a film, he was just all there. He commanded the entire space he was in."

"I particularly enjoyed when he played the role of detective; though he only played a detective a handful of times later in his career.

"Did you know that he originally was intended to be cast as Harry Callahan in *Dirty Harry*, the role that Clint Eastwood became known for? Sinatra had a developing issue with his hand that forced him to have to turn down the role.

"He also had to turn down the role of John McClane in *Die Hard*."

"What?"

"Yeah," she continued, barely taking a breath. I had to admit it was so wonderful to see someone so passionate about a subject. "Sinatra starred in the 1968 film *The Detective* as Detective Sergeant Joe Leland, which was based on the 1966 novel of the same name by Roderick Thorp.

"Thorp wrote a sequel to that novel that came out in 1979 called *Nothing Lasts Forever*, which also featured Detective Joe Leland. The studio was contractually obligated to offer the role to Sinatra, who played Leland in *The Detective*. But he had to turn that one down because he was seventy years old. Many other actors were considered for the role, including Clint Eastwood, Paul Newman, and Harrison Ford. Arnold Schwarzenegger was offered and turned down the role and opted, instead to star in *Twins* with Danny DeVito because he wanted to focus more on comedy.

"Bruce Willis was eventually cast, despite a conflict with the television show he'd been working on at the time, *Moonlighting*. He was able to do it, thought, when his co-star Cybill Shepherd became pregnant and there was an eleven-week break in production of that show. Joe Leland was re-written as John McClane, an everyman sort of guy. And the rest, of course, is history."

"Wow," I said. "I knew that *Die Hard* was based on a Roderick Thorp novel, but I didn't realize all of those things that led to it. And to think, an entire movie franchise for Willis was based on a series of hiccoughs or accidental changes along the way."

"It's interesting how chance or accidental things can lead to something pretty amazing," she said. And with that I felt an intense wave of emotion and attraction coming off of her.

She was really into me.

She was right. I was feeling something too.

But as beautiful and fascinating as she was, I wasn't ready for something so soon.

"It sure is," I replied. "It's funny that you bring up Bruce Willis as John McClane. I can't walk through an airport without thinking about the movie *Die Hard 2* where he's at an airport at Christmas, waiting for his wife to arrive, when he can't help but notice something strange going down.

"I spend a lot of time, myself, watching and observing people."

"Oh, so you fancy yourself a little like John McClane, then?"

We both laughed.

"Well, I have a bit more hair. But, yeah, maybe the observation aspects. Definitely not the heroics."

Of course, I had to pause and think about that a bit. I had gotten involved in several precarious and heroic situations over the past several years. More action in the past little while than I had ever seen my entire life. Maybe I was like McClane in that "everyman" sort of sense. No, I wasn't a cop, and I definitely wasn't ever a fighter, nor did I ever have any desire for action. But I did have a nose for trouble—especially now that my nose had a heightened sense—and had, lately, found myself in some action and adventures that might be adaptable into a Hollywood film.

"Oh, I doubt that. You've got that tall, dark, handsome thing going on for you." Nancy said, and put a hand on my right shoulder, giving it a bit of a squeeze. "And you seem to be in pretty good shape. I'm feeling some muscle under that shirt." She dropped her hand back onto the counter. "I'm sure if Hans Gruber or any of those other bad guys showed up, you'd be able to give them a run for their money."

Nancy's quick and fleeting touch thrilled me in a way

I had not been expecting.

"Uh," was all I uttered.

"Oh my god," she said. "You're blushing."

I felt the blood having rushed to my face.

"Uh," I repeated.

"That's adorable. And refreshing."

I shrugged, not sure what to say. Even though she'd only touched my shoulder for a moment, I could still feel the warmth of her hand there.

"I'm sorry, Michael. I'm usually not so forward. But there's just something about you that makes me feel so comfortable, and so relaxed." Her scent filled with regret and anxiety.

"I think it's my Canadian-ness," I quipped. "And speaking of which, I'm the one who should be apologizing. It is, after all, what we're known for."

She laughed, a sense of relief coming over her face that I could also smell, and the server arrived with our plates of breakfast.

"Ah," she said. "Perfect timing to break an awkward moment."

"Awkward is my speciality."

We both laughed.

"But seriously, Nancy, I'm actually enjoying chatting with you, as well. I'm glad we met."

"Well then," she said, raising her coffee cup toward me with her left hand. "Then I propose..." she looked down at her plate, then grabbed the toast off of the side of it. "A toast. To new friendships."

I laughed, picked up my own coffee cup and piece of

toast. "To new friendships."

We clicked our mugs together and then, for good measure, also tapped our pieces of toast.

"Bon appetite," Nancy said.

And then her eyes opened as if she just remembered something. "Oh yeah. I almost forgot. My blood pressure medication." She dug into her purse. "Go ahead, get started, Michael. Don't wait for me."

"You're the boss," I said, slicing into the pancakes—or should I say flapjacks—without bothering to apply any syrup, and bringing them to my mouth.

I wasn't as hungry as I normally get when I'm in the wolf phase and spent the previous night tearing around on all fours; but I was still hungry enough.

And these were good. Even without butter and syrup.

I loved to marvel at different tastes and flavors. There's something almost mystical about experiencing things on a much deeper plane.

I let the texture and flavor of the plain flapjacks roll about my tongue, trying to figure out the different ingredients that I could distinguish.

There was obviously egg and flour, milk and butter in this. Also, vanilla, and, it seems they used maple syrup for the sweetness rather than sugar. Nice touch. But there was also an interesting nuance that added an Asian sort of touch. Was that sesame oil? Definitely a nutty taste.

Nutty

Yeah, that was peanut oil.

They must have fried these in peanut oil.

I could smell it, now that I realized what it was, on my

plate. I focused on the scent coming from the flapjacks on Nancy's plate and could tell that hers, too, were fried in the same peanut oil.

Nancy, who had just sliced a bit-sized hunk of flapjacks with her knife, speared them with her fork and lifted it up to her lips.

"No," I said, my right hand shooting over to block the chunk of flapjacks from touching her mouth. "Don't eat that!"

A sense of confusion and startled fear shot through Nancy.

"What?"

I wrapped my fist around the flapjack on the end of her fork and slowly lowered her hand back to the plate.

"I'm so sorry, Nancy. I don't mean to be so forward. But there's peanut oil on these pancakes. They were fried in a mixture that contains peanut oil."

She looked at me, still shocked at how I had man-handled her food.

"Wow. And I almost ate it. Thank you, Michael."

"I'm just glad you mentioned your peanut allergy."

"You must have quite the sense of taste," she said. "Are you a chef or something?"

I laughed. "Hardly. I can barely whip up a bowl of Kraft Dinner."

"Kraft Dinner?"

"Oh, yeah, that's the term we use in Canada for Kraft Macaroni and Cheese Dinner. We call it Kraft Dinner or KD for short."

"More different term nuances." She mused. "I always

find that so fascinating."

"Me too."

"So, do all Canadians have such a refined sense of smell and taste? Or is it just the good-looking ones?"

The bartender approached. "How is everything?"

"Well," Nancy said. "My friend here with the exquisite sense of taste realized that my food had been cooking in peanut oil."

The bartender was genuinely shocked and appalled. "Oh my," he said. "I am so, so sorry, ma'am. The cook must have not seen my note.

"I'll get a fresh batch cooked up for you, a peanut-free one, of course. Or would you like something different?"

"I'm now thinking that the yogurt parfait might be nice."

"Of course. We'll get it right out. And I'll double check on that before we bring it to make sure it's completely nut free. And your breakfast, your coffee, is, of course, on the house."

"You'll have to cover his breakfast as well," Nancy said to him, hooking at thumb over in my direction. "After all, it was his keen sense of taste and smell that detected the peanut."

"Of course, ma'am. I'll be right back with your parfait."

He then rushed off to the kitchen.

"Thank you, Nancy."

"No, seriously, Michael, thank *you* so much. You saved my life. It's the least I can do. I know it's still early, but I feel like I owe you. Can I perhaps buy you a drink?

"Oh, No. It is early, and even if it weren't, I don't really drink that much. But thank you. The coffee and the flap-jacks were a wonderful treat. Thank you, Nancy."

Her yogurt arrived. There was no peanut scent associated with it. I smiled as she dug her spoon into it and took a mouthful.

"Are you sure? I would love to buy you a drink."

I sat looking at this attractive, energetic, and delightful woman who was obviously quite interested in me. This was good timing for my ego, I suppose, having been finally rejected by Gail after all of this waiting. It was flattering, but I wasn't yet ready.

A line from *Die Hard 2* came to me suddenly. It was from this scene in which a woman at a car rental desks who helps John McClane fax a fingerprint to a police colleague in New York offers that she'll be off shift in five minutes and would like to meet him at the bar for a drink. He responds by flicking at the wedding ring on his left hand and says: "Just the fax, ma'am."

Unable to resist a bad pun, I respond: "Just the flap-jacks, ma'am."

She laughed. She knew the line, was familiar with the movie.

"Nicely played," she said, laughing as she continued to eat her breakfast. "Mr. John McClane."

"I figured you likely knew the film. Being a big movie buff and all."

"Yeah, I got the reference. I suppose I also picked up on the subtle nuance that comes with that reference. I've come on a bit strong; and you're not interested. Are you, like John McClane, in that film, married or attached to someone? Did I misread that?"

"No. No. Not married. Not attached. I was just in a, er, a complicated relationship that recently ended. I'm still sorting out my feelings. Fresh wounds and all that."

Her feeling of compassion and nurturing warmth toward me was refreshing, comforting, and encouraged me to be a little more forthright than I normally would be.

"To be honest, Nancy, I think you're a beautiful woman. And fascinating. I actually am really enjoying talking to you. And I would like to get to know you more.

"I just worry that I'm too close to the previous ended relationship right now to be able to focus on something new. One reason I'm heading on this trip is to get away, have some alone time with myself, to figure things out."

She smiled, and the essence of disappointment coming off her was mingled with a mild sense of relief and further compassion. That attracted me to her even further. She was genuine and caring and considerate.

"You're a nice guy, Michael. Nice guys are rare. I respect that you've been so honest with me."

She sat pursing her lips and considering something. Then she reached down into her purse, pulled out a pen, and grabbed a napkin from the small pile in front of her.

She wrote something on the napkin and folded it over once.

"I've got to get to my flight," she said, downing her coffee and standing up. She took my right hand with her left and gently placed the napkin inside it. "Thanks for saving my life." Then she leaned over and gave me a quick and gentle peck on the cheek.

"I'll be back in a few weeks. Not sure when you're back, but just hang on to this, okay? Take your time. At any point, if you're ever ready. Just in case.

"Goodbye, Michael. It was a pleasure meeting you."

"The pleasure was all mine, Nancy. Goodbye."

She then walked out of the restaurant.

I looked down at the napkin in my hand, then opened it up.

Inside, written in pen, was:

Nancy Watson. 555-309-5462. Call me when you're back in town, John McClane.

Chapter Eight: Those Thoughtful Eyes Staring Back at Me as I No Longer Pretend My Ship is Coming

I think I have already mentioned I don't travel all that much. I'm also not a really good flier. Or, at least, not a good passenger on a flight.

So I find, when I'm on a flight, I constantly need a decent distraction.

After making my way to my seat, I immediately riffled through the pocket of the back of the seat in front of me, grabbing the in-flight magazine from the airline. When I pulled it out, I caught sight of a newspaper section tucked in the seat pocket between the in-flight magazine and the menu pamphlet.

The edge of a headline on this section caught my eye.

FEAR

I pulled it out. The full headline read: *FEAR STALKS THE STREETS OF L.A.*

It was a section from *New York Daily News* that had reprinted an article from the *L.A. Times*. I started to read it:

FEAR STALKS THE STREETS OF L.A.

In a move that is becoming more and more common in Trump's America, the rise of one particular hate and fear group is shaking up the people of many neighborhoods in Los Angeles.

The group was initially active only on social media, bombarding Twitter, Facebook, and YouTube with their thinly disguised messages of hate in their proclamations of unifying America, but they have now become active in the streets.

The *Proud Fighters for America*, or the PFA for short, started publishing letters to the editor in the *L. A. Times* and posting short videos from multiple different hijacked accounts on both *YouTube* and *Facebook*. Their claim is that America's open borders and acceptance of foreign cultures and religions and sexual deviants dilute the purity of the founding fathers. And that is what's responsible for the violence and divisiveness in the country. Their message is that they seek to fight fire with fire and to not relent and let the terrorists who are corrupting America from within continue. They have vowed to fight in the streets to clean and purify the unwashed masses of filth that are corrupting this fine country, the way that Americans have always fought for the liberty and freedoms they enjoy.

While none of the local police or investigative reporters have been able to trace the leadership of the group back to any specific person or identified groups, they appear to have been spreading and growing in numbers, especially in the last several weeks.

Unlike the mass public protests and marches of similarly minded groups, like the *National Alliance of*

American Brothers, this group doesn't appear to stage mass public gatherings. Instead, in moves similar to the *Freedom Party of Proud Americans*, they strike in a stealthy manner, in short, quick and emboldened attacks on various businesses and public spaces. Typically, these attacks are carried out while they wear novelty Halloween masks to hide their identities.

In addition to striking at the black, Hispanic and LGBTQ communities, they also strike at the sympathizers for such marginalized groups. So far, the group has claimed responsibility for more than thirty different attacks at convenience stores, restaurants, community centers and bars in Burbank, East Hollywood, Glendale, Del Rey, Monterey Park and Venice.

One message spray painted on the wall of a community center in Glendale included a combination of swastika and—

The article stopped there with a "continued on C4" note. But I didn't have a section C. I didn't have more than the cover page of the section I'd been reading.

I turned the paper over, curious about the odd happenings in Los Angeles and surprised that I hadn't heard about them. Although the whole thing didn't really surprise me. Not with how Alt-Right and other hate groups seemed to have come out of the woodwork since about mid-way through last fall's election.

The article had done a decent job of distracting me from my anxiety over flying. But now that there was no other section to keep reading, I focused back on where I was and what I had been previously thinking about.

I've always found flying stressful, particularly because, on virtually every flight I have been on, I've felt that I have to focus hard on keeping the plane in the air.

Yes, I know it makes absolutely no sense, that it has nothing to do with the physics that allows an airplane to lift off from the ground and fly. But, in the same way that, as a child, I always lifted my feet while crossing over train tracks—because you do that for good luck—I've always felt it was my duty to concentrate on thinking about the plane lifting, as if my mere thoughts were what could keep the plane in the air.

Okay, perhaps I don't do that much anymore as an adult; but I recall doing that from my very first flight when I was eight years old, and I traveled with my parents to Orlando, Florida to Walt Disney World.

I remember my Mom telling me to just go to sleep, because I had been tired from not sleeping, obviously in anticipation of the exciting next day, when we would be getting up early and flying to Florida and Disney World.

But I couldn't sleep. I didn't tell her that, of course. I couldn't sleep because it was my concentration on keeping the plane in the air that was preventing it from plummeting back to earth. That, and that alone, was doing it. I don't know, maybe it's a control thing. Because when you're a passenger on the airplane you're not, at all, in control. This perhaps gave that comfort and illusion of control.

And while I hadn't maintained that strict concentration on "holding the plane in the air" through an entire flight in years, I *did* feel it was my job to focus, during every takeoff and every landing of the plane. As if there were any relation to me focusing and sending positive vibes that made the takeoff and landing as smooth as possible.

And ever since I gained my heightened sense of hearing, I found airplanes particularly disturbing. Because, if I concentrated, I could focus in on what the pilot and co-pilot were saying to one another during the flight. I could hear the dialogue between them and the control tower.

And even though most of the words exchanged between the two pilots and air traffic control were routine and delivered in a monotone fashion, occasionally, they would say something with an urgency accompanied by the scent of worry, angst or even fear. And, while nobody else on the plane knew that something even slightly out of the ordinary was going on, I would be fully and completely aware. Even if it were a small thing that they were dealing with, I was in tune with it and could clearly feel the tension rising.

That, of course, didn't help an already nervous flier.

So I didn't really settle into my seat until after takeoff, until after we were well up in the air, cruising to an altitude where the airport and city below were like tiny little railroad models of a city and we passed through the lower level of clouds.

That's when I became reflective of this change in my life.

I pulled my earphones out of the breast jacket pocket inside my sports coat and stuck them into my phone. I found that, in the same way that the music helped me to not focus on people in a crowded room, like last night at The Algonquin, I could use the same technique to block the sounds from the flight deck from my ears.

Then I opened up the music app and searched through until I found the album *Fly by Night* from Rush.

I played the title track from that album, feeling it was appropriate as I stared out the window at the soothing sight of the floor of clouds that we were flying above, the illusion almost as if we were a large cruise ship hurling across a fluffy white sea.

I found that I always played that song from Rush on repeat whenever I was changing something significant in my life. I played it when I first moved away from home to attend University; even though it was only about an hour away from where my parents lived, it was a major change in my life. I was moving on to something different.

I, of course, played the song on repeat when I hitch-hiked to New York, following my dream of wanting to be a writer and to live in New York city, which I had fallen in love with from the Spider-Man comics I grew up reading.

And I was listening to it again now.

No, I wasn't leaving my home in Manhattan.

But I was flying away, I was partaking in a change in my life. The flight to Los Angeles for an extended visit was symbolic, to me, of the change I was making in my life, to the chapter in my life that I was being forced to close. A chapter, with Gail, that I had always imagined would be an entire book. I had always felt we were destined to be together; I had always imagined the two of us staying together, getting married; perhaps even having children (although, admittedly, I wondered, apart from my penchant for the occasional bad dad joke, if I had what it took to be a parent). But I had imagined us being together and growing old together.

I suppose, with this new chapter in our lives, in our relationship, and knowing how close we were as friends, we would likely always be friends. I couldn't see not spending time with her, not sharing things with her. So maybe we *would* grow old together, but we'd grow old together as dear friends.

It still made my heart ache just to think about it. It still burned and hurt; because, despite knowing it was over, despite Gail being so plainly clear about her intentions, I still yearned for her; I still thought about her non-stop.

Meeting a beautiful woman like Nancy and seeing how it was entirely possible for me to actually be interested in someone else; to be interesting to someone else, was definitely eye-opening and helpful to me. That I was attractive, that I was desirable, that I wasn't "dead yet" when it came to relationships—was a good thing. It was a positive experience. I patted at the note tucked in behind the passport in my breast pocket. Who knows if I would call Nancy when I got back to New York? Who knows if a relationship might actually work out? But the possibility of knowing that something like that might happen was enough to help me realize it was time to move on.

Admittedly, it made me wonder about relationships in general.

The reason Gail and I broke up in the first place was because I hid my curse from her. I kept it a secret. I lied to her. That deception was ultimately what ruined our relationship, and, as part of a series of lies and betrayals that Gail had experienced, led her to the position she was in now.

She couldn't trust men; or any man for that matter. Including me. She'd been betrayed, lied to, hurt too much, just enough to not want that any longer.

And, despite my deception, Gail had figured out the secret of my lycanthropy. She had figured it out, kept it a secret and yet still accepted me. If I had told her about it myself, perhaps we'd never have gotten to where we were now; perhaps we would have worked it out. But that point was moot, because I had deceived her. And despite her lack of trust in me, I knew I could trust her completely, whether in human or in wolf form. And my wolf form understood that Gail was a trusted and honorable person too.

What would I do if I met someone? If I ended up going on a date with someone like Nancy and then started to see her seriously? Would I tell the woman about it? And at what point?

I don't think there are any books out there where you can find that sort of advice.

Dear Abby, I might write. *At what point in a relationship* does it make the most sense for a lycanthrope to reveal his animal nature? Is it something you do on a second date? Sincerely, Lonely Wolf Boy.

Dear Lonely Wolf Boy: This isn't something that you tell a woman on a second date. It isn't something you tell her on a first date either. It's something you simply never tell a woman. Here's why. You're a freaking wolf. An animal. A creature. The fact that you expect to have a relationship with a normal human woman is simply out of the question. We all have seen, through experience, that cross-species relationships put too much strain on a couple. So don't go there. Find a nice wolf woman to spend time with, to run through the fields with.

I shook my head at this imagined back and forth.
A nice wolf woman.
Now where the hell was I going to find someone like that?

Chapter Nine: Chatty Cathy the Limo Driver

When we arrived at LAX, my "awaiting driver holding a sign with my name on it" cherry was popped. While I have seen such things at airports plenty of times before in my extremely limited time spent in airports, I have never had one for me.

I'm talking about one of those drivers you'd see standing in the arrivals section, holding a sign with the last name of the person they were there to meet. Of course, there were now almost as many drivers holding up glowing tablets or iPads with the name boldly and clearly visible in giant black capital letters.

I'd never paid much attention to them as I would walk past but had always wondered who they were for. My original assumption was that they would be for celebrity guests visiting from out of town; but I'd never seen any name that I recognized.

In this case, though, I paid a lot more attention; because I knew that there would be a driver waiting for me.

When the plane had landed—after I spent the appropriate amount of superstitious time focusing on making sure we came in for a smooth landing of course—and we were given the all-clear to turn on our cellular devices, I turned mine on to a greeting from the show runner who was supposed to be my ride to the hotel.

Something has come up. Can't make it to LAX. Have arranged for a limo service to get you. See you on set tomorrow.

There were half a dozen of these folks with signs at the bottom of the escalator where we arrived, more than half of them dressed in the stereotypical garb of the limo driver. I spotted my guy holding a tablet with the name ANDREWS on it almost immediately.

It's funny how we see our own names so easily in a crowded mess.

They leap out at us, as if the text weren't normal text, but somehow highlighted or pulsing in a way to draw our attention.

My name virtually screamed out at me.

My guy was a large black man, mid fifties, dressed in a sharp-looking pinstripe black suit. He even had one of those black driver caps that you sometimes see. Prior to even spotting the sign I caught a whiff of recognition from the man who obviously recognized me; most likely from a photo that Anne had sent to the show runner which was likely relayed during the booking.

I walked over to him and smiled, sticking out my right

hand.

"I'm Michael Andrews," I said.

He lowered the sign and thrust out his own right hand. "Pleased to meet you, Mr. Andrews. My name is Andwele-Gahijii Abiyoe."

"Wonderful to meet you, er, Andwell..." I paused, unable to pronounce the name properly.

"Most people just call my Argyle," he said, beaming a huge smile at me.

"Argyle?" I said, returning a smile at him. Funny that Nancy and I had just been talking about the *Die Hard* movies. Argyle as the name of the young driver who picks Bruce Willis's character up at the airport in the first movie in the franchise. This guy was a few decades older and had a handsome chiseled face and a body that was definitely familiar with the gym. He looked nothing like the young, skinny and happy-go-lucky character from the movie. "You mean like...?" I started to ask.

But he finished my sentence. "The young black driver from *Die Hard*. Yes, exactly like that. I picked up the nickname many years ago when I first started this job. That was years before I started working out; I looked more like that actor then. It didn't hurt that I developed a reputation for liking to chat a lot, just like that character."

I laughed. "I had just been thinking about that movie. Well, not the first one. The second one. It happens to me virtually every time I travel by air."

"The two first films in the *Die Hard* franchise are among my favorite Christmas movies."

I liked this man. I thought we were going to get along

quite fine.

He then reached for my carry-on bag. "Please let me take your bag, Mr. Andrews."

I smiled politely. "It's okay, Argyle. I've got it. And, please, call me Michael."

"Very well, Michael," he said, and then turned, gesturing in the direction we should take. "This way, please."

Argyle led me out to where he had the short black limo parked.

Popping open the trunk, he took my bag from me and placed it inside, then opened the back door for me and I got in.

To be honest, even though it happened from time to time, particularly when I was doing things related to the movie versions of my books, I still wasn't used to the white glove treatment. That was something for other people, for celebrities and Hollywood stars, not for someone like me.

But I figured I should at least enjoy the moment while it lasted. After all, it wasn't every day that you were chauffeured around Los Angeles.

As the limo pulled away from the curb, Argyle turned.

"There is cold water in the console between the seats, if you would like, Mr. Andrews. And this morning's versions of the *L. A. Times,* the *Los Angeles Daily News* and *Los Angeles Sentinel.*"

"Thank you," I said. "And, please, call me Michael. I insist."

"Yes, of course. I keep forgetting.

"I read about you when this assignment came in. It's an important thing to understand a bit about my clients so that I can anticipate their needs.

"You're in town for a movie shoot for *Tome of Terror* which is based on your book."

"Yes," I said. "My agent thought it would be good for me to get out of New York for a while and do something a little different."

"You were in a rut?" Argyle asked.

"Yeah, something like that." Even though he was genuine in his question; he wasn't just being polite—he really cared about the answer—and he was also natural and easy to talk to, I wasn't about to get into the situation with Gail.

"Ah," Argyle said. "It must be related to a woman."

I grinned but said nothing. How the heck did he know? Did Argyle have an uncanny sense of reading people or something?

"It is a woman, isn't it?"

I laughed. "Bingo."

"Thought so."

"How did you know, Argyle? I haven't said more than a dozen words."

"I've become adept at being able to read people just through the inflection in their voices. I could tell in the way you responded to my question. A very subtle shift in your tone. Being a driver, I can't really spend much time reading facial nuances or body language—so I've learned to pick up on the changes and inflections in a person's voice.

"It is definitely a handy skill that I have honed through years of practice and experience."

"Well, you're a natural at it, Argyle. You picked up on that quite effectively."

"It's what I do," he said and grinned that infectious grin he had given me when we first met inside the airport.

Only a moment in silence passed before he spoke again.

"If you're looking for something interesting to do, I know of a few spots that are slightly off of the beaten tourist path but will be near where you are staying."

"I'm all ears, my friend."

"If you're into live music, there's an act playing tonight at The Hotel Café. It's on Cahuenga Boulevard just off Hollywood Boulevard. You get in along the side of the building, in an entrance off the alley. It's one of the best live music spots for up-and-coming indie musicians.

"One of my favorite local musicians, at least when she's not traveling and doing Hallmark holiday movies, is the pianist, Alicia Witt."

"Don't think I've ever heard of her."

"My wife introduced me to her music. She's not as well-known as a musician, but she has an amazing array of songs. You might recognize her from a few things she has appeared in over the years. She was on the television shows Two and a Half Men, Twin Peaks, Friday Night Lights. Oh, and last year she made quite a splash on an episode of The Walking Dead."

I watched The Walking Dead but wasn't familiar with

the other ones he'd mentioned. "Haven't seen most of those shows."

"Let's see. She played the teenage daughter on Cybill. Do you remember that show that featured Cybill Shepherd in the nineties, not long after the stint on Moonlighting—you know speaking of Bruce Willis. See, things can all be connected. In any case, Tom Wopat, Luke from The Dukes of Hazard, was also on that program. Witt played Cybill's teenage daughter.

"She has been in a number of movies, too. She had a part in *Two Weeks Notice* with Hugh Grant and Sandra Bullock, and played opposite Al Pacino in *88 Minutes*. Oh, and, of course, she was also on one season of Law & Order: Criminal Intent."

I wasn't much of a television watcher, but the cross-references put an image in my head; I remembered enjoying the Cybill sitcom when I was younger.

"She's a redhead, isn't she?"

"Yes."

"Yeah, I think I know who you are talking about. I recognize her as an actor. But I had no idea she was also a musician."

"The reason I bring her up is that if you want a real treat, I know that she is playing at The Hotel Café tonight. It's definitely worth dropping in and checking out."

"Thanks, Argyle. I appreciate the tip."

"Oh, I've got plenty of other tips and suggestions, my friend."

"I'm all ears."

"Okay then. Now, I know you write thrillers that have

a lot of disturbing murders in them. And you mentioned that you've watched *The Walking Dead*. Does this mean that you are a fan of perhaps darker things?"

"Stephen King is one of my favorite writers."

"How about beer? Do you enjoy a good beer?"

"I'm not much of a drinker, but I do like to sample things that are produced locally. Local music, local coffee, local beer and wine, I suppose, can also be part of that."

"Okay, then. I'm going to suggest a place that not only has some interesting locally produced beers, but they also have a decent small menu of similarly crafty food items. But the most intriguing thing about the place is the décor and the theme; I think it's based on the fact that the place is allegedly haunted.

"Inspired by that, and a delight for old horror films, the owners have incorporated a very eerie theme to the place, complete with skeletons and scythes and candles glowing within fake human and animal skulls.

"It is quite the macabre spot, and certainly something to behold. Who knows, it's the type of place that just might inspire you to write an odd and eerie murder scene for one of your next books.

"It's called Skull Crusher Brewery, and it's just off Highway 110 heading through South Los Angeles in Gardena.

"I can guarantee you'll see nothing like it anywhere else."

"It sounds like quite the place," I said.

"If you're not as daring and want to try out an excellent selection of local beers, might I suggest a small and unassuming bar not all that far from Playa Del Rey.

"It's called Gulp Restaurant and Brewpub. There are three locations, but the one with the most character, and the most characters, is the one in Playa Vista. Not far from where I live, which is how I found out about it.

"It's far cleaner and far more mainstream than Skull Crusher, but they spotlight quite a few local and innovative breweries on their thirty-six taps. And if you go there, be sure to ask for local regular Lex. Lex usually sits at the bar and knows so much about the local beer, local culture and local music scene. Well worth the visit."

"Thank you, Argyle. That is quite the wealth of information you have passed along in such a short time. I'm hoping I can remember it all."

He let out a quick infectious laugh. "Oh, don't worry. In that console beside you there's also a set of my business cards. It has my cell phone number on it. Please don't hesitate to use it at any time if there's anything I can ever do for you while you are in town."

"That's quite generous of you. Thank you, my friend."

"It is my pleasure, Michael. My pleasure indeed. I do aim to please, after all."

I sat back in the seat and enjoyed the fact that Argyle was the one driving and not me. I liked him. He was easy to talk to and loved to share. He reminded me, in fact, of Buddy, a traveling salesman friend I had met and gotten to know when he'd picked me up hitchhiking my way to New York all those years ago. Buddy loved to chat—although his chats were more of a non-stop monologue; but he was entertaining and informative and had proven to be helpful to me over the years. Particularly if I think about the way his car had appeared just as that wolf had leapt out from the forest on the side of the highway and begun to attack me. Had Buddy not shown up, I might have been that wolf's meal rather than this hybrid mammal I have evolved into.

"Los Angeles is definitely a fun and exciting place to be," Argyle said after perhaps less than a minute of silence. "There is so much to explore. I recommend you enjoy the riches of as many neighborhoods as possible. People think of this city as one large bustling megacity, but it's really a unique blending of so many distinct and unique neighborhoods.

"But I will tell you one thing that you need to be careful about."

"What's that?"

"The recent activities of the PFA. The *Proud Fighters for America*. Have you heard about them?"

"Yeah. In fact, I recently read a bit about them in a newspaper article."

"They have become far more active, particularly in the past month. You can't be too careful where you hang out because they strike quickly and ruthlessly. Just be mindful."

That's twice this group had come to my attention in the past few hours. I'm not one to believe in premonition, but, heck, I know that there are strange things operating within this world—the wolf blood flowing through my veins, for example—so I wasn't one to immediately dismiss such things.

I'm a writer, after all.

I know a blatant smattering of foreshadowing when I see it.

Chapter Ten: The Highs and Loews of Hollywood

Argyle dropped me off at Loews Hollywood Hotel, which was right off the main strip of Hollywood Boulevard.

By the time we arrived, he had educated me in the fact that, despite California and Los Angeles being known for the palm trees, only a single type of tree was native to the region. Most of them were ornamental imports, with a massive effort that boomed in the 1930s. In 1931, the forestry division of Los Angeles had planted more than 25,000 palm trees and put over four hundred unemployed men to work.

He also informed me that Frank Sinatra—interesting how he had also come up earlier in the day—has stars in three different categories on the Hollywood Walk of Fame; one for film, one for television, and one for music. The same was true for other stars from that era, including Bing Crosby, Dean Martin, and Mickey Rooney. Gene Autry is the only person to have stars in five categories. A walking encyclopedia, Argyle explained that in order for a star to obtain a spot on the Walk of Fame, they must be nominated and go through an annual application process. The application needs a sponsor who will agree to pay the $40,000 for the star which covers the construction, installation, and maintenance for the star; and, if the celebrity is still alive, they need to be in attendance, ideally, bringing along a bit of a fanfare to the unveiling ceremony.

Before I left the limo, I had to ask him if he was possibly related to Buddy Samuels, that trivia-spouting traveling salesman friend of mine. The two seemed like they'd been cast in the same mold.

"Not that I'm aware of," Argyle said. "Of course, stranger things have happened, my man."

I thought about how Buddy had been the one who drove me in to the Big Apple, and Argyle had been the one to deliver me to Hollywood; each of them filling my noggin with trivia, statistics and insight, delivered in the friendliest way. Each offering assistance that went above and beyond.

"Indeed, they have," I agreed.

"Enjoy your stay in LA. And listen, Michael. Like I said, you have my card. Do not hesitate to call me if you need anything. Anything at all."

As I watched the limo pull away, heading north up North Highland Avenue, I figured I'd likely be seeing him again. I hoped I would see him. He was a good guy. And then I just stood there for a moment, marveling at the view of the famous sign in the Hollywood hills that was clearly visible up in that same direction.

I checked in to the hotel, made it up to my room,

dropped my bag, took my sports coat off and flopped on my back on the king-sized bed.

I was exhausted. Flying took a lot out of me.

And, with the time difference, after my six-hour flight, though it was 3 PM back home it was just a little after noon local time.

I laid there on the bed, thinking I might have a quick nap. But my mind was racing like wildfire; I was in Hollywood. I was here to be on the set of the second book of mine to be made into a movie. But not just to visit the set, but to take an active part in the production. Although, admittedly, I had no idea what a script consultant did, it was still a pretty thrilling premise.

After about ten minutes, realizing I wasn't going to sleep, I got up, went into the bathroom, splashed some water on my face, then grabbed my sports coat and left.

By the time I got to the elevator I had ordered an Uber to take me to the set and only needed to wait about a minute when I exited the front lobby doors before it arrived.

The info pack Anne had provided me that contained what I needed to know about the set—which was still upstairs in my laptop bag—had me scheduled to be on set first thing in the morning tomorrow, but I figured it never hurt to get there a day early and introduce myself. Why not meet some of the cast and crew members and take the time to become accustomed to things a little? It couldn't hurt.

As we moved through the streets on our way to the studio in Culver City, I marveled at the sights, where I was, why I was there, and the location I was heading to.

As we drove down palm-tree-lined boulevards, I remembered the details Argyle had shared to me about their import to this area and smiled.

I think I held that smile on my face the entire drive to the studio, and it might have even grown larger as I took in the gates to the studio. But the grin fled my face the way a delinquent rock-throwing young boy flees the scene a split second after his rock connects with the glass of the window not too long after I arrived there.

"Andrews," I said to the security guard at the gate to the sprawling studios which went on for about ten city blocks, looking like a giant fortressed compound. "Michael Andrews."

The guard himself was as imposing as the large white walls surrounding the studio grounds; and his face was an odd shade of pale that I hadn't yet spotted in the locals here so far. "I don't see your name on the list anywhere," he said. He was impatient with me and I could tell he thought I was a liar, likely a tourist trying to sneak into the studios.

"Could you double check your list for *Tome of Terror*? I'm the author of the book it was based on."

I smelled the irritation growing on him when I said that. It was partially because I seemed to be telling him what his job was; but partially because I sensed he had a lot of writers, or wannabe writers, trying to get past these gates.

Some of the folks who worked at the studio and were coming and going through the entrance were giving off

similar scents of irritation. One of them was more empathetic in nature. But I can only imagine how many people
desperately wanted to get into this place.

"I told you I already looked."

"Maybe it's under my agent's name. Mack Halpin."

He glared at me; it was a look I would have felt the
chill from even if I hadn't been able to smell and hear the
fine-tuned way I can. His steel-wool blue eyes would
have scoured through the thickest of skins.

"I don't have a Michael Andrews here. And I don't
have a Mick Halpin."

I knew he was lying and didn't know the second name
I'd just offered; and not just from the fact he got Mack's
first name wrong. He was convinced I was some sort of
fraud.

"I—"

"Excuse me," a gruff male voice from my right-hand
side interrupted. I recognized it coming from one of the
empathetic smelling people I'd picked up on. "Did I hear
you say you were Michael Andrews?"

I looked over at the man, who was white, middle aged,
with a bit of a Jeffrey Dean Morgan look to his eyes and
cheekbones, short white hair and a thick dark beard. He
carried with him a scent of red maple wood shavings, the
tangy scent of white glue, along with a bit of tomato, Di-
jon mustard and pastrami, from the sandwich in the
white takeout bag he was holding.

"Uh, yeah," I said.

"I thought I recognized you," he said, putting out his

hand. "Pleased to meet you, Michael. I'm Craig Tomp-kins. Lead Carpenter for *Tomes of Terror*."

I shook his hand. He had a firm grip; strong, calloused hands.

He turned toward the security guard.

"Hey John. This guy is legit. I don't think we were ex-pecting him on set until tomorrow, though. You'll likely find him on the list for tomorrow through the next couple of weeks."

The guard's heightened aura of confrontation had set-tled down when Craig approached. He grimaced at me, but it was more a show of dominance than an actual feel-ing. Then he turned and grabbed a second clip board and consulted it. I could smell that he found my name even before he acknowledged it.

"Yeah. He's here." He looked up and glared at me again. "But he's not on the list for today."

"Can you please add him as my guest for today?"

"Yeah. Just need some ID."

I handed him my passport, and he set about copying something down onto the clip board. "Thank you, Craig."

"Don't mention it. So, what brings you to the set a day early?"

"Well, I was here. And, admittedly, I'm pretty pumped about the whole thing. I've never been a script consultant before, and I figured it might be good to famil-iarise myself with the location the day before I officially start. Besides, I've always had a thing about being late; I'd rather be two hours early for something versus being one minute late."

Craig laughed. It was a unique laugh; husky and deep, like his voice, but it carried a jovial nature to it that was as pleasing as the matching disposition that exuded out of him. He came across as a down-to-earth sort of man who enjoyed life, enjoyed people, enjoyed all the moments.

"Early bird. I get it."

"Okay," the security guard said, hanging me a plastic nametag with a metal clip on it. "Here's your security pass tag. You need to wear this somewhere visible at all times.

"Will do," I said. "Thanks."

"Thank you, John," Craig said. Then he turned back to me. "C'mon, eager beaver, let me give you a lay of the land 'round these parts."

Craig then gave me a mini tour of the studio grounds on our way to the main building for our film project. He pointed out where television shows like Jeopardy and Wheel or Fortune were shot, as well as Lorimar-Telepictures, responsible for about two hundred different television shows and movies. He highlighted many of the programs he had been involved in, in the various roles and tasks he had taken on over the years, before he reached his current role of lead carpenter. He had worked as a scenic carpenter, for example, on *Print of the Predator*, the other Maxwell Bronte novel of mine to have been adapted into a film.

I also learned that he, like me, was originally from Canada. He grew up in British Columbia, on Canada's west coast, in a rural community, enjoying all the outdoors activities of hunting, fishing, skiing. He had fallen in love with carpentry when helping his father build a large two-story utility shed in their back yard. He started working on the set of some smaller productions filmed in the Vancouver area, often referred to as Hollywood North. That eventually led him south, where he slowly worked his way up within this studio. He had also been offered opportunities to move even further up, but he had been less interested in management positions because he preferred to have a more hands-on and interactive approach.

When he had been working on *Print of the Predator,* he had taken an interest in the fact it was based on a novel by a Canadian author. So he had picked it up to give it a read and then gone on to read all the rest of my novels. He was a bit of a fan, had even seen my appearance on *Late Show with David Letterman* a few years earlier.

"Are you still with that hot babe who appeared on that show with you?" he asked, flipping me a wink. He had been referring to Gail, of course, who had accompanied me to the set of Letterman, and been incorporated into a short bit on the show during my appearance. Of course, while Craig, and the rest of the other viewers of that show had seen a bit of banter between Gail and I and David, none of them had witnessed the deadly fight involving Gail and I and another werewolf that ended up happening shortly after backstage while the rest of the show was still recording.

"No," I said. "In fact, we weren't actually *together* back

then, either. Dave was just having a bit of fun with me. Gail and I were just friends. We are still just friends."

It was something that I said a lot, over the years, to plenty of people. But it was something that was starting to sink in. I had always said it while maintaining a bit of a hopeful feeling that, eventually, things would come around and we would return to being lovers, to being a couple. But it was becoming painfully clear that I had been holding out for something that just wasn't in the cards.

"That's too bad."

"Yeah. Yeah. That's really too bad."

As he walked along, Craig reached into the white bag he'd been carrying and pulled out two halves of a hunk of crusty subway style of bread that was crammed beyond capacity with a couple of inches of shaved pastrami that was bursting out on all sides, the way a portly midlife crisis man's midsection fatty flesh might spill out around all sides of a Speedo brand swim brief. "Hope you don't mind if I eat this in front of you. I've got to eat this before I get back to the set. Lots to catch up on."

"No. It's fine. Go ahead."

"Actually, are you hungry? Do you want the other half of my sandwich? These guys make the best deli sandwich in Culver City." He then opened his mouth large enough to sink his teeth into it.

The smell of that sandwich was even stronger outside of the bag. It smelled amazing. I realized that, apart from a few cookies and pretzels I'd had on my flight, I hadn't eaten since breakfast. That breakfast with Nancy. Thinking about her made me smile. Perhaps there was some hope for a love life after Gail. But thinking about that morning also reminded me how long it had been since I'd had any food, and I really was hungry.

"You mean that's only half of the sandwich?"

He nodded, his mouth still full.

"No," I said. "But thanks for the offer."

There was a pause while he swallowed his first bite.

"You sure? I don't mind at all. I wasn't all that hungry, I just really had a hankering for Johnnie's Pastrami. It's quite a hike from the studio, but I think I needed the walk as much as I needed a taste of their legendary sandwich."

"Well, when you put it that way, how could I possibly resist? Sure, I'd love the other half."

He handed me the other half of the meat-loaded sandwich and while I was in awe of how it was held together in a similar physics-defying miracle of a guy who should never be caught dead in a Speedo®, that's where the similarities stopped. The more you looked at it, the greater your sense of hunger. Whereas with the old guy in the tight swimwear, well, the more you looked at it, the more you regretted the fact that there are some things you can never unsee.

I took my first bite of the pepper-encrusted, coriander infused smoky meat masterpiece, and, admittedly, I'm not sure if I can remember the next minute or so of conversation.

But I'm pretty sure we didn't have any conversation; that's how absorbed we both were in that magnificent sandwich.

We continued walking, without exchanging words, as we finished off the shared marvel of the sandwich world. A few times, as we walked, Craig wordlessly pointed out a few interesting sights along the way with a subtle elbow gesture or a nod, including a few big-name Hollywood and television personalities that were easily recognizable. They walked past just like any person on the street would, a few of them nodding or smiling as we walked past. One addressed Craig by name.

I couldn't imagine any of them being able to walk down a crowded city street in the same nonchalant way. They would have been mobbed by adoring fans. But here, on a closed studio lot property, they could move about without the trepidation and anxiety that likely came with just wanting to get by.

Lyrics from the Rush song "Limelight" came to me. It was a song in which the band's lyricist and drummer, Neil Peart, reflected on his discomfort with the celebrity life; particularly given that all he wanted to do was his job as a musician to the best of his ability, and then just enjoy living as an average person who blended into the crowd. I'd never really understood how Peart must have felt when he wrote those lyrics until just now, as I got to see a few larger-than-life celebrities getting to have that sense of normal that the rest of the world takes for granted.

"Well, that was amazing," I said, after swallowing down my last bite.

"The sandwich or having just walked past half a

dozen Hollywood big names?"

"There were celebrities?" I asked.

He laughed, then pointed out a building up ahead on our right. "Okay, this is us."

I took a deep breath as we went inside from the bright afternoon sunlight into the comparatively darker studio building. This would be the first time I would be setting foot onto a real Hollywood production studio for a film being made from one of my books. I had briefly been to the set from the previous film, but that had been one of the on-location scenes and it was more of a cordial token "author visit." This was a studio in Los Angeles. This was me coming to the set not for a brief visit, but to spend a few weeks in the role of script consultant.

I wish I could have held onto that moment. The thrill and wonder of being on that studio lot, comfortable with a new friend I'd just made; the smoky, peppery taste of the pastrami sandwich I'd just eaten still on my lips and tongue.

Because what happened shortly after that was pretty much all downhill. Well not all of it; but the things that mattered to me in the moment.

As we got into the studio and started making our way about, I was reminded of being backstage in the theater; because that's a bit of what walking around the set area was like. There were risers and unfinished rough backings to the front of set fixtures that were made to look like living rooms, bedrooms, kitchens, and offices; at least on one side. They always made me think of those false front facades that were popular in the Old West. I was taken back to some of my earlier days working backstage at my university's theater group, and it also made me wonder what might happen if I'd kept up my interest in the theatre. Would I have written screenplays instead of novels? Would I have continued to experiment with the short stint of acting I had tried out and quite enjoyed, in a few of the smaller studio theater shows from back in the day.

Along the way, Craig introduced me to several other crew members who were, mostly, quite pleasant and personable and gave off a friendly and welcoming scent, particularly after learning I was the author of the book for this film adaptation.

As we made our way through the maze of set structures, I imagined what it might be like to come to work at a place like this; if my current role of script consultant might lead to the opportunity of doing more work like this; combining my love for writing with my long-lost passion for theatrical performances. Would working on movies bring the same thrill that the theater did? Did the thrill of the theatre have more to do with the live audience everyone—actors, stage crew, technicians—was collaborating on? Or did that heightened emotion come from the act of working on creating and performing an imaginative act, a three-dimensional storytelling experience? Would I get those same highs from working on a movie?

I should have known, before we rounded that last set structure, because I could already smell the anger, impatience, and tension exuding from one specific male. The scents of most of the others nearby contained hints of trepidation and fear. Even Craig's scent began to taint, in just the slightest of ways, toward nervousness.

At some other time, I could blame the fact I was in the phase furthest from the full moon cycle and my senses were not at full capacity. But not today. It was more likely I was simply moved by the emotions of my university theater day memories and the wonder of being on a Hollywood set.

Because when we rounded that corner, I should have been on alert of what to expect, but it caught me completely unawares.

I don't think I could have been more surprised, in fact, if someone on the other side of that last set façade we passed had been hiding in wait to jump out and slap me in the face with a rancid trout.

"Who the hell is this?" a high and whiny nasal voice said in a loud voice. It shockingly came from a surprisingly short and rotund bald man with a chunky face, bulbous nose and long white beard who was thrusting an accusatory pudgy finger in my direction.

If there hadn't been what looked like a permanent scowl etched across his face, he might have passed for a Santa Claus left in the dryer too long. It took me a second to connect the voice to the person, because of the complete mismatch between voice and appearance. He looked more like someone who should have a deep voice, perhaps a throaty voice. I quickly surveyed the room to see if I was being punked and if this guy was in cahoots with someone else playing a game of ventriloquism.

But I wasn't being punked. The anger had been coming from this man, whose level of annoyance matched the vile with which he had directed his words, and that stumpy-fingered hand, at me.

"JP," Craig said, "This is Michael Andrews."

JP? Did I hear Craig say that right? Oh yes, that white beard, that look. Of course, this was JP Heartschwinger, the esteemed and multi-award-winning director hired to work on this film. According to the press I had read, he was one of the hottest directors currently in demand for thriller pictures, whose previous handful of films had all been box-office sensations. I had only seen a few pictures of him, which must have been photoshopped, or taken at very construed angles—or maybe the photos were of a much younger and slimmer man—because none of them relayed the almost grotesque fatty layers of the man's face. Nor just how short he was. Tom Cruise would have towered over him the way Hagrid towered over Harry Potter and all of his Hogwarts friends. He might have been able to look down at Danny DeVito, but not by much.

"So? Why the fuck should I care?"

Craig was as taken aback and shocked as I was.

"Er, he is the author of the novel *Print of the Predator.*"

JP scowled in my direction. The combined odor of anger, annoyance, impatience, and intolerance he was firing in my direction on all cylinders increased as he stared at me.

"Andrews," he muttered. "Andrews, Andrews, Andrews. You're not supposed to be here until tomorrow."

He turned to the tall and beautiful blonde assistant to his right, whose scent relayed a strong confidence; she seemed to be the only person in that room who wasn't afraid of him. "Velma, what time was he supposed to meet with me?"

"10:30 to 11:00 AM."

"Strike that from my calendar. That gives me half an hour back. Book in my foot massage in that spot. I've met him. Check that off my list. I can tell him, right now, what I had planned on saying tomorrow."

He then looked back to me.

"Listen Andrews. It might have been your book, but it's my work of art now. It's my film, my script, my cast, my crew; and I won't tolerate another disruption on my set from an unwelcome outsider. You're only here because of an obligation the studio made that is out of my hands to give you a bullshit superficial title, and a grandiose tourist role on this set.

"The fried egg sandwich I had for breakfast today is going to have more of an impact on the artistic direction of this film than you ever will. So make sure you check your New York Times bestselling writer ego at the door. You might be able to hack your way through print media. But this is a multi-dimensional production, and something you know bupkis about.

"I'm the king and grand master of this little empire. And if you ever get in my way, interrupt me again, or if I hear that you have attempted to offer any of your pedestrian opinions on the script, or this production even to the sandwich cart girl on this lot, you'll be sent packing so hard your head will still be spinning when you land your ass back in New York.

"Capisce?"

I stood there, likely with my lower jaw extended so far down that I might have been able to tap it with the tops of my toes if I had been barefoot.

The set was completely silent as the air filled with a chorus of scents of discomfort. Not surprise, though. Nobody in the room, except for me, was at all surprised, suggesting this was a typical outburst from the man; something they had all become entirely used to. There was a scattering of sympathetic vibes coming from a few of the people there, including Craig, whose scent was also giving off an air of disappointment and regret at having put me into that position.

It hadn't been his fault, of course. He had been eager to greet me and enthusiastic about introducing me to the cast and crew.

"I understand," I said after a moment of that awkward silence. "I'm sorry."

"You better be."

He then directed his attention to Craig.

"And you. Bringing him here? Who the fuck do you think you are, you glorified Bob Vila? Bob the fucking Builder, more like. You're giving studio tours when you should be working on the art gallery set. Is it finished yet?"

"It is," Velma offered before Craig could reply. "We have it on the schedule for you to review at 4:30 today."

"Fine. Just let me tell you this, Mr. Carpenter Boy. I

better love it. Every single square inch of it. Because if I don't, you'll be lucky to get a job sweeping sawdust."

Craig nodded silently, his scent filled with disappointment more than ridicule. I suppose that he, and the others, had become used to this type of behavior and words coming from the little man.

But it was bothering me.

How could this monster of a person be attacking Craig? I was perfectly okay to be put in my place when he was deriding me; but this attack on the well-intentioned Craig was infuriating.

I had been about to open my mouth in defense of Craig, but he cast me a quick sideways glance that said *don't*—the message, if not already clear by the look on his face, came through with every fiber of his scent. I picked up a very distinctive sense of: *Don't. It'll make things worse. Just let it go. Just let the storm pass.*

It was a good thing I had plenty of practice riding out Mack Halpin's tirades; because I choked those words back and stood there in silence, while the beady-eyed little man took turns glaring at me and at Craig.

After another few beats of silence, he threw his arms up in the air.

"Oh fuck! Now I've got a headache. I can feel my blood pressure ready to explode. I need to lie down in a dark room. Velma, bring me my pills."

He then stormed off with a dramatic flair, and the cast and crew that had been standing in baited silence continued to move about their business, their emotions relaying that this, too, was already a typical occurrence they had been used to.

"So, that's JP," Craig said with a wry grin on his face. "I should have known better. I thought maybe, given your role, the fact that you're from outside the industry. he might have treated you differently than he treats everyone else on this production."

"Well, at least he's consistent. I'm sorry that I got you in trouble with him."

"Oh," Craig laughed. "That's nothing. It's just the way he is. His bark is far worse than his bite. That's got to be the tenth time I've been threatened with being fired, or demoted, or thrown off the set. I think the only person I haven't seen threatened in that way would be Velma."

"She didn't seem frazzled by him at all."

"She's a tough cookie. Holds her own quite nicely."

I could tell that, on top of the basic admiration and respect he held for Velma, he was sweet on her.

"C'mon," he said. "Let me go find the show runner who has been assigned to you."

Chapter Eleven: A Woman with Definite Talent, Charm, Humility, Compassion, Humor, and Witt

A rgyle was right. Alicia Witt was an amazing presence.

She owned the entire room.

No, she didn't own it—*own* is too harsh of a word for the experience—so much as she embraced and nurtured it.

And that's not just an expression.

I smelled the nurturing and compassionate essence exuding from the beautiful red headed woman who sat alone on the small stage behind a keyboard. When she moved and played the keyboard, it wasn't so much an instrument as it was an extension of herself. And that's exactly how she treated it. Even when hammering out a vigorous rhythm that required intense quick strikes of the keys, she demonstrated an element of caressing and loving to the ebony and ivory topped instrument.

And I could feel the conjoined reaction to her performance in the heartbeats, breaths, and scents coming off my fellow patrons in the club.

They weren't just listening attentively to her music; they were absorbing the entire experience. Their heartbeats were practically beating to the rhythms she shared from the stage.

Even between songs, when Witt would share a little story or a few words about the song she was about to perform, the audience was with her, following the narrative, attending to everything she said, sipping their own cocktails when she sipped—she alternated between sipping from a tall glass of water and a tumbler of bourbon—and hanging on her every word.

And I was too. It was a welcome change of pace, scenery, and experience for me.

After what had turned out to be a disappointing and embarrassing afternoon on the movie set, despite lead carpenter Craig's kind spirit and generosity, I had gone back to the hotel even more morose.

I'd been recently rejected by Gail, after holding on to years of this hopeful feeling we might get back together. And then faced a humiliating rejection by the director of the film. And here I'd thought working on this movie set might be a distraction, some sort of new start for me. Heck, for a short time when Craig was walking me through the one warehouse building, my university years theater flashback even had me imagining working in this area.

But I'd found out what the role of script consultant really meant. It was a token, symbolic role, and didn't really mean any involvement or active participation. I didn't want symbolism, or window dressing. I wanted something to sink my teeth into. Something to help keep me from sitting alone and just dwelling on Gail.

That's when I had remembered Argyle telling me about the Hotel Café, and that Alicia Witt would be playing there tonight.

I figured getting out, experiencing something new, would be just the thing I might need to distract me from the disappointment and overall feeling of sadness.

The Hotel Café was an intriguing and cozy little club. You had to get into it from an alley entrance, which added to the charm of the place. Relatively small inside, with stylish decorative curtains, a long bar in the corridor led to the small room I was sitting in. There were six small round tables, and a modest dance floor that led to a foot-and-a-half-tall riser that was the stage platform boxed in by red curtains.

I sat by myself at one of the little round tables just off to the left and a few feet back from the side of the stage. I'd given up the two other chairs from my table to the strangers on my right; a friendly and amorous group who were obviously personal friends of the performer, based on the way she regularly interacted with them and called them out between songs.

But one thing that was so unique about this woman is how she could acknowledge and address her friends without making the other patrons in the space feel left out. She was inclusive and sweet in her approach, so gracious for the hearty and energetic applause at the end of each song and took the time to make eye contact individually with everyone there.

She was at home in front of the keyboard she sat behind. And she radiated a warmth, love, and appreciation for the audience that I'm sure I would have been able to feel even without my enhanced wolf senses.

She finished an upbeat sounding yet hard-hitting song that Witt said was her "girl power" song *About Me* to raucous applause, beamed a glowing and beautiful smile with a warmth that she radiated to every single person in the room, wordless smiled and waited for the clapping and cheers to abide.

"This one is off of *Revisionary History*," she said, then started in on a slower song. The first word of the song began in perfect time to the first note.

I'm not looking for
What you think I am,
I should let you down gently.

Nothing I can do to lose my mind.
You're too close to reaching
What I never want to find.

You can look but you won't find me I'm
Already gone
You can't tell I hide it well and I
Keep moving on
I'm already gone.

And that was it. I was gone. Taken right into the moment. I was listening to those words as if they were Gail speaking to me. I couldn't stop, and didn't even try to prevent, the tears that started blurring my vision and streaming down my face.

I kept listening, though, feeling the music, feeling the moment, feeling the complete and utter compassion and care that Witt poured into the song.

But also feeling as if this was a message from Gail to me. In some bizarre and supernatural way that the universe is connected—and God knows, I should understand that better than anyone, with the supernatural wolf blood running through my veins—this song was Gail, still back in New York, and speaking to me in words she could not find but needed to express.

She had tried to tell me, but I wasn't listening to her. I wasn't listening to what she had been trying to tell me for almost two years. Because I was attending too much to her feelings and emotions for me which I could easily sense; but not attending to what she needed to do for herself.

This song was speaking to me. In the deep and meaningful way that I wouldn't let happen.

Can't sit still and I
Can't run fast enough
Nothing's ever come easy.

Hard to hold the dam from breaking free.
And all the lies I've left behind
Come pouring out of me.

At this point, I could sense a subtle shift in Alicia Witt's emotions. She had noticed me sitting there quietly bawling. I couldn't see more than the blurry image of her on the stage, but I felt the care, concern, worry, and compassion pouring out of her in my direction. She was genuinely empathetic to me.

It felt like she was channeling Gail.

And, again, as the rest of the song came out and she finished, it wasn't Alicia Witt singing so much as Gail speaking directly to me.

You can look but you won't find me I'm
Already gone
You can't tell I hide it well and I
Keep moving on
I'm already gone

Didn't know what we were getting into
No one ever does until it ends

You can look but you won't find me I'm
Already gone
You can't tell I hide it well and I
Keep moving on
I'm already gone

Tears were still freely flowing down my face as the song ended and the crowd cheered. I was sad, finally acknowledging that things were over with Gail; finally starting to accept them.

It was a beautiful and bittersweet moment.

Alicia offered her thank you to the crowd, but I could still sense the concern and worry she was subtly pushing in my direction. She then seemed to pick up on the fact that there was some comfort in that moment's catharsis for me.

"This next song," she said. "Is off that same album. And this one I would like to dedicate to someone here. You know who you are. I call this song *Friend*."

I felt her intent directly at me.

The song started up. It was another lovely ballad.

It was another song where Gail seemed to address me via Alicia.

It spoke of the type of love that two people can have that is deep and meaningful and something that would always be there for one's entire life; a love that was truly without end. But it was also a complicated type of love; one that was far more platonic in nature. It was of acknowledging the power and strength and uniqueness of what the other person brought to one's life and wanting to have that person as an ongoing companion, but just not in the traditional sense of partners and lovers.

It spoke to me of what I believe I had been ignoring from Gail.

The song seemed to come at the perfect time right after the previous one. Like the delivery of just the right appetizer before the main course of a meal.

Somehow, Alicia must have sensed what I was going

through. I understood, based on the essence of spontaneity that she'd given off immediately prior to playing the song, she had not intended on playing this song here at this point in the set, but later. On the fly, she had inserted this song here because she somehow felt it was what I needed at this moment.

And she was right.

The song ended with the lyrics that seemed to kick me into the proper frame of mind.

I would always love Gail.

She would always love me.

But she didn't want, couldn't want, the depth of the type of relationship I wanted to have with her. She wanted me around; she cherished having me in her life; but she needed to keep it at a distance to be her own person. She could never be one half of something; she could only be a whole person; but also needed me and my love in her life.

You're a road I never cleared a path for,
It's safe to say you made your own way over,
You're a gift I'd never dare to ask for,
I'm just askin you to stay.

'Cuz I don't wanna be your burden,
I don't wanna weigh you down,
I don't wanna make you hurt, I just wanna stay around.
I don't wanna turn you on, this ain't no start, no happy end.
I don't wanna be your promise, I just wanna be your friend.

The song finished, and fresh tears streamed down my face. But they were more tears of gratitude. Some way, somehow, Alicia Witt, a musician I had never really known about—not in any real sense—even just a few hours ago, had connected with me, felt something I needed from a person on the other side of the continent, and delivered it to me.

As the flow of tears subsided, I could see clearly now and spotted her glancing over at me.

"Thank you," I mouthed quietly, and nodded my head in her direction.

"You're welcome," she said under her breath before taking a sip of her water. Nobody else could hear her, of course, except me.

Those two songs, played back-to-back, created such an incredible purging moment of all the pain, anxiety and grief over a lost relationship I'd been holding onto for these past few years. It was as if the music, the musician, the moment of being alone so far from home, that last in person conversation I'd had with Gail, all of it, had come crashing through. I'd been able to release it all, without shame or fear of judgment. A moment made possible due to a chance encounter with a limo driver's personal rec-ommendation that I go see this musician performing live.

For the rest of the show, with those high emotions acknowledged, affirmed, and then released, I could thor-oughly enjoy the musician's performance on its own merits. No, I wasn't over Gail, but I was on my way to finally accepting our relationship for what it was, rather than what I wanted it to be.

Witt continued to delight and fulfill the room, with every audience member seeming to hang on her every note, her every lyric, her every word between songs. And she was basking in their glowing adoration.

I had been to plenty of live concerts before, but never had I seen, heard, and felt such a sense of community, mutual respect, love, and adoration.

This was a magic moment. Something to behold.

But I imagined that this might just be what it was like whenever or wherever Alicia Witt performed.

She got to her closing number, *Anyway*, which was another one of her post-break-up songs, that started off slow, and then evolved into a hard-hitting, and fast-moving song. It became like an affirmation of accepting the end. The audience was moving to the hard-hitting song, and it seemed the perfect one to close with.

She finished, to roaring applause, thanked the crowd as they continued to cheer, stood up, bowed, put her hands up over her mouth—I found it so endearing that she seemed overwhelmed with their positive reaction; I mean how could she *not* know the effect she had on her audience?—and then slipped backstage through a thin crack in the red curtains.

The audience wouldn't stop. About a minute later, she slipped back out onto the stage, nodding, shaking her head, with a beautifully radiant smile on her face, and then sat back down at the keyboard.

"Thank you so much," she said, as the crowd finally calmed back down. "I know it's still summer, but soon summer will be gone. And the season kind of sneaks up on you. And even though every year I try, I often find that I'm—"

"I'm not ready for Christmas!" someone from the other side of the room shouted.

Alicia laughed—it was an infectious laugh that couldn't help but make you smile—and nodded her head. "Yes. That's right. I'm not ready for Christmas!"

Half of the room roared out a huge cheer.

Then she played a song that was obviously the one the audience member had shouted out and she had just repeated. That became apparent as the song opened.

Like the song she'd finished her set with, this one started off slow, and then, when she hit the chorus, it really picked up and became a rockin' tune. The crowd went nuts. I actually found myself laughing through the song. This was, obviously, the not-safe-for-radio version of the song that had a few explicit lines in it.

I found it such a fascinating and hilarious juxtaposition to hear someone who had such a sweet and genuinely soft demeanor sing that she needed a *fucking holiday* in the middle of a Christmas song.

The song finished, and we all stood up, cheering and clapping enthusiastically. The combined heightened passion and energy I could smell off the fellow audience members, the quickened and thrilled heartbeats was, to me, like another layer of the applause. I might have been the only one who could sense it, but Alicia seemed to also have picked up on it, even without any supernatural wolf abilities. She stood, took another few bows, told the audience she loved us, blew a few kisses, and then slipped off backstage to our continuing rapturous applause.

About a minute after we all sat down, as I was finishing my drink, Alicia slipped out from behind the curtains and came over to the group at the table beside mine. She took turns hugging them all and exchanging greetings with them; I tried not to listen but couldn't help overhearing. Three of them were dear friends—two of the others were partners of those friends that Alicia hadn't met before. She chatted with them while I admired the interaction of a group of people who were close with, admired, and cared for one another.

As she was chatting with her friends, a small group of fans clustered on the other side, eager to speak with Alicia.

One of the women from her group of friends pulled a now empty chair from the table on the other side and told Alicia to sit with them so they could buy her a drink. "Of course," she smiled, "But just give me a minute. I want to say hi to folks and thank them for coming. You know what I'll have to drink." And then she excused herself. She addressed the first person lined up in front of the stage. "Thank you guys so much. I'll be right over to chat with you. Just give me one minute, please." And then she stepped over to my table.

I stood up as she came over. Admittedly, I was a bit star struck. No, I wasn't all that familiar with her as an actress, but I had just watched one of the most masterful intimate and passionate performances ever; I was in awe of this amazing woman.

"That was incredible!" I said. "You, and your music

are amazing."

"Thank you," she said. "I really do love playing for people. I'm glad you enjoyed it."

"No, thank you, Alicia. I'm so glad I came out tonight." I said, and I offered my hand. "I'm Michael."

She took my hand and gave it a warm shake, then a fresh wave of warmth and compassion radiated off her. "How are you doing? Are you okay, Michael?"

I was a stranger, she had a group of friends to hang out with, there was a crowd of fans bustling to speak with her, and she approached a stranger she'd witnessed bawling at a table by himself. Talk about an empathetic gesture.

"Yeah," I said. "Recent breakup with someone really special. It was…hard. Your music really helped."

She nodded. Deeper empathy radiated out from her in my direction.

"I've had my share of pretty bad breakups myself, Michael. I channeled a lot of that into some of my songs. It can be a cathartic experience."

"It was cathartic hearing those songs."

"I'm glad it helped."

"It really did."

I felt myself tearing up again.

Alicia sensed that and stepped forward, wrapped her arms around me in such a loving and comforting hug. Her compassion, empathy, and concern were as warming as the friendly and soothing embrace.

"Thank you," I whispered repeatedly, as she held me. "Thank you."

She stood back, both her hands on my shoulders. "With every end, with every goodbye, we learn something about ourselves, Michael. We add a layer to the richness of our lives.

"You'll get through this. It's okay to spend some time mourning the loss of something special. If you have ever tried journaling, that might help. I know that when I write, it helps me."

"Thank you," I said again, smiling. "Yeah, I write."

"Good," she said, "It's good to express those feelings, to get them out. I find it helpful. But be careful. I know it's tempting to hang onto all those things that were good about the relationship. And it's okay to remember and cherish them. But don't hang on too tightly to them. That can continue to cause more harm, more hurt than good. And not allow you to move on. Not allow you to love yourself again. Love yourself first. Love regardless of the circumstances. Starting with love, staying with love."

"I quite love the way you put that. Your perspective."

She let out a nervous laugh. "I'm sorry. I don't know what came over me. I just stood here lecturing a stranger in his love life. I didn't mean to be so forward, so meddling. Nobody wants to hear me blathering on and giving them advice about love."

"No, don't be sorry. You did it with the most noble intentions, with kindness." I could, of course, read the genuine compassion in her intention. "And it actually helped. More than I can properly express."

"I'm glad to hear it." She then gave me another quick embrace. "Be good to yourself. Take care, Michael."

"Thank you, Alicia," I said.

She turned and moved over to the people that had lined up to speak with her.

As I sat back down and picked up my drink, I sensed an underlying eagerness Alicia had to just chill with the friends at the table who were waiting, somewhat impatiently, for her to finish her obligatory fan greeting. But that was a subtle aura compared to the essence of appreciation and adoration the woman had for her fans that beamed off her.

Yes, she wanted to hang out with her friends; but she also wanted to express her appreciation to the people who came to see her perform and had hung back and wanted to share an enthusiastic word with her.

She lived for sharing her music, her talent. She basked in the connection it gave her with others.

And she was making a positive difference.

She had my adoration, my respect. And I knew she had those things from both the friends who waited at that table and the line-up of fans eager to speak with her.

The music, the songs, the experience, had been cathartic, valuable, and much needed for me. But also experiencing the reaction from fans, witnessing the interaction she was now having as she attended, without distraction, to each of the people she was speaking with, was important.

This was something a writer never really got to take part in. There were book signings, and interactions with fans. But reading is a more personal and introspective experience, whereas music was communal.

But witnessing something like this, being able to experience the immediate reaction of fans to a performance, also heightened my own sense of worth as a creative person, as a writer.

No, I'd never properly get to experience anything like the magnificence of what I had just watched, just felt; but I knew that when someone read one of my works, we were having a connection. I was reaching them; and in a way that was unique to each individual that came to that page.

I grinned as I continued to watch Alicia interact with the beaming fans, her energy and enthusiasm to speak with them never wavering.

And I was thankful for the two things that this experience had offered me. An acceptance of my status in Gail's life; and a clearer understanding of my role as a writer.

I finished the last swallow of my drink and stood up.

Argyle had been so right about this.

But it was time to move on.

What was that other place he had been telling me about?

Skull Crusher Brewery. I definitely needed to check that out. And that beer bar. Gulp.

As I left The Hotel Café, I resolved to go visit both of those places.

But not tonight.

Tonight, I needed to go back to my hotel room, put a few tracks on repeat—maybe some Phil Collins; maybe add some Alicia Witt songs to that playlist—grab a few more drinks, have a good cry, and continue to purge these feelings out of my system.

Thursday, June 15, 2017

Chapter Twelve: The Scent, and Lack of Scent, of a Woman

T he next day on the movie set, the day that I was supposed to be there, was a much better experience. Better, of course, if you consider not being reamed out by one of Hollywood's hottest directors in front of nearly a dozen cast and crew members.

JP Heartschwinger was his typical short-tempered, overly demanding, and rude self. But not once did he have any sort of monstrously ugly hissy fit on me. In fact, we actually had a brief discussion that bordered on civil. Okay, to be honest, the conversation bordered on civil on one side, while the other adjacent nations might have been condescension and mockery. Not to mention, the country we were in was narcissism, and we were sitting in the capital city of arrogance, of which JP was the grand high Poobah.

The conversation we'd had, was a fifteen-minute monologue rather than a discussion. It was mostly JP asserting himself to be the best of this, the biggest of that, the most of something else, and the greatest of that other thing. He took credit for accomplishments that I'm pretty sure he had nothing to do with on previous blockbuster films, such as discovering and making a star out of celebrity names who'd been well known years before he'd ever worked with them. The thing about his grandiose misalignments with reality that was so striking was that most of them flew directly in the face of well documented facts and details that were already widely known and completely contrary to his statements. It was almost as if he were daring the person or group listening to him to challenge his authority or uniquely fictional version of reality.

What frightened me the most was that all the while, as I listened to him ramble on, boasting about his various accomplishments—the real ones sprinkled in along with the imagined ones—was that he actually honestly believed the bullshit he was spewing was real. There wasn't a single iota of the usual scent I picked up when someone was lying; not even a trace of the typical essence of fear that came when a person was consciously trying to deceive others.

Nazi propagandist Joseph Goebbels said that if you tell a lie big enough, and you keep repeating it, people will eventually believe it, and it will become the truth. Their truth, at least.

I had never met anyone like that in my life; or, at least, not since I had gained my extra-sensory abilities that allowed me to determine the emotive scents that often gave away a person's underlying feelings despite the masks we often put on.

And I never thought I would meet a person who would make the country's current president look so humble and honest. I'd never met that former reality television show host turned politician, but I worried, had

I ever been in his presence, if I might detect the exact same essence from him.

It might have been when JP was explaining to me how he had been the genius behind Maxwell Bronte's major character flaw, the one thing that propelled him to be an antiquities collector. Bronte, was, of course, my creation, and had existed in multiple books, an adapted film, and a television movie pilot, and that trait had already been explored in detail in all of them.

"Here's the genius of my interpretation of Maxwell Bronte which is going to make this movie the pinnacle of any of the other films or books," JP said, stroking his chin and looking at me, but not really seeing me as anything more than an audience ready to praise and admire him. "He was an orphan. Given up at birth. Though he had been adopted at a very young age, and raised by a set of loving parents, and thus has no memory of those earliest moments, he still holds this feeling of rejection, of inadequacy, of there being something missing. It was this that led him to collect antiques. It's this continued subconscious feeling of looking for something—that missing connection to his blood parentage—that drives him to collect, and, ultimately, to solve crimes.

"He can gather things around him; he can solve crimes, help others. But none of these things will ever satisfy that fundamental lacking that over-rides his entire being."

I sat there and nodded silently at him, not bothering to tell him he was practically quoting, verbatim, a line of dialogue right out of my novel *Tome of Terror*.

There was virtually no point in sharing, with this emperor, the fact that he was buck naked; perhaps it might be because, on top of having no clothes on, he was also sporting a delicately thin skin.

Apart from that meeting, I got to chat with several extremely talented members of the crew, and a few of the supporting cast members. They were all friendly, and gracious with their time, most of them similar in disposition to Craig, who took on the role, more actively than the show runner who was supposed to be my official escort.

I had shared with Craig how much I had enjoyed The Hotel Café the night before; that it had been a place recommended to me by Argyle. I mentioned the other two places Argyle had suggested I check out—Gulp, and Skull Crusher Brewery.

He hadn't ever been to, nor heard much about the brewery, but said he was familiar with Gulp; as it wasn't all that far from where he lived.

At the end of the day, Craig dropped me off on Inglewood Boulevard, which was not too far from the neighborhood he lived in. He offered to take me directly to Gulp, since he knew where it was and was familiar with the place, but I was quite fine with wanting to do some more walking and exploring.

Consulting the GPS on my map, I decided to head south on Inglewood and then head down South Centinela Avenue and over to Bluff Creek Drive. That route would be a picturesque walk and would take me past a few interesting spots, such as the Yahoo and YouTube Space complexes, the Hercules Campuses which contains multiple shooting studios, and titans like Google. I'd also pass the Spruce Goose Hangar where mogul Howard Hughes built his Spruce Goose aircraft in the 1940s.

I was not wrong about the fascinating walk. It was a

beautiful and hot late afternoon, and I was making my way along the drive and simply enjoying spotting so many of the iconic technology companies that had taken up residence there.

Not to mention, of course, the view of the bluff that ran along to the south, slowly gaining in height the further I walked. Along the way there were interesting sports fields and a tennis court and a playground and a dog park.

Based on the directions from the GPS on my phone, I knew I had to turn right and head north on South Seabluff Road, which was just past the spectacular view of Loyola Marymount University, a campus that was nestled on top of that hill.

It was just a couple of blocks up Seabluff where I had to turn left on Pacific Promenade. I made a mental note about the interesting looking little coffee shop called The Coffee Bean & Tea Leaf; but I was much too warm to think about a hot beverage.

No, as much as I wasn't that much of a drinker, I was certainly looking forward to a cold beer in a frosted glass to ease my thirst.

I found Gulp at the next corner. It boasted a small patio out front and inside there was a long narrow bar area with plenty of high-top tables throughout. An auditory layer of pop music nicely coated the restaurant, and there was enough of a crowd to create a soft rumble of blended conversations.

I walked over to the bar which was filled to capacity except for one seat.

To the left of the one empty bar stool was a spot where the servers likely picked up drinks from the bartender.

And to the right was a blonde woman in a dark blue dress with white polka dots who was engaged in a conversation with a man and a woman at the end of the bar and someone else who was standing beside the bar holding a drink. I wondered if the seat might belong to the gentleman who was standing, so I stood there, waiting to see if he would return to that seat.

Neither he nor any of his companions took notice of me. They continued to engage in their conversation. I could tell, from the scent coming off them, that they were deeply focused on the back-and-forth exchange taking place. They were discussing something about the local football team, tossing stats and speculation out like color commentators. They hadn't even noticed this stranger walking into their midst.

I wanted to ask if the seat was taken but wasn't successful in getting their attention.

The female bartender, a stunningly attractive woman with Hispanic features and long straight hair dressed in a black tank top with the stylized name of the place Gulp written in all lowercase letters across her left breast, smiled at me from across the bar.

"Sit wherever you like, Hon."

I pointed at the empty stool and then at the blonde woman in the blue polka-dot dress to my right. "I was wondering if you knew if this stool is empty or if it belongs to someone from this group."

"Nope, it's free and clear, sugar," she said to me and whisked a thin round cardboard coaster over to the spot then tapped her palm onto the top of the bar. "Help yourself." She slid a menu and drink list onto the bar and then also hooked a thumb over her left shoulder at a board on the wall across from the bar. "The drink list is here, but it's also written up there. Just let me know what you might like. My name is Kortney."

I slid onto the bar stool, and only taking a cursory look at the menu, said, "Thank you, Kortney. What do you recommend for a nice thirst quencher for a Canadian who is not used to this beautiful hot weather?" Yes, even though I lived in New York and it had a similar climate to the one I grew up in, I always thought it was more effective to stick with my Canadian roots rather than mention the metropolis I now lived it. It had a slight better effect in the grand scheme of things.

Americans tended to be nicer to Canadians than to Americans from other parts of their own country. Perhaps it was because, by default, they looked at us like younger, more innocent siblings.

There was a twinkle in her beautiful dark eyes, which came with a genuine feeling of empathy towards me. Maybe it was the mention of my Canadian heritage that warmed her to me. But a smile from a beautiful woman like that certainly warmed my heart.

"I would recommend that you start off with a Boo Koo. It's a nice West Coast style IPA from a California brewery called Mother Earth."

"That sounds delicious," I said.

She beamed another smile at me; yet again the smile bounced off my heart strings. Wow, Kortney was quite a beautiful woman. Was I now noticing attractive women more since I had resolved to try to get over and move on from the stalemate I had been in with Gail? First Nancy, and now Kortney? Was it because I was in Los Angeles where everybody is apparently stunning and beautiful?

Or was it something else?

But regardless, it felt good to just relax and enjoy the moment.

And, if the truth be told, to enjoy the simple pleasure of looking at Kortney as she moved behind the bar, filled up the glass with the beer I had ordered while already multi-tasking and talking to another customer down the other side of the bar.

When she finished filling the glass, she slid it onto the coaster in front of me and then stood there, waiting for me to taste it.

"Let me know if you like it, Sugar. If not, then I'll pull a different one for you."

I lifted the frosty glass to my lips and took a tentative sip. The beer was hoppy and had an interesting floral aroma to it. Of course, with my heightened senses, I could detect subtle elements of pine and fruit even more as I took a sip.

It was stronger than I was normally used to but had a pleasant and refreshing citrus taste not unlike orange juice.

"It's delicious," I said to Kortney. "Excellent choice."

"Did you get a chance to look at the menu and see if there's anything you like, Sugar?"

"No," I said. "Not yet. But I have complete faith in you to pick something for me. Something a bit more than a snack but not a full meal."

"Okay," she said, smiling again. The smile combined with the playful enthusiasm scent she gave off told me that this was a part of her job that she enjoyed. Sizing up and trying to connect a patron with exactly the right order, whether it was a drink or something off the food menu. It allowed her to stretch her own strengths and abilities with reading people. Because even though she appeared to be just a regular bartender, I could tell she was operating at multiple levels based on a few subtle clues that only someone with my special ability might be able to pick up on. She was acutely aware of every single person in this bar — attending to multiple stimuli, numerous elements of body language and gestures. And it was well beyond the standard "smart serve" or whatever they call the training that bartenders and waiters needed to have. This was an acutely refined sense of people; combined with a genuine caring for them. Kortney had a bead on every single person here, was aware of their level of drunkenness but also their general disposition. And even though she wasn't the supervising manager on duty, she was adeptly in charge of this room.

She reminded me, in some ways, of Gail. Of that first time I had met with Gail while doing research for a book, and how, over drinks which turned into dinner, I was aware that, like me, she was paying attention to all the details of the other people in the bar. She was closely observing and attending to almost everyone there.

So yes, Kortney reminded me of Gail.

But the coolest part of that was that I wasn't uncomfortable or feeling in any way strange about that. I was okay with it. She reminded me of one trait I admired most in Gail, but it wasn't bothering me, it wasn't making me morose or verklempt or any of those things. It was merely an observation that I quite enjoyed.

Gee, perhaps that giant waterworks cry I'd had both during the live performance at The Hotel Café and afterwards listening to those Alicia Witt songs had really purged the whole heartbreak from my system.

I did, in many ways, feel like a fresh and whole man again.

Dammit. Mack seems to be right, yet again.

"Do you have any allergies that I should be aware of?" she asked.

I shook my head. "Nope. All free and clear. Except, maybe for arsenic. I do have an adverse reaction to that."

She gave off an instant odor of confusion as she wrinkled her brow at me. But, as her brow slowly unwrinkled, she beamed that beautiful, white-toothed smile at me again, and the odor changed to one of amusement.

"Ahh, I get it. A joke. Arsenic."

"Most people don't get that one."

"That's likely because of your dry delivery. It sounds like you're saying something legitimate rather than joking. So, I'm sure most people don't understand or are trying to make mental notes about what food on the menu might have that substance in it."

"Er, none I hope."

"I'm sure it throws most people for quite the loop."

"That, it might."

Kortney shook her head and then stood back, a serious look coming over her face again. "Okay, so, just to be clear; and no bad dad jokes about it, you don't have any allergies?"

"Not a one."

"Good. Okay, let's see. I'm a really huge fan of the Artisan Sausage Plate, but it can be quite filling. The pan seared salmon is to die for but is far too much to eat based on what you just said. The Bahn Mi Chicken Sandwich is delicious; there's a nice play of flavors off the jalapeno, the cilantro, the cranberry mayo and the pickled veggies. But, again, I think that'd be too much, particularly with the accompanying fries.

"No, I think you will be satisfied with the Greek Flatbread. It comes with artichoke, sundried tomatoes, spinach, Kalamata olives, Italian cheeses and goat cheese. It'll likely hit the spot and it goes really well with the IPA you're drinking."

"Sounds great to me," I smiled, picking up my beer and taking another sip.

"Super, Sugar." She leaned over and keyed the order into the small computer screen to my right. "It'll be out in less than fifteen minutes." Then she slipped down the far side of the bar to attend to a customer as if sensing that he needed something with some uncanny extra-sensory perception. I wasn't above believing she could have such abilities. I had them; in the past few years, I had met at least a couple of others who had some sort of paranormal abilities—including another werewolf. But, even if I hadn't, it would be foolish of me to think I could be the only one walking around with some hidden secret powers and abilities.

I took another hearty sip of the beer.

I wasn't a big fan of beer, but this one was growing on me. It didn't taste as strong, not nearly as dank, bitter, and hoppy as it had with my first sip. Or maybe it was Kortney's beautiful smile that was growing on me.

Whatever it was, I was a-okay with it, and with this moment.

Again, Argyle had been spot-on in recommending places.

As Kortney busied herself with helping customers at

the far end of the bar, I continued to enjoy the sheer pleasure of just looking at her, admiring her. But then I became self-conscious and didn't want to appear to be a creep, so I turned my attention to the ongoing intense conversation of the blonde woman beside me and the three guys and one other woman that were part of her group.

They were making plans for attending the next home game of whatever team they were discussing, and the intensity of their previous discussion was winding down. The guy who was standing at the end of the bar with his drink walked back to a table a few feet away from the bar and sat down with the older woman and man seated there. It appeared as if he had just joined in on this conversation on his way by.

I looked at this blond woman, the short haired dude on her right, the dark-haired woman beside him and the guy in the business suit who sat beside that second woman. It appeared, based on the comfort that they all felt, not to mention the essence of familiarity that they gave off, that they were all regulars at this bar.

They all obviously knew one another and likely slipped into intense conversations like this about sports, politics, or Hollywood gossip on a regular basis. I was able to tell that they were situational friends who all regularly hung out at the bar and perhaps didn't even know one another outside of this place. This spot, this neighborhood bar, was like a home away from home for them where they could hang out with the extended family of others, who, like them, frequented the bar. This spot, like some sort of proverbial Cheers, was a place that they took comfort in. In familiarity of the same faces, the same people that they would see again and again. The familiarity would extend, of course, to linked events, such as the football game they had all decided to attend together, the guy in the business suit having assured them he had access to the best tickets at the lowest possible price.

But, for the most part, I deduced they were only ever really together here at this neighborhood watering hole.

It was this locale that brought them together; that was the heart of their family connectivity.

It was an interesting element to observe, and one I squirreled away in those mental notes to be used in a future writing project.

And then I thought about Gail and how the two of us might have noticed these nuances in our own ways and enjoyed both observing and reflecting on the subtle cultural ques and nuances of such a group of people. I quite liked that aspect of when Gail and I hung out together.

I took another sip of my beer and chastised myself. I had been enjoying the moment, sitting beside a bunch of friendly regulars, enjoying observing a beautiful female bartender with class and charisma completely in her element and owning her role—and I had to go and bring myself down by thinking about Gail.

Why couldn't I just move on and appreciate this new place, this new experience?

When Argyle had told me about this place, he had mentioned this guy named Lex who was a regular here and knew a lot about the local culture, the local scene. Argyle had been batting a thousand so far with his recommendations; so, it made sense for me to see what new things Lex might introduce into my life. It would certainly provide a welcome distraction from constantly reflecting back on Gail.

I drank down my beer quickly, again noticing that the overpowering bitter taste wasn't as strong as it had at first seemed. Maybe I was getting used to it. As expected, Kortney spotted the empty glass and moved back toward this end of the bar.

"Can I get you another one, Sugar?"

"Yes, please."

"Same one, or do you want to try something else?"

"This one was delicious. Didn't realize I could like an IPA. But I'm all about trying new things. You haven't steered me wrong yet. What should I have next?"

She smiled and stroked her chin, looking over at the taps, and though my ability to pick up on her scent was a bit muted now—maybe I'd drank that beer down a little too quickly—I could tell she was taking the responsibility quite seriously.

"I think I know what you should have next. It's a bit of a step up from that last one." She slid over to the taps, grabbed a small tumbler and filled it about one finger high with a brownish amber beer. She slid it in front of me. "Try this one. It's called Space Dust. It's from a brewery in Seattle."

I lifted it up to my lips, and the scent was even stronger than the last one. The taste was also bitter and hoppy, but it didn't hit me quite so dramatically as the last one had. Perhaps I was becoming used to this style of beer.

"I like it," I said. "Yeah, let that be my next one."

"Excellent." She grinned and grabbed a larger glass and started filling it.

"So, Kortney," I said, as she handed me the beer. "I've heard that there's a regular here that goes by the name of

Lex."

Kortney's disposition immediately changed. She became more cautious, concerned, reserved. It didn't show on her face, though.

"Lex?" she said. "Yeah, Lex is a regular here. Why do you want to know?"

At that point I could also sense the woman on my right pick up on the conversation; her heartbeat altered enough to indicate she recognized the name, and she was suddenly attending to our conversation. Perhaps Lex was her boyfriend, or husband?

I took a long pull from the glass and drank down about a quarter of it.

"Well," I said. "The guy who recommended that I come here suggested that I ask for Lex."

"For what?" Kortney was still on edge, concerned, perhaps even protective of this Lex person. Who the heck was this guy, and why was her disposition suddenly so different? The woman beside me was still attending to the exchange between me and Kortney.

"Apparently, Lex knows a lot about the local culture. The music scene. Fun places to check out, like this one."

Kortney's sense of panic reduced slightly. That or the beer was getting to my head; because her scent wasn't coming across as powerfully as it had been before. Similarly, my bead on the woman on my right who was definitely interested in and attending to our conversation, was also muted a bit; but her own disposition seemed to calm back down.

Who was this Lex? And why did they both seem a little jumpy about me asking after the guy? That was the type of thing that got the writer in me interested in learning more.

Kortney's face also visibly relaxed.

"I see," she said. "Well, if Lex shows up, I'll let them know you were asking for them."

"Thanks." I took another long sip from my beer. Beside me, the woman with the piqued interest returned her attention to the football related conversation she'd been engaged in with the others.

I sipped my beer, noting that, with each drink, the harsh-hitting bitter tones seemed to become reduced.

Another bartender, one I hadn't noticed before, moseyed in from the kitchen area. He was a good-looking male with short brown hair and a thin dark beard, who looked a little like Justin Timberlake. Smelling of confidence and a husky rich aftershave, he slid down the length of the bar, squeezing past Kortney who had moved on to attend to another patron, and called to the blond woman beside me.

"Hey, Dree," he said to her. I could sense, off of her, a mild sexual attraction to this fellow, which wasn't surprising. He was quite the hunky specimen, admittedly pleasing to my own heterosexual eyes.

"Hi, Max," she said in a breathy voice. "Making up any new drinks lately?"

The woman in the blue polka-dotted dress, whose name I now knew was Dree, spun around on her stool to face straight to the bar; like a spotlight fixating to her target, Max. I hadn't had more than a cursory look at her before. But I noticed now that she was rather cute; suede blue eyes and rosy round high cheek bones that enhanced her lovely smile. The smile was focused on Max, but I was fine with just appreciating her beauty as an observer.

"Yeah, I've got this cocktail I've been working called a Smokey Tonic Fashioned. It's a smoke infused gin and tonic but with the ingredients of an Old Fashioned added into it. Want to give it a whirl?"

"I'm game," she said and then, noticing that I was listening to their conversation, flipped me a quick wink.

"Max is one of the best bartenders in this city," she said. "Watch this."

I observed as he set about making the drink; fascinated with the intense concentration he put into the process. He focused on the drink and nothing else; it was, to him, an exquisite piece of art that commanded his full attention.

Beside me, Dree was as intent on watching Max as Max was at focusing on the drink. I took the opportunity to take a bit of a longer look at her, appreciating the way her long blonde hair framed her cute face so wonderfully.

When he finished, he slid it in front of her. The liquid in the glass was a dark and hazy gray; it didn't look at all palatable.

She lifted the glass to her lips and took a quick sip.

"Wow," she said, putting it back down on the bar. "That is a strong one."

"What'd you think?" he said.

"I'm not sure," she said. "Let me take another sip."

She took another sip; and this time I could tell that she was not at all a fan of the beverage. It was difficult to get a bead on her emotions, because there was a layer of deception to it. I was picking up on the sense she didn't want to say something negative and hurt Max's feelings, so she was trying to cover it up.

"It's really strong; not a drink for beginners," she said.

"This one's definitely for the pros."

She turned to me, an obvious ploy to deflect the conversation away from what she really thought of it.

"How about you? Smoke?" she said to me. "If you like peaty, this is one for you."

I grinned, reaching for the drink. How could I resist those cool blue eyes? "I'm not much of a seasoned drinker, that's for sure. This IPA is likely as hearty and as hazy as I would normally go with a drink. But what the heck, I'll give it a whirl."

I lifted the glass up to my lips, took a quick sip of it and immediately choked on the overwhelming taste of the thick and peaty smoke. I put the glass down, surprised that I didn't spit the harsh toxin back up.

Both Dree and Max laughed.

"Uh, no," I said to them both. "I don't think I'm the right customer for this particular concoction. Just pour me a nice tall glass of ice-cold water any time. That, I can handle."

Max shook his head, took the drink back and pressed his lips together. He wasn't insulted. Instead, he seemed committed to want to give it another shot, change up the recipe slightly. "It is an acquired taste," he said, walking down the side of the bar.

The blonde woman beside me laughed again and briefly touched her left hand to my shoulder. "I'm so sorry," she whispered to me. "I didn't mean to put you on the spot like that. But I just wasn't sure how to tell him I wasn't a fan of it. I hate letting people down."

"That's okay," I said. "I'm a bit of an amateur when it comes to hard liquor. Even without the smoke in it I don't think I would have been a good candidate for a straight up gin and tonic, or whatever that drink was."

She laughed again.

"I'm Alexandria," she said.

"Alexandria? I thought I heard Max call you Dree."

She laughed again. "Yeah. My full name is Alexandria. Dree is one of many incarnations of it."

"Well, that's intriguing. How'd that come about? Alexandria is a lovely name."

"I suppose. It's a long name, but one I never actually liked; hated, even, my entire life. Whenever my family moved to a new town—which we did a lot because my father was in the military—I could change the name up and try to take on a new personality, a new persona. Perhaps that compartmentalizing is something that helped me move on and not miss the friends I had made at the previous towns we lived in so much. Because it wasn't me, you know. She was still there, not missing her friends. But the new me was here now, fresh, and clear of that longing.

"So, in one town I might be Alexa, and in another, I might be Dria. And then, in the next one, I'd flip to Alexis. I've actually found it useful to slip on a new persona, give things a fresh start."

Yeah, I thought. A fresh start. That's the entire reason I was here in Los Angeles, wasn't it? At least, that was part of Mack's grand plan. I nodded silently as she continued, enraptured by listening to her talk.

"The folks at this bar call me by many names. To some I'm Alexis, to others, I'm just Al.

"Or even Alex?" I asked.

Another beautiful smile that shot straight to the center of my chest and warmed my heart graced her face. "Yes, sometimes Alex. And then there are those who call me Xander. A few call me Andria."

I nodded.

"I went through a phase where, every second move, I went by Lexie. I quite liked that one."

"Lexie. That's cute." I thought the name matched the lovely pixie-like nose, the high round red cheekbones and the hint of dimples that reminded me a little of Jennifer Garner.

"Yeah, I think that's why I returned to that name more than once. I haven't used that in years, actually. But to most of the staff and regulars here, I'm Dria or Dree."

"Ah, I see," I said.

"But I'm also known, to many folks, as Lex."

"Lex?"

"Yeah," She laughed. "I'm the Lex you'd been asking about.

"Lex," I said. "I'd assumed Lex was a guy."

"That's one of the reasons I like that name," she smiled. "That and the fact it reminds me of my brother Davy.

"There was this one time, during the phase in my life when I was going by Alex that little Davy, who couldn't pronounce things properly—I mean, there was NO WAY he could ever say Alexandria—would try to call me 'Alex.' But instead, he would always just say the last syllable. One of my friends, who was a fan of the Superman comics, thought it was neat that that it sounded like he was calling me Lex as in Lex Luthor, Superman's biggest foe.

"As Davy continued to get older, he kept calling me that. I suppose it also fit that I was in one of my Tomboy phases.

"And I liked the fact that the name was ambidextrous, interchangeable, or gender agnostic. Lex can be a man or a woman. Like Pat. Like Leslie. Or Kerry. You hear it and you can't be sure if it's a man or a woman. And it shouldn't matter. A person is a person, regardless of how they identify. I hate when people make assumptions about someone because of the chromosomes they were born with.

"A popular name like Lex has that about it. But so do other shorter names, like Dree, even. Because a name like that doesn't limit me to just the one. It doesn't reduce my status to female, which can sometimes be quite demeaning."

She paused and was quiet. I realized, for the first time during her explanation of the name that I was getting very little signal, a muted sort of input of the extra-sensory perceptions that normally come to me. I had picked up on some feelings of discomfort from sharing, with a little bit of longing and missing something, perhaps. It was odd for my senses to be so muted.

"In any case, that's a bit of a long story. I'm Alexandria. Or Dree. Or Lex. Pleased to meet you." She put out her hand.

"Well, nice to meet you Lex," I said, taking her hand. It was warm and soft, yet firm. It might sound cheesy to even admit this, but there was the briefest tingle of something that felt like electricity exchanged between us as my hand fit so comfortably into hers. The feeling of touching her was both sensual and familiar. There was a hint of sexy and playful stimulation where our skin was making contact. But it was also oddly comfortable, like she and I had known one another before. As I continued to grip her hand, I again tried to focus on her heartbeat, her breathing, the smell of her, trying to conjure up where I might have recognized her from, but couldn't come up with anything. My senses remained muted; her scent, emotions, the sounds and smells of the room itself, felt out of reach. Sure, I was at the time of month when my enhanced senses were the most subdued, but this was something more. Maybe the jet lag, combined with the alcohol, particularly the smoky gin I'd just tried, were having an effect on me.

"I'm Michael. But maybe, in the spirit of shortened and modified names, you can come up with a shorter version of that; and something more interesting than just Mike."

"Yeah, Mike is just too plain for a guy who looks the way you do."

Woah. If I didn't know any better, I'd say she found me attractive. Of course, I didn't know any better, because I was having trouble sensing much beyond normal human sensations right now.

"Hmm," she said, a playful glimmer coming across her beautiful blue eyes. "How about if we call you Kal? You know from Mike-kal." She spelled out the three-letter word. "But also, Kal-el was the name that Superman had been born with. So you can be the Kal to my Lex."

I smiled. Superman. Considering the fact I often ended up using my enhanced powers to help others, I thought it was funny she had no idea just how accurate she might be in using that nomenclature. Of course, I didn't want to think of her as the arch enemy, because this interesting and funny woman rather intrigued me. Not to mention,

I'd been more of a fan of Spider-man rather than Super-man. But it didn't mean I couldn't appreciate the gesture. She'd created a nickname for me that tied us together. I know it's a silly thing, but I found it quite thrilling.

"That works for me."

"Excellent!" She grinned, and her smile sent a tingle down my spine. She then lifted her cocktail up with her right hand. "Here's to new BFF's Lex and Kal."

I clinked my drink against hers and we both drank heartily from our glasses, finishing them.

Kortney swept in and grabbed the glasses, already having a replacement of Lex's cocktail ready. "Same for you, Sugar? Or do you want something else?"

"Surprise me, Kortney," I said. "Maybe something local. I'm quite enjoying the local surprises I'm discovering here."

Kortney flashed a knowing smile at me. "I can tell. Glad to see it." She then went over to the taps to pour me another beer.

"So, what do you do, Kal?" Lex asked me.

"I'm a writer."

"A writer?"

"Yeah."

"Have I ever heard of you?"

"I doubt it. But maybe you've seen a film based on one of my books. *Print of the Predator*."

She grinned, and I picked up a vibe of familiarity from her as Kortney slid the glass in front of me. "This one's called XPA from a brewery in Santa Monica."

"Thank you." I picked up my drink, offering another toast to Lex, and we clinked glasses again before taking the inaugural first drinks from our respective glasses.

"Oh yeah. *Print of the Predator*." Lex said. "I know the movie. It was a thriller. It had Ryan Gosling in it. I didn't realize it was based on a book."

"Yep. That was mine. In fact, I'm in town to be on the set of a second movie based on another one of my books." I paused, suddenly feeling awkward about being so boastful. Sure, I was proud of what I did, and, despite the disappointment of learning my role on the set was a token title with little involvement, I was still pretty pumped to be here, and a part of it. I tried to pick up whether or not she found my bragging annoying but realized that I was having trouble getting a read on her. I paused, focusing on each of my senses one on one. The other conversations, which I normally had to focus on blocking out, were distinctly muted. The scents and emotions of the other patrons and staff were similarly dulled.

I looked down at my beer, realizing I hadn't had this much to drink in a long time. I was feeling a bit of a buzz for sure. But the muted senses I was experiencing was actually quite refreshing.

I was attracted to this beautiful blonde woman in front of me. But I could not easily read her heartbeat and emotion. I couldn't tell if bragging about the movie was putting her off or not. It was actually a wonderfully liberating experience.

I took another drink of my beer.

"I'm not much of a reader," Lex admitted. "I'm more into sports. I'm a big fan of football. But I really love music. Live music, especially."

Lex and I continued to chat about music, about the different styles we both liked. About some local venues she had gone to, including The Hollywood Bowl, which was just north of where my hotel was, and the Hotel Café, where I'd seen Alicia Witt performing the night before. She was intimately familiar with those locations, having seen plenty of musicians at each of them, and so many other venues, over the years.

She had even seen one of my favorite bands, Rush, live a handful of times. Heck, the fact that I'd met an American female who not only knew about Rush and liked them but had seen them live suggested I had found myself a real catch.

We fell into a comfortable conversation, mostly just the two of us. Occasionally Kortney and Max and the other regulars who Lex had been previously engaged with, and whose names I mostly can't remember, even though she had introduced us, joined in.

I jokingly started to call Lex Norm, referring to my observation that this friendly group of patrons and bartenders reminded me of that feeling from the television sitcom Cheers. Lex was definitely a core regular patron like Norm, but I couldn't quite get a peg on the others; though Joe, which I think was the name of the guy sitting on the other side of Lex, occasionally spouted out sports, music, television, and history trivia, and so he would have to be Cliff, the know-it-all mailman character.

Lex shared that she worked as a project manager for a software company and enjoyed her work, but didn't find the work, or the people at the office, all that appealing. She much preferred socializing with friends, and Gulp was one of several establishments where she was a regular.

"Wait a minute," I'd said, learning she was a regular

at more than one bar. "You mean you're Norm at multiple places like this?" I brought my hands up to both sides of my head in loose fists, then pushed them off the side, expanding my fingers as they moved away, while making a soft explosion sound, in the "mind-blown" gesture.

After Lex learned I was originally from Canada, she started referring to me as her new Canadian friend. Some of the others at the bar made a few jokes related to my country of origin. Comments about Rush, hockey, poutine, Celine Dion, and the overuse of the word "sorry" came up from time to time, particularly when I did something Canadian, like actually apologizing. At one point, a Bryan Adams song came on in the background music, which prompted a comment. From time to time, a snicker from one of the regulars followed after I had said the word "about" in a conversation.

Lex let out the cutest giggle, the first time that happened and repeated the word, but pronounced it like the word "boot."

"I don't say it that way." I said the word a couple of times, not at all hearing the long and drawn out sound the others claimed was rolling off my tongue.

"Yeah," Lex said, the most beautiful smile coming to her face as she giggled again, reaching out and placing her hand on my arm. "You do. A-boot. It's so adorable, Michael."

"The name," I said, "Is Kal."

"Of course," she laughed. "Speaking of which, we need to capture this moment, this partnership of superpowers. Kal and Lex. Let's get a selfie."

She pulled her phone out, leaned over to put her head close to mine and spent a minute fussing about, not able to get the right angle. I didn't mind her being that close and relished in the moment and in the wonderful rich and intoxicating smell of her hair, even with my senses muted.

"Here," I finally said, pulling my phone out. "My arms are a lot longer. Let me take it."

I positioned the phone at an angle. She nestled in even closer to me, our heads touching. "No, a little more to the left," she said. "Okay, up just a bit. There, that's it."

I took the picture, and we looked at it.

"That's such an awesome pic!" she said. "Text it to me, so I can say I met this famous writer." She then gave me her number, I sent the picture to her, and she confirmed receiving it by messaging back "BFFs."

That was twice she'd used that abbreviation. I suspected it meant something positive but hadn't a clue what it actually meant. To me, it sounded like it might be a type of sandwich, like a BLT.

"What does BFF mean?"

She giggled. "Best Friends Forever. This is a pic of Lex and Kal. Not enemies, like in the comics but BFFs."

"Huh. BFFs. Neat."

She laughed, shaking her head. "So much to teach you, my Canadian friend." She then reached over and touched my arm again, like she'd done before we did the selfie.

I felt a warmth and a tingling sensation whenever Lex reached out to touch me like that; something she seemed to do every time we shared a laugh. It was a sensual and fleetingly thrilling touch that I yearned and longed for as the conversation moved on and we enjoyed more drinks, appetizer style plates of food for sharing, and talked and joked and laughed.

As the evening continued, and I was feeling more and more buzzed, I realized Lex was holding her liquor extremely well.

I, on the other hand, was not.

But, admittedly, it was nice.

Here I was, crushing on a beautiful woman who I was pretty sure was into me—but, with my senses muted and unable to properly pick up on the emotions from her scent, her heartbeat, or any of the usual ways by which I could "read" people, we were just two normal people having a normal conversation.

I had no additional powers guiding me through the moments. No shrouded underlying ability of navigating a conversation to my advantage.

And it was something I liked.

Tremendously.

Lex and I were getting along quite brilliantly, chatting, laughing, sharing, getting to know one another.

I suspected she was into me in the same way I was into her. But I had no additional way to verify that. I had become so used to having that advantage for all these years that I forgot what a regular conversation was like.

It was like walking a tightrope without a net.

And the adrenaline rush was an amazing experience.

It was liberating.

I remember, somewhere in the easy and comfortable back-and-forth with Lex, thinking back to my encounter with Nancy at the airport. Yes, she was beautiful; yes, she was funny and intelligent and a good conversationalist; and yes, we had hit it off quite brilliantly.

But I had this advantage of being able to read her.

I realized it had been unfair. For both of us.

With Lex, who was also beautiful, funny, intelligent, and a good conversationalist, I had no such advantage.

It felt more natural.

More real.

After several more rounds, where I could tell my own speech was getting a bit slurred, I realized I should probably stop drinking, and call it a night. When I glanced at the time on my cell phone, I noticed it was already close to one in the morning.

We had been sitting and chatting for over six hours; even though it felt like maybe an hour.

Things were going well with Lex, but I didn't want to do or say something in my drunkenness that was embarrassing. I thought it might be best for me to call it a night.

"Okay," I said, regretting leaving such a wonderful conversation. "I've got to be on the set early tomorrow morning. I'm going to pack it in."

I called for Max to come settle the tab and quietly gestured, without Lex noticing, that I wanted to also pay for Lex's tab. Max nodded, understanding. As he was totaling our tabs together, I looked back over at Lex.

The look of disappointment on her face was clear.

"Do you really have to call it a night?"

"Yeah. But I had such a great time getting to know you, Lex."

"Me too, Kal," she grinned.

As I signed for the combined total of our drinks and the various appetizers we'd shared I realized we hadn't had nearly enough food. Well, I hadn't had nearly enough food to absorb the alcohol flowing through my system. Lex seemed to be holding her own quite well. I added on a fifty percent tip to the total, partially because the math was easier, and partially to show my ultimate satisfaction for the experience. The staff here was top notch, the cocktails and beers were unique and flavorful, the food was delicious, and the company was world class and a delightful surprise.

As I stood up, Lex stood as well, and we hugged our goodbyes.

As she was pulling out of the hug, but remaining close, her hands resting on my shoulders, she whispered. "I really hope you're single."

I paused, looking at her. Yes, this made it very clear she was as into me as I was into her.

But the question threw me.

I had been single for several years, but hadn't considered myself single; because, in my mind, I was there for Gail. I had always been there for Gail.

In all these years since our breakup, sure, I had been attracted to plenty of women. But I'd never made any sort of move for anything more than friendship with any of them. Because I'd been holding onto the possibility that Gail would eventually come around.

I'd behaved, for all intents and purposes, all these years like I was in a relationship, was taken.

Not so much this evening, of course.

As I stood there my arms still loosely around Lex's hips, her hands on my shoulders, I felt—despite not having that insightful wolf-sense—I could easily lean in and kiss her. I also realized I'd spent several hours with Lex and had not once thought about Gail.

A feeling of guilt rushed through me.

I stood there a moment, opened my mouth, but said nothing.

"*Are* you single, Michael?"

"Uh, yeah," I said. And then added, and I'm not sure why. "Mostly."

Even without my enhanced senses, and despite the alcoholic buzz I was feeling, the hurt look on her face was clear.

"You really should figure that out, my Canadian friend," she said. And with that, she tilted her head up and planted a soft warm kiss on my right cheek. "Goodnight."

She then turned and walked toward the restroom, leaving me standing alone at the bar.

I looked over at Lex's friends, a slightly different medley of them than the ones who had started off in the late afternoon. A couple of them were looking over at me; they had obviously overheard the exchange. One of them quietly said something, and despite the sound of the music and boisterous conversation and my muted senses, I still heard her words quite clearly.

"Not cool, man. Not cool."

I turned to look at Lex, but she had already disappeared into the women's restroom.

I stood there a moment, head down, and then moved toward the exit, consciously trying to make myself as small as possible, wondering if I looked as much like the weasel I suddenly felt I was as I slunk out the door.

Friday, June 16, 2017

Chapter Thirteen: Muggers in the Night, Exchanging Victims

The momentary fresh blast of cool evening air cleared my head a bit, which I appreciated. But I didn't have a chance to stand out there for long, because a line of cabs had been waiting right outside of Gulp.

I got into the back of one, giving the driver the name of my hotel in Hollywood. As he took off down the street, I marveled in how I could barely detect his heartbeat or any emotive scent.

As he drove, I thought about Lex, how attracted to her I had been. And how, the entire night, I hadn't thought about Gail. Well, at least, not until those last few awkward moments. It had been the first time in years that, when speaking to a woman I found appealing, Gail hadn't crept into my mind. Until that last minute, of course, when I had pretty much blown it, by suddenly acting like there was someone in my life.

It felt like I had been getting in my own way for a long time by over-thinking. I meet an interesting woman that I find attractive, and I'm reminded of Gail, either from one of the similarities, or perhaps even differences. And then those thoughts prevent me from appreciating what is in front of me. Over-thinking. Over-feeling. Of course, something else, that hadn't occurred to me was the over-sensing.

Being able to read people's emotions, moods, reactions, through their heartbeats and the subtle scent they give off has been extremely useful to me; I've definitely leveraged it to my advantage in various negotiations and interactions. It, along with heightened strength, speed, and agility, has also helped me in the encounters with "bad guys" I have confronted.

But what if my reliance on those senses has dulled my ability to enjoy or appreciate the unexpected, the unknown?

If I'm able to tell, by the scent she is giving off, by the change in pulse of her heartbeat, that a woman is into me, it's like always having the answers to an important test plastered in large bold letters right front of you, where you can't miss it. You can't not see the answer, and, thus, you're unable to determine if you actually knew the answer of your own volition, or you were cheating.

As the evening and hours of conversation with Lex continued, my normally over-active senses continued to be dulled by the alcohol, the jet lag, the combination of things perhaps. Who knows? It's not like there's any sort of manual. Not for the first time I reflected on the fact that there was no *Werewolves for Dummies* style guidebook I could depend on.

I had become so dependent, over the years, upon relying on those additional sensory inputs that having a real and normal conversation with someone, had been a unique and enjoyable experience.

Until Gail had come to my mind.

Which made me suddenly feel like, just sitting there and talking for, what, for six or more hours, with Lex, had been a form of cheating.

Why had I said that? She had gone from being so into a tender and intimate moment to looking like I had slapped her in the face and insulted her.

My response had hurt her.

Because I was mooning over a woman in a city thousands of miles away who had made it clear, multiple times, that we were just friends?

The lyrics to that song from Alicia Witt the previous night came to mind.

I don't wanna be your promise, I just wanna be your friend.

That's what Gail and I were. That's what we've long been. And yet I was still standing in my own way.

I resolved to call Lex in the morning; explain myself, ask her to forgive me. To see if we could meet up again for another drink.

That, admittedly, was a scary thing.

As I sat there, I wondered if I should just text her now.

No, that would be too forward of me. Too assuming.

But she was up. Why not do it now?

No. Too forward. Too eager. Too desperate. Wait until the morning.

I shook my head.

I had never been good at this. I suppose I became a little better at direct and in person interactions with people, with my heightened senses, because I could read them, but not as good when over the phone or when I couldn't leverage that sense advantage. And, prior to being bitten by that wolf, I had interpersonal skills so weak that I couldn't negotiate my way out of a wet conversational paper bag. My fear of doing or saying the wrong thing and offending someone made introverts look gregarious.

And I'd proven it with Lex tonight when I offended her.

Should I call her or text her?

Should I apologize now, or in the morning?

And I should also apologize for walking out of the bar without saying goodbye, shouldn't I?

No, her last words to me before she headed for the restroom were goodnight. She didn't expect me to be there when she returned from the restroom. She was disappointed; it was over. The moment was ruined.

Unless she'd been hoping I would still be there, to explain things to her—to work things out.

Damn.

To call me confused would be an understatement of magnificent proportions, like referring to the results of last year's Brexit referendum as a minor parting of ways for the UK.

I needed to think. Get some fresh air. Maybe take a walk. And I couldn't do that in the back of this cab.

When I asked the driver how far away from the hotel we were he said it was still about a five-minute drive. I figured that might be just a long enough walk to clear my head and think more about what I was going to do. What

I was going to say to Lex when I called her in the morning.

"Do you think you can let me off here? I'd like to walk the rest of the way to the hotel. You know, clear this alcohol-filled head a bit with fresh air."

"Sure, no problem."

He pulled over, and, as I was paying using the touch screen mounted to the back of the seat in front of me, he let me know which way to head.

"We're facing north on North Highland Avenue. Keep walking in this same direction. It's about a dozen blocks. I'm sure you'll recognize once you get to Hollywood Boulevard, and the hotel is about a couple of blocks past that, on the left."

"Thanks," I said, keying in a generous tip and completing the transaction.

The cool night air hit my face as I stepped out of the cab and immediately made me feel better.

That cool air was refreshing as it flowed over my skin. I immediately noticed the difference in not being able to smell the air the way I normally would, with my senses so muted. But I still enjoyed the refreshing sensation.

Out of habit, I picked up my phone to check on the app how long the walk might be, but the screen was dark and wouldn't come on.

It was dead.

That decided, for me, that I wouldn't be calling or texting Lex.

I slipped it into my back pocket and started walking.

With the debate of whether or not I'd call Lex to apologize now moot, I enjoyed the sights, and got a kick out of some of the names of the streets I was passing. Streets I'd heard about or were part of television shows or songs, such as Melrose and Santa Monica Boulevard.

North Highland was a wider street. Two lanes moving in either direction, with a boulevard in the middle through most of it, some with the palm trees that I now knew, thanks to Argyle, had been imported to the area.

The walk was good for me, for my head. Though I was still quite drunk, I managed to walk mostly in a straight line. The cool night air helped clear my head a bit, and occasionally I picked up on a sound or a scent that came from my more enhanced, heightened wolfish awareness, like it was trying to punch through the drunken cloudy fog in my head. One of those scents along the way was fresh urine from where someone must have relieved themselves within the past hour or so, because it was distinctly fresh and was strong enough that, even without that bit of enhanced powerful scent poking its way through, I'm sure I still would have smelled it. While I was glad for that fleeting return of my heightened senses, I wasn't pleased to note that the guy who had relieved himself must have recently digested a meal that was some sort of medley of asparagus, Brussels sprouts, onions, and salmon. If anything, it relieved me that the sensation and awareness came on strong, then retreated back behind the murky fog again.

As I walked, my thoughts kept playing in those highlight movie reel style clips—applicable, I suppose, as I was walking towards downtown Hollywood—reviewing various parts of the later afternoon, evening, and night, spent with Lex. Our conversation was animated and filled with laughs; she was fun, spirited, and playful. She seemed to get along well with all the regulars and the staff at the bar, being a good friend to them all. And, of course, she was beautiful. Long flowing and curvy blonde hair, those beautiful round high cheekbones, those lovely blue eyes. Combine that with her personality, classic sense of charisma and charm, and it was no wonder I was a babbling idiot in that moment where I should have, in retrospect, just leaned in and given her a quick kiss.

Not that I would ever be so forward upon first meeting someone; no matter how attracted to them I might be.

I was just crossing the intersection of North Highland and Sunset Boulevard, tickled at another street I recognized, Sunset Boulevard, when my fleetingly returning senses alerted me to someone in peril.

It was a whimper and the disturbing sound of flesh hitting flesh combined with the mingled scent of fear and intense anger that reached out through the fog and seemed to grab me by the throat.

I looked in the direction the slight shifting feel of wind on my face told me had carried both the scent and the sounds, and saw what those sensations usually accompanied—a mugging taking place, in the parking lot on the other side of Sunset.

There was a group of four people. Two of them were holding a guy by the arms from either side while a third one was throwing punches at his stomach and face.

Upon closer inspection, it looked like the three guys, dressed all in black, also had masks on. They immediately reminded me of the masks from *The Purge* movies.

One of them was the plastic pale white face with rosy cheeks, and the other was a rubber face twisted into a huge sick Joker-like grin.

I instinctively tried to get a better gage on the situation via sound and scent, but I was pulling nothing. The fog had returned. I reached to my back pocket for my phone, thinking it might be best to call 911, rather than try to take these guys on in my drunken state but I remembered it was dead.

The group hadn't noticed me standing there, and the thug was continuing to mercilessly beat on the one guy, who looked to be a middle-aged black male.

Considering the amount of alcohol in my system and my reduced super powered abilities, I shouldn't have done what I'd done.

But then again, maybe the alcohol also reduced my inhibitions.

Or maybe it was instinct that kicked in, as I rushed toward the group, and yelled out. "Hey, no fair. Three against one. And you didn't even give him a mask."

As I ran at them, the guy throwing punches turned — he was wearing one of those blue LED light masks with crosses over the eyes, and the fog shifted enough that I caught a quick sense of his scent of anger and hatred quickly shifting to surprise.

I threw a hard round-house punch at him with everything I had in me.

I would normally pull my punches, knowing my enhanced strength might kill a person with a single blow, but it was the weakest time of my monthly cycle, my powers seemed dulled by alcohol, and, as I mentioned, so were my inhibitions.

His head snapped to the side, and he went down.

Even without my heightened senses I knew he was unconscious.

One down. Two to go.

I turned to the others. "Who's next?"

The other two guys immediately let go of the man they'd been holding and came at me.

Normally, I would have been able to dodge and deflect their clumsy attack quite easily and take them out.

I had done it enough times.

But the alcohol coursing through my veins seemed to hold those abilities at bay the way these two had just been holding their prey.

I feigned a punch then shifted, in what I felt was a deft maneuver to punch the guy in the white mask in the stomach with my right hand, while kneeing the one in the smiley mask between the legs.

But I failed miserably.

Not only did I not dodge their punches, but I didn't get a single hit in.

A punch from Whitey caught me on the top right side of my head, and a split second after Smiley landed a punch to the side of my throat just above the collar bone.

I stumbled back a half step, and Smiley threw another punch, this time to my solar plexus that sent me stumbling back a couple more steps.

"Hey," I said. "That smarts."

Whitey threw another punch, but this time, a combination of my stumble, and an additional backwards step, to catch my balance, resulted in him missing.

Behind them, I could see the guy they'd been beating on slowly shuffling away. Good. Hopefully I'd be able to distract these guys long enough that he'd get away to safety. Maybe even call 911. Because I started doubting I was going to be able to hold my own.

"Missed me, missed me," I chortled at Whitey. "Now you've got to kiss me."

I'd learned that mocking and insults often set my opponents back a bit with a combination of confusion and anger. I could normally sense from their change in heartbeat or emotive scent, that I was having an effect on them.

Of course, I wasn't able to read anything. Not to mention, the masks were hiding any emotion I'd normally be able to see on their faces.

And, on top of it all, neither one of them said a single word. That, combined with the masks, was frightening and eerie in and of itself.

But I played the only cards I knew.

As I stepped back, I tried again to get a reaction.

"So, what's with the masks? Is it that you're both so terminally ugly that you even have to wear them after dark?"

Smiley rushed me in a heads-down tackle move. I dodged it and threw an elbow into the middle of his back as I stepped aside. He stumbled, off balance, and fell to the ground behind me.

"Or is it because you're ashamed to show your face knowing that a single guy is about to take out all three of you?"

In a similar forward crouched tackle position, Whitey launched himself at me. As I moved to step out of the way, the back of my foot connected with Smiley's leg. I realized, as I was being tackled, that he hadn't missed me; it had been a ploy to get into a duo attack position. Smiley was on his hands and knees behind me so that as Whitey piled into me, it threw me back, the backs of my knees catching on the man behind me and off balance.

I fell back, my left shoulder and the back of my head connecting hard with the pavement.

They both piled on top of me, holding me down while kicking and punching at my face, stomach, and sides.

During this pummeling, I noticed that the guy they'd been beating had gotten away. He was nowhere in sight.

Well at least I'd accomplished one part of my attempted mission. The entire melee wasn't a write-off.

"Fellas," I said. "Don't you think you're coming on a little strong here? Maybe before we get so intimate you could at least buy a guy a drink."

My jibes had no effect; not that I could sense, anyway.

And they remained completely mum, not saying a single word, or even making grunting noises as they threw punches and kicks at me.

One good thing about the effect of the alcohol in my system is how it numbed the sensation of pain a little.

As another blow stuck me particularly hard in the stomach, I yelled out, joking seeming to be my only defense at this point.

"C'mon. No fair. I had a lot to drink last night. You hit me like that again and you're going to make me pee all over myself."

A couple more punches struck me in the face and the side of the head. Another one struck me dead center in the left eye and my vision from that one turned to a red hue.

I felt a wave of darkness start to shroud my vision and I realized I was blacking out as additional blows struck me in the head, chest, and stomach.

As the black blanket started to envelope me, I thought I heard a voice yelling out from somewhere nearby.

"Stop!"

The punches stopped, and the darkness receded a bit as I shook my head and tried to look past the guys piled on top of me. That same voice called out.

"Get up and step away from him. Now."

My vision was still blurry, and I could only see out of my right eye, but as they moved back, I made out a full-figured person—male, based on the voice—in what looked like a blue jumpsuit standing in the parking lot a few feet away.

"That's it." The voice said. "Make one false move and I'll take you both down. Don't try me. This guy is a good friend of mine. It's late. I've had a long day and closed some pretty tough deals. Don't make me close you out, too." The man laughed at his own joke.

It was a laugh I recognized.

As my sight cleared, I took in the middle-aged stocky white guy in a pale blue business suit and tie—not a jumpsuit after all—who looked like a cross between Lou Costello and Buddy Hackett, with a handgun clasped between both hands fixed on Whitey and Smiley.

I'd never before seen his resemblance to that second actor; maybe it was the angle I was seeing him at; maybe it was the alcohol; maybe it was the beating to the head and face I'd just taken. But that second actor's first name was how I knew this guy.

It was Buddy—Buddy J. Samuels—my traveling sales-man friend.

What the hell was he doing here?

"Hey, Mikey!" Buddy smiled at me. "Welcome to the jungle. Looks like I got here just in the nick of time, huh?"

I tried to sit up—apparently too quickly—and that's when the darkness swirled back in a double time march and everything went black.

Saturday, June 17, 2017

Chapter Fourteen: An Extended Rest in the Arms of Morpheus

So, you're finally awake." Buddy's voice was the first thing I heard as consciousness returned to me. It was accompanied by a low pulse throbbing of pain like the super-boosted bass of an annoying jerk's car stereo parked outside.

"Looks like you needed quite the extended rest in the arms of Morpheus, my friend." The sound of his voice ramped up the throbbing pulse of the bass.

I tried opening my eyes, but the brightness of the room was too intense; inviting what felt like a cacophony of Buddy Rich, Neil Peart, and John Bonham going to town with their drumsticks slapping at every possible surface on the inside of my skull.

"Oh," I said in a low moan, and the effort and sound from inside my head was like that first trio had invited Keith Moon, Dave Grohl, and Phil Collins to accompany them.

I didn't dare sit up, for fear that these half-dozen percussionists might invite Ringo Starr, Stewart Copeland,

and maybe even Animal from *The Muppet Show* to join in.

"Here," Buddy said, suddenly right beside me and pressing a chalky round pill tablet between my lips. "This'll help." His hand came behind my head to prop it up a bit as the cool edge of a glass came to my lips; it was water to wash the pill down. The cold liquid was good, refreshing. I raised my right hand to the bottom of the glass, tilting it further, releasing more water into my mouth and down my throat.

"More," I said. And then the darkness returned.

When consciousness came calling again, I was able to open my eyes without inviting a cast of legendary drummers to do consecutive drum solos on my skull. That was a good sign.

I was in a hotel room, but not the one I had checked into. The layout was completely different. And it didn't smell like the same hotel. Buddy was sitting in a chair beside my bed and looking at me over the pages of a magazine.

"You feeling any better now?" Buddy asked.

"Yeah," I said. "A lot better, actually." It was good to say something without the sound of my own words attacking my pain receptors. Though there was a numbness in my head, likely the effect of the painkillers Buddy fed me, my enhanced senses had returned. I could detect the lemon scent of the detergent from the sheets of the bed I was in, the slight lavender of the fabric softener. It was definitely not Loews Hollywood Hotel. Their laundry had more of a honeysuckle fragrance to it. I also easily picked up Buddy's musky aftershave mingled with his distinct smell of sweat, and the fact he hadn't showered in at least a day. Also coming through was the familiar sound of his heartbeat, the murmur of voices from other rooms in the hotel, the movement of people and traffic on the street outside. All of those underlying background sounds and smells I'd become used to were there. They were still a little muted, dulled, perhaps, by the painkillers, but they were definitely there.

"Where are we?"

"The Roosevelt. The Hollywood Roosevelt. Right on the strip. Not the Roosevelt I sometimes stay at when I'm in New York."

I smiled. "Of course."

One curtain was open, revealing bright sunlight streaming into the room.

"So how long have I been out?"

Buddy paused, his heartbeat picked up a bit; and though I was finding it hard to read his emotions—something I occasionally had a problem with when it came to him—he was giving off a sense of nervousness.

"Well," he said. "You haven't been out the whole time. You've been in and out of consciousness on and off. You don't remember, do you?"

"Buddy, how long have I been out?"

He looked down at his wrist, consulting his watch, then pursed his lips together, and started tapping the tips of the fingers on his left hand with the index finger of his right, obviously doing the math.

"Maybe thirty-two hours. No more than thirty-four."

"What?"

"You really needed the rest, my young friend."

Holy crap. I missed an entire day being on the set. And Lex. I'd wanted to message Lex.

"It's Saturday?"

"Yep. But I do have to say, the rest did you a heck of a lot of good. I've heard people use the term 'beauty rest' before but have never seen it make such a dramatic difference.

"Right after I chased those thugs off, your face was all swollen and bruised. It looked seriously nasty. I almost didn't recognize you. Your one eye was so puffy you couldn't even open it.

"But now, less than forty hours later, the bruises and swelling have receded significantly. I've never seen anyone heal so fast."

Buddy didn't know that, along with my enhanced werewolf strength, and senses—not that they'd been working very well that night—came a significantly advanced metabolism. My constitution and ability to heal and recover was heightened, strengthened. It worked more actively during those monthly cycles where my body transformed from human into canine, the mammal transmogrification seeming to force a bit of a reset on my system. My scratches and bruises seemed to fade the way the lines on an Etch A Sketch would when given a quick shake. Each change to wolf and then back to human was like an additional flip or shake. The healing ability persisted throughout the entire month, even though my other abilities were somewhat lessened. It was just less aggressive. It was like an Etch A Sketch given an accidental bump or nudge. My health, in general, was quite robust and hearty. Apart from a few sniffles, sneezes, and coughs, I hadn't caught any sort of major cold or flu bug since becoming a werewolf.

"How did you get me here?"

"You don't remember coming here, do you?"

I shook my head. It was mostly darkness since I saw him standing in the parking lot with a gun.

"After the hooligans in the masks ran off, I revived you; but you were really out of it. Bombed out of your head, to be honest. You didn't say much, weren't answering any of my questions, but, apart from a bit of a beating, and the alcohol you'd been swimming in, you seemed to be okay.

"I've helped enough drunken stumbling friends after a night of debauchery make it home safe that I'm an old pro at it. You weren't speaking more than a few incoherent words; which meant I wasn't able to find out what hotel you were staying at. But I was able to get you into my car and drive us back to my hotel.

"You don't remember any of that? You don't remember sitting up to eat the food I've been ordering in? Any of that?"

I shook my head. "No."

This realization startled me. I didn't have any solid conscious memory of my time as a wolf—except for some fleeting snippets of sights, sounds, and smells—but I'd never experienced that sort of blackout as a human. It was disconcerting.

"I don't know, Mikey. Maybe it was good that you were so inebriated. You know how when someone falls, if they tense up, they end up hurting themselves a lot more, but a drunk guy just goes over and is fine? Maybe the same thing happened with you. You were so pickled that you didn't tense up as they were hitting you. Maybe that helped reduce the damage. I don't know. I'm not a doctor, and I don't even play one on TV."

He stopped to laugh at his own joke.

"I didn't know you carried a gun."

"I just started about a year ago. And I only take it with me when I'm out after dark. A guy has got to protect himself, you know."

"No, I don't know."

I wasn't a fan of civilians owning guns. Handguns, at least. Weapons meant to hurt other humans. I'd grown up in a rural part of Ontario where shotguns and rifles, meant for partridge, rabbits, ducks, deer, and moose were a way of life. Those kinds of guns had never bothered me. But it never made sense for non-hunters to have guns; especially not the assault rifles or handguns typically used by the military and armed forces.

Most of the people I had encountered over the years who owned guns were the bad guys; those who used those weapons not to defend themselves, but to attack or hurt other people.

"Well, if I didn't have that gun, what do you think might have happened to you the other night? I'm a damned good negotiator, but those freaky masked guys didn't look like they were ready to be reasoned with."

"Good point." I conceded. Buddy having that gun had saved my skin. "I'm glad you showed up when you did. And that you had that gun. Thanks, Buddy."

He nodded.

"So, those guys. How the heck did you get mixed up with them? Seriously, Mikey, I thought I was walking onto a filming of the next movie in the *Purge* series when I came upon you."

"I was just walking back to my hotel. I saw them beating on a helpless man. I stepped in, managed to surprise one of them, and take him down. The other two jumped me. I think the guy they were beating up when I got there escaped. Did you see him?"

"No. Just you and the three masked guys. There were the two on top of you, and the third one was just getting back up when I arrived."

"What happened after I blacked out?"

"I told them to scram, to skedaddle, to beat-it. They took off like a bunch of whippersnappers who'd just smashed a school window. Didn't say a single word. Not even a 'yoicks we've been busted' or anything."

"I noticed that about them, too. They were eerily quiet."

"And seriously, what's with those creepy masks?"

I thought about that, then remembered the article, or at least part of the article I'd been reading on the plane and the discussion I'd had with Argyle.

"I think those guys were members of the PFA."

"The *Proud Fighters for America*?"

"Yeah. I'd read an article recently that mentioned they

wore masks when engaging in their stealth attacks on people and businesses. It must have been them."

"I don't know much about them, but I do remember hearing an NPR radio broadcast about them. Apparently, they originated right here in the Los Angeles area. All I can say is, glad I had that gun in my glove compartment."

"Glad you came upon us when you did."

He nodded.

"I think I've lost count of the times you have showed up completely out of the blue and saved my skin in the nick of time."

Buddy nodded again. His heart skipped a beat and there was a brief flash of nervousness before he recovered and pushed out a more playful scent.

"Yep," he grinned. "That time you were being walked through that alley in the South Street Seaport area of Manhattan. Or the first time we met, in the middle of the night on that lonely stretch of highway in upstate New York."

"That first time, your car appeared just as I was being attacked by a wolf. You scared him off."

"Yep. If I hadn't arrived when I did, you might well have been a goner."

I grinned. Yeah. He saved me. We talked about that almost every time we met. How couldn't we? It was quite the memorable first meeting. And the beginning of our long-term friendship. But it was also the genesis of me developing my lycanthropic wolfish abilities. Something in that wolf's saliva had gotten into my blood, infused with my DNA, infected me with this curse, this tremendous ability. Buddy hadn't just saved my life; his accidental interloping had entirely altered the course of my life.

Despite my relationship with Buddy being perhaps the longest-term relationship I had as an adult he did not know about the side-effects that wolf attack had on me. I didn't transform into a wolf until the next cycle of the moon. I'm no scientist, but that's likely because whatever from the wolf that had infected me likely had to work its way through my bloodstream, infuse itself, over time, with my DNA.

"You seem to attract trouble, Mikey."

"And you have a knack for appearing at exactly the right time."

I caught another very brief whiff of nervousness coming off of him.

"Seriously, Buddy. I'm on the other side of the continent. How is it that you showed up, here in LA, at the right place, and just the right time? Again?"

"I'm in LA half a dozen times a year. I travel a lot. I spend three quarters of my life on the road. You know that, Mikey. New York, Los Angeles, Chicago, Houston, Phoenix, San Antonio, Philadelphia, Nashville. All the biggies.

"I'm back and forth through these cities so often. The odds are actually quite good I would be here when you were here. It was bound to happen that, no matter what larger city you visit, I'll either be there at the same time, or likely within a week or so. Do you know how many air miles and hotel points I have racked up? How much of this grand nation I have seen through the windshield of my car? I could likely fly and stay in hotels all across the US of A for free for a full year and still have points left over when the year is done. I could likely tell you which highway or interstate I'm going down if I were still blind-folded. Willie Nelson might sing about being on the road again, but he's got nothing on Buddy J. Samuels.

"I got into town Thursday morning. I was supposed to be out of here, leaving for Houston yesterday. It's a lit-tle more than twenty-two hours to drive, so I usually do it in two days. You're the only reason I stayed on. I couldn't leave you."

"I appreciate that."

"But now that you're up and conscious again, and do-ing better, I need to try to get myself on a flight to Houston so I can be there for my Monday morning meet-ing. And then rent a car for the rest of the stops on my tour."

"So sorry you had to go to so much trouble, Buddy."

"Think nothing of it," Buddy said. "I've had to change my travel plans more times than Elizabeth Taylor and Richard Burton have tied the knot and gotten divorced. More times than Trump's businesses have filed for bank-ruptcy. More times than Canadians like you apologize in an hour. Changing plans is a way of life. I've learned, over the years to just-"

I said the next line in harmony with him, because the line, borrowed from Del Griffith from *Planes, Trains and Automobiles* had been one he'd used repeatedly over the years.

"*Go with the flow.*"

"That's right," Buddy said. "*Like a twig on the shoulders of a mighty stream.*"

"Well, thank you. Again, I'm in your debt."

"Oh, don't worry," Buddy said, laughing. "I'm keeping track. I'll come to collect when you least expect it."

"You always *do* show up when I least expect it."

"It's too bad I don't have more time with you here, though. I've got so many things to share with you about LA and Hollywood. Maybe I can catch you after I finish my trips to Houston, New Orleans, and Oklahoma City. I'll be returning to LA the second week of July. How long are you here for?"

"I fly back to Manhattan on the third of July."

He pursed his lips as he shook his head.

"That's too bad. There are so many local fascinations to relay about this area. Trivia about the stars on the Walk of Fame; the ghosts that allegedly haunt this hotel we're in right now; the reason the film industry ended up here from its origins on the east coast; the fact that the palm trees here are all imports. So many things."

"Actually," I said. "I have already learned about two of the things you mentioned. You don't happen to have a cousin who goes by the name Argyle, do you?"

Buddy's scent gave off a scent of confusion.

"No. Why?"

"Just a guy I met; a limo driver whose penchant for sharing trivia might rival yours."

"Well," Buddy said. "Rival might be too strong of a

word, don't you think? I mean, I doubt he could keep up with the master."

While Buddy had been the most verbose, trivia-spouting person I'd ever known; a man who never tired of hearing himself talk, Argyle was no slouch in that area. I wondered what seeing the two of them in a face-down might look like. But I decided to let that pass.

"So, when everything went down that night—the masked guys beating me, you pulling a gun on them, me being so beat up—did the police not get involved in some way?"

"No." Buddy said. And a mild yet steady wave of nervousness exuded from him. "No police. It was over. You were safe. They were gone. And had masks on. What good would descriptions be?

"There was also no way I was taking you to a hospital, either. You looked beat up, but still in one piece. Heck, I think the booze in your system did you more harm than those hooligan's fists. And you know how much I like to avoid the authorities and their endless questions. That's not good for anybody. And not good for me, either. I mean, I'm not saying this is the case, but the gun I'm carrying might not actually be registered, you know."

I nodded. Ever since I developed the habit of using my enhanced abilities to carry out vigilante justice, I was leery about the authorities myself. Sure, they were there to protect and serve, but the last thing I needed was to be held in a jail cell during that time of the month, then being discovered as a lycanthrope and to spend the rest of my life locked away in some secret government lab being studied and poked and prodded until I died. No thank you. Give me my freedom.

I was evasive of the authorities because I was a werewolf. What reason, then, was Buddy so shy when it came to the police?

We were both quiet for a moment. I tried reading Buddy's nervousness, but it dissipated. A slight curious odor came from him just before he spoke his next words.

"Who is Lex?"

"What?"

"Lex. You didn't speak much when I was half carrying you to the Uber, into the hotel, or in those brief conscious moments where I managed to get either more painkillers or some food into you.

"But a few times you mumbled some things. The only clear words I could make out was the name 'Lex.' At one point you said you had to call Lex, needed to apologize. To explain things to her.

"Who is this mysterious Lex?" He had a big Cheshire Cat grin on his face when he asked. "You gettin' a little tail while you're in town? Finally moved on from Gail? Decided it was time to pack those heart bags, move them on to a new town, park those boots under another woman's bed?

"You know, *every new beginning comes from some other beginning's end*. You might recognize that phrase from a pop song from a few years back; 'Closing Time' by Semisonic. The song writer, Dan Wilson, was quoting the Roman Stoic philosopher Seneca."

Buddy kept rambling on about Roman philosophers

and other songs the same writer had co-written with the Dixie Chicks, but I zoned out of his flow of verbal diarrhea.

Because I was thinking about Lex.

It was Saturday. I'd missed my chance to reach out to Lex on Friday morning.

To apologize to her.

To explain my idiotic reaction and see if she would give me another chance.

I pictured her sitting at the bar beside me, that beautiful smile and the way those playful light blue eyes twinkled as she laughed. I reflected on the fun we'd had just talking about music and movies. Talking, and sharing, and enjoying the hell out of one another in a way that made all those hours pass far too quickly. Then I remembered the look of hurt and disappointment on her face as a result of the last words I'd spoken to her.

Oh, Lex.

I'd blown it.

Chapter Fifteen: I Just Met You. This Is Crazy. Had Your Number, Didn't Text You Lately

A few hours later, once I convinced Buddy I'd recovered enough to not need a babysitter/fairy god mother, or hairy wolf mother, or whatever you might call that protective role he played in my life, he made arrangements to fly to Houston and packed up his stuff. He dropped me off at my hotel room on his way to the airport, but not before giving me a warning in his usual jolly tone.

"Try to stay out of dark parking lots at two in the morning, would ya?"

Back in my hotel room, I noticed a large bouquet of flowers on the desk with a little note on it.

Feel better soon. Mack.

What the hell? How did Mack know what had happened?

I shook my head, plugged my phone into the charger

at my desk and waited for it to have enough juice in it to power on. The text message indicator showed there were a dozen unread messages. Two of them were from Lex.

The first one had come in at 11:40 AM on Friday.

Had a really fun time last night. Have you figured out if you're single or not? Would love to see you, Kal.

The second one, which came in at 9:12 PM on Friday, was a single word.

NEVERMIND

Damn.

The other text messages were from Craig, my new friend from the movie set, Anne, Mack's assistant, and Gail. But the voicemail indicator said I had seven messages. Maybe they were from Lex.

I poked the indicator then punched in my code to retrieve the messages.

"First message," the female AI voice on my phone said. "Friday, 10:01 AM."

"Michael, it's Craig. Is everything okay, man? Don't mean to bother you but JP was actually asking for you today. There was something he wanted to discuss with you about one of the characters. And, as you know, he can have his moods. He's in one of them now. Hope you're okay and that you're on your way here. Call me. Let me know."

I hit the button to delete that message and move on to the next.

"Next message. Friday, 11:15 AM."

"What the hell, Andrews?" It was Mack Halpin. "You were a no-show on the set. And I have to find this out by getting a call from Heartschwinger himself? Do you have any fucking idea what this sort of bullshit does to my reputation? I pulled a shit-ton of strings to get you onto that set, you ungrateful cockwomble. Oh, goddammit, my blood pressure..." he was saying as he obviously slammed the phone down.

Mack wasn't a fan of cell phones and quite enjoyed having an old-fashioned land-line telephone that he could dramatically slam onto his desk when he was pissed-off. Which was often.

I deleted that message.

"Next message. Friday, 1:14 PM."

"Where the fuck are you, Andrews?" It was Mack again. "Don't make me cancel a shit-pile of meetings to hop on a plane and come down there to fix your little red wagon. I swear, you better damn-well be dead in an alley somewhere to have just fucked off without a single word to anyone."

I deleted that message.

"Next message. Friday, 1:41 PM."

There was just silence, the sound of a breath being released. Then it ended.

I entered the code that would relay the number associated with the message. It was Lex's number.

I hit the button to listen to it again.

Silence. Breathing out.

Rewind.

Silence. Breathing out. Was that a breath of exasperation?

I listened one more time. Then I moved on to the other messages, hopeful another one would be from her.

"Next message. Friday, 2:45 PM."

"Michael. It's Craig again. I'm worried about you, man. Heartschwinger is storming the lot looking for you. I think he called your agent back in New York. Really hope you're okay. Give me a call, let me know."

Delete.

"Next message. Friday, 6:18 PM."

"Do you have any idea," Mack began, "how incredibly unprofessional and incompetent this makes you look? But more than that, it's how it makes me look. I couldn't give two shits if you want to flush your pansy hack ass writing career down the toilet by dicking around and being elusive. You've done it before, and it was mildly cute, Andrews. But not this time. This time you're toying with my reputation with Holly-fucking-wood. And I won't stand for it. I won't stand for it at all, you ungrateful, incompetent waste of space. Everyone has a right to be stupid, to do stupid things; but you, Andrews, are overtly abusing the privilege. There is no excuse. No fucking excuse at all for the bullshit you're putting me through. Except, maybe, that they found your dead body while dragging the Hollywood Reservoir."

"Next message. Saturday, 1:14 AM."

"Hey Andrews," My heart leapt into my throat at the sound of the familiar female voice. But it was not the voice I'd been hoping to hear from. It was Gail. "Was just thinking about you and wondering how Hollywood is treating you."

It was disconcerting hearing Gail's voice. I didn't want to think about it.

I deleted the message.

"No more new messages," the female AI voice said.

I flipped over to the text messages, saw a few concerned notes from Craig, similar in tone to his voice mails. And then a number from Anne Lee, Mack's assistant. Her first one was a worried note letting me know Mack was on the phone with JP Heartschwinger and she was worried about me. To call or text and let her know where I was and if I was okay. There were a couple of follow up ones; they were like Craig's texts of concern and worry. Anne Lee was a kind, gentle, and loving soul. I never understood how such a sweet and kind person could work for such a vicious and cut-throat hard-ass as Mack the Knife, but I was always thankful for the way her kindness and thoughtfulness balanced out the rough edges that came with Mack.

One of the later texts from Anne was her letting me know she'd heard from Buddy J. Samuels who explained I'd been beat up and was recovering, still unconscious. I looked up at the flowers sent from Mack, knowing he likely knew nothing about them. They were from her; trying to make it look like a subtle apology from Mack for the messages he had left me.

But I knew better. Mack would never apologize; would never come close to apologizing. That was all her, all Anne.

Yet again, I was grateful that he was my agent, was the one fighting for me. Because it was that ruthlessness and bullheadedness he exuded that likely got me into more than half of the great deals and offers I had experienced in my writing career.

But I wasn't concerned about Mack. I was thinking about Lex. And her last text to me.

I opened it up and looked at it.

NEVERMIND

I re-read her first message to me again. It was so sweet, so hopeful. Then came that call from her. The one with no message. Just a short outtake of breath. Disappointment? Maybe I was reading things into it, and into what I thought we'd had the other night. But I was pretty sure she was into me. She had kissed me on the cheek after all. She had asked if I was single.

Which I'd messed up.

And then, I went MIA. Not only did I not call her the next day, but I hadn't responded to her inquisitive and hopeful message. I had let her call go to voice mail.

Another virtual slap in the face.

I had to call her. I had to explain what happened.

Or should I text first?

I keyed in: *Sorry I didn't message you. I can explain* and pressed send.

The little indicator below my text showed the "Delivered" status.

I stood there staring at my phone.

And waited.

And waited.

I wanted to sit on the bed and moved as far as the

charging cable would allow. But it wasn't long enough. I unplugged it and sat on the end of the bed.

I saw the little multi-dot indicator that meant she was typing something; and I took a deep breath.

Her message appeared.

Too little. Too late.

My heart sank. I had blown it. But I needed her to understand what had happened. That I hadn't been ignoring or avoiding her. It hadn't been my fault.

Well, technically, it had been my fault. I'd walked into the situation. I should have known better, with my limited powers at the time, that I would have gotten my ass kicked. But how could I have just walked by and let them beat the crap out of that helpless man?

I needed to call her and tell her what had happened.

As the phone rang, I felt my mouth going dry. It rang several times before she picked up.

There was a brief split second of silence. Well, not exactly silence. Music and the sound of people chatting in the background spilled forth. But no voice. No Lex. Then the call disconnected.

I tried again. The phone rang multiple times. Then it went to voice mail.

Lex's recorded voice came on: "It's your dime." Then the beep.

"Lex, it's Michael. It's, uh, Kal. I need to talk to you. To explain what happened. I wanted to call you, but..." I paused, took a deep breath. "Listen. I'm going to call back in a minute. It's easier to explain to you rather than in a message."

I disconnected, then sent a text that read: *I just left you a voice message. Will call back in one minute to explain. Please pick up.*

The "Delivered" indicator popped up.

A moment later, the little dots indicating she was typing appeared on the screen. Then her message.

kk

Good.

I sat and stared at the phone. Checked the time at the top of the phone. It was 6:19 PM.

Scrolling back up, I looked at the selfie Lex and I had taken and which I'd sent her, how close our heads were, gently touching, as we'd leaned together and grinned for the shot. I looked at her response to it.

BFFs

"Best Friends Forever." I said aloud. "I hope we can be more than just friends, Lex." I thought about Gail, about the longing and yearning I'd had for so long for our friendship to evolve back into something more. But wishing and hoping wasn't going to make that happen.

Lex and I had enjoyed one another's company. She was charming, spirited, fun, and an interesting person to talk with. And she was beautiful.

I really wanted to see if this could work out.

I took a deep breath, noticed that a minute had passed. Then called.

It rang twice before she picked up. There was a brief moment where I could hear the background sounds of the restaurant or bar where she was at. My enhanced hearing was back to normal, and I could make out Kortney the bartender's familiar voice in the mix of background chatter. Then she spoke.

"This had better be good, Michael."

"Thanks for taking my call, Lex." I thought about the multiple things I needed to apologize for and to explain. I thought I would start at the beginning. "Listen. I'm so sorry. The other night at the bar, I really felt something between us. We were just clicking, you know. Everything. It was good. And then, when you asked me if I was single, my mind went back to someone. Someone in New York."

"You *do* have someone? A girlfriend back home?"

"I did. But, it's not like that..."

I stopped. The line had gone silent. Dead. She'd hung up on me?

I looked down at my phone. No. She hadn't hung up on me. My phone had died. The little bit of a charge from plugging it in had ran out.

"You've got to be freakin' kidding me!"

I scrambled over to the desk, plugged the phone back into the charging cable and waited the minute or so—which felt a little more like an hour—for the phone to have enough juice to power back up.

It only rang once; no, not even a full ring. It went straight to her voice mail.

"It's your dime."

I disconnected. Called again. It went to voice mail after

the first half ring again.

"Dammit!"

I called again. Again, it went to voice mail.

I hastily typed in a text and sent it.

My phone died.

The "Delivered" message never came.

I texted another message and hit send.

Tried calling you back.

Again, no "Delivered" message appeared.

That, plus going straight to voice mail told me she'd either blocked my number or put her phone in "do not disturb" mode. There was no reaching her by phone.

But I did know where she was.

I unplugged my phone again and headed for the door.

Chapter Sixteen: It's a Small Skull-Crushing World After All

On the way to Gulp in the Uber I called Craig to let him know I was okay, to apologize for not getting back to him, and to explain what had happened.

"Oh, we know," Craig said. "Everyone on the set knows. JP made a big deal out of it after your agent called and shared what had gone down. It was quite the about-face. He'd been storming around bad-mouthing you in his melodramatic way, calling you every possible insulting name in the book. He already hates script writers. But novelists, he was saying, are the lowest of the low. He was spouting off about how a meddling novelist from the first movie he had shot based on a book had ruined his first movie, screwed him out of the Academy Awards nomination he deserved. I think he also expressed how novelists likely kill babies and drown puppies when nobody is looking.

"Then, after the call from your agent's office, he launched into gossip mode. He started sharing how you'd been ambushed and beaten half to death by a gang of thugs from the Proud Fighters of America. How they likely have a vendetta against this studio, not only because JP Heartschwinger is a Jew, but because Schwinger Films was praised at being an inclusive company, openly hiring, and promoting people from the LGBTQ community, and a large percentage of Latino and Black employees.

"He even tried to explain that the attack was likely made on you because you're not even an American. You're a Canadian who is taking work away from hard working folks born right here in this country.

"I've seen him do this sort of open gossip-spreading with the entire cast and crew before. To be honest, I think he's hoping to leverage this for some pre-release publicity for the movie. He wants this to get out to the media. Wants people to start talking up the film this early in the production cycle. The papers have been running stories about the PFA for months now, and so are eager to find anything to print about them.

"JP's not an idiot. He's good at manipulating people, and the media. And he's running full tilt with this one."

"Wow," I said, wondering about the repercussions of having to speak to the police about the attack if it were to be well-known. I preferred avoiding having to deal with the authorities. But at least I was a victim and not caught in some vigilante action where I'd been the one who cleaned the clocks of those scumbags. "So I suppose he's not pissed that I'm not on the set today."

"No. Nobody was expecting you back for several days anyway. And that, of course, makes JP's mythology that much better. The more days you're unable to be up to coming to the set, the better for his message."

We exchanged more small talk and I shared that I had been doing better and would likely be back on Monday. We finished our conversation just as the Uber arrived at Gulp.

I thought I could pick up on Lex's faint scent as I was walking in the doorway, but it didn't get much stronger when I went inside. The stool at the corner of the bar where she'd been sitting the other night, the one I learned was her stool, was occupied by a guy in a business suit. The faded scent suggested she had been here but had left recently.

Standing there, I picked up on the odor of contempt and disdain. It came from a few folks I'd recognized as regulars that Lex had introduced me to, as well as Kortney, the bartender.

Kortney was standing at the corner of the bar, opposite where I'd been sitting Thursday night, and scowling at me. Even if I had not been able to smell her disgust for me, the cold icy glare would have gotten the message across.

"What's *he* doin' here?" one of the regulars on the other end of the bar whispered.

She was shaking her head as I walked up to the bar.

"I thought you were a nice guy," Kortney said. "Can't believe how wrong—"

She stopped and a look of shock came across her face along with a scent that matched. She'd noticed my black eye, the swelling and bruises that, though significantly healed, were still evident.

"What the heck happened to you?"

"Maybe Lex saw him outside and gave him what he deserves," Max, the other bartender who had just popped out of the kitchen, said.

As much anger, hostility, and vile feelings the staff and several of the regular patrons were exuding toward me, it impressed me just how much they cared about this woman.

"That's what I was trying to explain to Lex when my phone died," I said. "I got mugged in a parking lot on my walk back to my hotel the other night. I was completely out of it, barely conscious while I was laid up and recovering. I wasn't able to call her."

"Oh, Sugar," Kortney said, "I'm so sorry. But there's still that whole girlfriend thing, you know. Getting beat up doesn't take that away. You were leading the poor girl on."

"That's the thing," I said. "I don't have anyone. Haven't for years. I couldn't possibly be more single."

"Then what the heck was that the other night? What does 'mostly single' mean?"

Kortney hadn't even been around when I'd said that. Obviously, these folks shared a lot with one another.

"I've been single for years. But, all that time, until only recently, I've been stuck thinking about that someone that I should have been over a long time ago.

"For the longest time, I never..." I paused, not sure how to continue. I never what? Never saw another woman the way I saw Lex? Never thought I would actually meet someone who would make me stop thinking about Gail? I never expected a moment like I'd had with Lex could ever happen? Sure, all of those things. But how to explain to a group of Lex's protective friends? Because even though this was a conversation between me and Kortney, I knew the others, including Max, were all attending to it.

"I haven't dated in a long time. Never been good at it. I'm sure you can tell I'm far from a smooth player. But I really like Lex. And I suppose I was nervous. I suppose I was a little afraid, too. I tripped over my tongue. I'm not...I'm not really all that good at this. And I can't really hold my alcohol all that well."

She smiled. "I noticed." The last remains of the residual anger and contempt from her morphed into a deeper sense of sympathy. I picked up a similar vibe from the others who were listening in.

"But you've got to know," she continued, "that girl is right pissed with you."

"Can't say that I blame her. Do you know where she went to?"

"She has several regular hangouts. Prince O' Whales, Mo's."

One of the other male regulars piped in. "Brennan's."

My head was spinning. How could someone spend so much time in so many different bars? Did she have a caring family of regulars at each one? Those questions, of course, added to the mystique and the growing infatuation I had regarding Lex, this woman of many names, this woman of many places.

"But I think," Kortney said, "based on the look she had on her face after you hung up on her..."

"My phone died."

"I was just teasing you, Sugar. I think she needed to get to a place that was further away. A spot that is perhaps darker in nature, to fit her mood. I suspect she was in a Skull Crusher sort of mood."

"Did you just say Skull Crusher? As in Skull Crusher Brewery?"

"You've heard of it?"

I nodded. "Yeah, I have."

I had planned on visiting there anyway, thanks to a recommendation from Argyle. And in the odd 'it's a small world' way that things seemed to be connected lately, I suspected that's exactly where I would find Lex.

I lifted my phone to open the Uber app so I could punch in the address and saw that it had died.

Naturally. I hadn't left it plugged in long enough.

"Do you have the address?"

"The cabs know the place, Sugar."

Kortney was right. The cab driver was familiar with Skull Crusher Brewery and said it wouldn't take more than half an hour to get there.

The driver wasn't chatty, and I even picked up a tinge of nervousness he had toward me. Was it because of the beaten-up look of my face? No, as I took in more of the scent, I sensed more than he was afraid of me.

I was happy to sit in the back seat in silence and think

about what I would say to Lex when I found her. If I found her, I had to remind myself, because I didn't know for sure if she would be there.

The driver had the radio on, an easy-listening pop station. During one of the short news breaks a story came on reporting an increase in frequency of attacks associated with the *Proud Fighters for America*. More than a dozen stores in four different neighborhoods had been firebombed the previous night. The attacks caused an estimated four million dollars in damage. All the businesses hit were owned by visible minorities. And a symbol that had become associated with the PFA, described as a large hard-angled capital letter A was spray painted in red at each of the crime scenes.

As the story played, the driver's anxiety peaked.

"What is the world coming to?" I said, when the news clip finished. "What's wrong with these people? Where did they come from?"

"They've always been here. Just not all that visible."

"You think so?"

"I *know* so." He replied. "The world has always been dangerous for someone like me. I thought, when I left South Africa, I would leave all of this behind. Apartheid ended; but that didn't change what it was like for me there. The way they looked me at. The way I was treated.

"I came to America with visions of equal opportunity. With the belief that if you worked hard, you could rise and make something of yourself. That racial discrimination would be a thing of the past in this great nation where slavery had been abolished and where segregation was a thing of the past. Sure, on the surface, it might have looked safe, and equal, and free for a long time. But the tentacles of white supremacy are long, and have been creeping below the surface, unseen, for years. Just waiting for the right time to become visible.

"The PFA are a radical and violent group. But they represent an ill and injustice that makes America not all that different from South Africa. The two nations are twins, born of the same mother, suckled by the same breast of tainted white milk."

He stopped and got quiet, and his fear and anxiety rose.

"I'm sorry," he said. "I apologize. I didn't mean to go on like that. Please forgive me."

I didn't respond right away. How could I?

"No. It's okay." I finally said. "I mean, it's not okay. It's wrong. Not what you said. What you said, I get it. I understand. What's happening is wrong. And it's wrong that you should even think you have to apologize."

He nodded, and the scent he gave off, though still nervous, was now slightly relaxed.

I can only imagine the disappointment he must feel; must have to live with every day.

And I understood, a little better, the nervousness and the fear I smelled off him when I first stepped into his cab.

It wasn't that I might be a member of the PFA. It was that I might just be yet another one of those people who was compliant, open, and accepting on the surface. Another person pretending to hold a belief in equality while harboring the residue of the white supremacy that flows through the very bedrock of the western world.

We were both quiet for the rest of the ride, listening to the smooth jazz streaming from the radio station. I found it interesting that the sound of the music seemed to act like a calming salve on my driver's heartbeat and tension.

I thought about the effect Alicia Witt's music had had on my very soul when I was hearing it at exactly the right time I needed it. If I hadn't experienced that, would I have been open to the possibilities of what things could be like with Lex? Would I be pursuing her in the way I currently was in order to make things right?

As the cab dropped me off in front of a pair of warehouses, I wondered about what I was doing.

Did I have any right to be chasing Lex down?

Would she see this as an aggressive move? Something completely out of line? Perhaps even interpreted as stalking her?

No, I told myself. I just wanted a chance to explain what happened, and why I hadn't been able to call her. And that I had been hoping to see her again, if that was possible.

And if, after hearing what I had to say, she was out, I'd leave her be.

So, no, this wasn't stalking.

There was nobody in sight down either stretch of the street. Both warehouses in front of me were nondescript, with no signs or markings on them except for a spray-painted skull-and-crossbones on the warehouse on my left with the letters SCB scrawled underneath them and

an arrow pointing into the alley between the two buildings. I noted that the "bones" under the skull were beer
bottles. Clever.

The scent of the traffic of sweaty bodies filled the alley,
and the throbbing sound of bass came from the warehouse on the left. Even without my acute sense of sound,
I'm sure that would have been plainly evident.

I thought I'd picked up pick out Lex's scent among
the smell of numerous strangers. It was faint. Residual.
Like she may have been here recently. I took that as a
good sign and headed down the alley.

Chapter Seventeen: One Belgian, One Stout, One IPA

Moving down the alley toward what appeared to be an entrance while the shadows deepened and stretched out as the sun made its decent in the western sky, the alley was rather disturbing.

Not that I was nervous about descending dark alleys. I had, after all, been down a fair share of alleys chasing bad guys. And my heightened strength, speed, and agility, not to mention my enhanced senses gave me a huge advantage over normal folks.

No, I wasn't afraid someone might jump out of the shadows and attack me. Because I'd be able to smell them, detect their emotive intent, hear their increasing heartbeat, well before the attack came.

I was fearful of speaking with Lex.

Because, assuming she accepted my apology, listened to what happened, and understood about the incident in the parking lot the other night, and about my odd reaction to the question about being single, what would I say to her?

The fact is, I wasn't a smooth talker. Had never been

good at the whole relationship thing to begin with.

Not to mention, Lex lived in Los Angeles. I lived in New York.

What was the point of trying to have a relationship like that?

And that's not even considering the whole lycanthropy issue.

It's what initially ruined my relationship with Gail.

No. I can't blame the fact I was a werewolf on the failed relationship with Gail. It wasn't that. It was that I kept it from Gail; lied to her about the whole thing. She had even figured it out, on her own. But it had been the mistrust, the fact I'd lied to her, that she couldn't get over.

Even if Lex and I worked this initial misunderstanding out and figured out this distance thing, too, what then?

Would I fly to be with her in LA, or have her fly to be with me in New York only during those times of the month where I was human and not morphing into a wolf?

See? There I go again. Immediately and automatically moving toward deception.

But how the heck is anybody going to accept the fact that I'm a walking myth; a virtual impossibility? And how do you tell someone about that?

I'd only ever shared that secret with one other person. But that was out of necessity. For her own safety. Gail had pulled it together on her own. I knew two people, both female, who had known and accepted me as a werewolf. Heck, both of them had actually spent time with me when I was in wolf form, too.

So, it obviously wasn't an impossibility.

But I had to stop myself. Here I was, again over thinking. Over planning. Progressively imagining a fantastical future with a woman I'd just met.

I hadn't even yet apologized to Lex.

First things first.

As I arrived at the metal door, it opened, and a massive man who was at least six inches taller than me dominated the entrance. He was bald, handsome, and had muscles on top of muscles. He looked quite a bit like The Rock, actually. I'm sure *he* had no issues when it came to confidence, and women.

"ID," he said.

I handed him my New York Department of State photo ID.

He took a cursory glance at it. His scent revealed a complete disinterest. He didn't even attend to the details on the card. It was clear I looked older than twenty-one and was just going through the required protocol.

"Been here before?" he asked.

"No. This is my first time."

"Welcome to Skull Crusher Brewery," he said. "Three rules. No ties. No dancing. And no credit cards." He gave the entire spiel without intonation or inflection.

I nodded. "Fair enough."

"You got cash?"

"Yep. You take Canadian Tire money, right?"

His face and scent gave off an air of confusion, and his automaton style patter broke. He paused, actually looking at me for the first time.

Not sure why I was goofing around with the big guy. Maybe I just wanted to nudge him out of his boredom and routine. Canadian Tire money was a loyalty program from a Canadian retail chain that was a substitute for legal tender printed to resemble actual bank notes. They were given out on purchases as a percentage of the overall sale in denominations of 5¢, 10¢, 25¢, 50¢, $1 & $2 and accepted for Canadian money at par. There are likely few households in Canada where there wasn't a stash of Canadian Tire bills stuffed into some kitchen junk drawer, toolbox, or glove compartment. I knew he wouldn't know what I was talking about.

After looking me up and down he spoke, this time in a more human sounding tone. "We don't take foreign currency."

"American cash, then."

"Another rule," he said. "No wise guys."

I nodded. "Check."

He opened the door to let me in, but not before sizing me up one more time. Despite the shadows of the alley, he seemed to spot my fading bruises and black eye.

"No fighting, either," he said. "And don't puke on the floor."

Inside was dark, dank, and loud.

It smelled of a combination of spicy hops and sweet roasted malt, of worn warm leather, of cedar and oak, of odd combinations of chocolate and coffee and banana and metallic sulfur, of the skunky remnants of spilled beer and sour sweat, both fresh and baked into the very walls of the place.

The throbbing beat of heavy metal music was so over-powering that I had to consciously block it out. It masked a lot of the other noises, of conversation, heartbeats, and the sound of screams of terror. I started at that, but immediately recognized the screams weren't coming from people in the place, but from movie reels. I looked up to see, projected onto the ceiling, what looked like an old eighties X-rated horror movie scene of a voluptuous naked woman writhing on a bed and covered in blood. It was difficult to tell if she was moaning in ecstasy or horror, and if the blood was hers or belonged to someone else.

I looked away in embarrassment.

There were skulls everywhere. Glow in the dark skulls painted on the dark walls, plastic and plaster ones fixed to tabletops, walls, sections of the ceiling. Metal skull heads were on the top of every single tap pull behind the bar. There were skeletons on the ceiling, and even a pair of them at the end of the bar looking like they were engaged in copulation. There was a refrigerator in the shape of a large stand-up coffin to the left of the bar with a "Bottles to Go" sign above it. Beside it was a skeleton in an old wooden wheelchair, one hand-less arm propped up as if waving at the patrons walking through the front door.

The room was packed with people sitting at a combination of small high top square tables and slightly lower beer barrels converted into tabletops.

A secondary room off to the right of the bar had

"PHANTOM THEATER" in glow-in-the-dark chalk capital letters above the entrance. Above that were more skulls and skeletons and dripping zombie faces drawn in chalk alongside sketches of iconic horror figures. Among them were Jason's hockey mask from *Friday the 13th*, the one Michael Myers wore in *Halloween* and the screaming skull mask from *Scream*.

The masks reminded me of the Proud Fighters of America I had encountered the other night and I felt a bit of a shudder. If I encountered any of them tonight, I could certainly handle myself. But remembering how quiet they were when they were attacking gave me the creeps.

The smells were powerful, and I tried to focus in on the scent I remembered from Lex. It was faintly there in the background, but there was nothing immediate. Like she had been here recently but wasn't currently present.

I stood there, debated turning around and walking back out.

To go where? To take cab ride after cab ride to the other bars and restaurants Kortney mentioned that Lex frequented? To actually become a stalker?

What was I doing?

I was chasing a woman across the city; a woman who'd made it clear she didn't want to hear from me. Blocking someone on your phone, cutting them off from being able to communicate with you was a pretty not-so-subtle sign of a person's intent. So why was I still pursuing her? Because I wanted to let her know my perspective? Properly apologize? What was the point? I had blown it.

We'd had a nice moment. We'd shared some time together. Things had felt right, and we'd established a connection.

And then I'd blown it.

Well before I had been beat up into unconsciousness and was incommunicado.

I'd blown it when she asked if I was single and I'd hesitated.

Letting her walk away after she'd kissed me on the cheek was a mistake. I should have said something right then and there.

But what?

Hell, I'd never been good at this.

Heading out on this wild goose chase was useless.

Because I doubt, even had she been here, that I'd be able to say the right thing, anyway.

I looked over to a single empty stool at the bar and walked over to it.

The bartender, a guy in a black mesh tank-top and with more ink on his arms, shoulders, chest, neck, and face than untouched skin, caught my eye and gestured to let me know the stool was free.

It was too loud for discussion. He slid a printed beer menu in front of me and I tapped at one of the first ones, *Massacre IPA*.

He nodded and then moved to pull the beer while I hopped onto the stool.

I'd come all this way, and she wasn't here. Or, she had been here, but she'd already left. So, no Lex. No luck in my love life. Which was too bad, because I'd really thought we had something.

But I was here already, and I wanted to experience new things. And this was such a fascinating and bizarre place. Perhaps I could absorb a bit of the atmosphere here and store some details for potential use in a forthcoming novel.

Just as the throbbing heavy metal music stopped, I heard a woman's voice shout out.

"There is a huge penis on your forehead!"

I looked over to see a middle-aged white woman being pulled to a crouch by a tall male friend with glasses and a thick head of gray hair. "You're standing in front of the movie," he said, hauling on her arm. "Get out of the way so people can watch!"

The crowd let out a chorus of cheers as the two hunkered their way over to the other side of the bar.

Then the next song started up, and the room throbbed with the pulse of the base as everyone returned to what they'd been doing.

Oh yeah. I'd definitely be taking inspirational notes about the stuff that went down in this place for my writing.

"How about this *Screaming Skulls Blood Orange Wheat*?" I said to the bartender at one of those rare moments between songs where a person could maintain somewhat of a conversation.

"Coming right up."

Though I wasn't much of a drinker, I enjoyed the beers

this brewery created. The flavors and tastes were as unique as the names. I could tell the brew masters here put as much consideration and curation into the beers they produced as who ever decorated the place put into the macabre and over-the-top horror theme.

I probably should have had one of those sampler axe handles with holes drilled into them to fit four of the smaller five-ounce glasses I'd seen other people ordering.

The food here was delicious; I'd enjoyed one of their hickory smoked Appalachian BBQ brisket sandwiches, and it was good to get some food inside of me. But the food wasn't enough to absorb the alcohol from the beers I had already consumed. Not to mention the painkillers that were still in my system from earlier. Mixing them likely wasn't the best idea.

As the bartender was sliding my latest order onto the bar in front of me, I did a quick tally of the beers I'd already had before this one.

Massacre IPA.

Summer Nightmare on Main Street Saison.

Skull Crusher Sour Stout.

Deadly Grounds Coffee Infused DIPA.

Skunky Swamp Thang IPA.

Demons of Darkness Belgian Dark Ale.

That was six before this one. I consulted my watch. It had been just under three hours.

I really should consider slowing down.

But I had to admit the buzz was nice. It helped take a bit of the edge off. The residual pain from the beating I'd taken; not to mention the disappointment at having blown it with Lex.

It was also, of course, dulling my enhanced senses a bit. Not nearly as impactful as the drinks I'd had the other night; but they seemed a bit muted, which helped from having to concentrate so hard to block out the throbbing pulse of the music.

The latest song, a heavy metal sounding beat with no lyrics, just the occasional high-pitched male scream every once in a while, finished and there was barely a second of silence before the next song started. This one, unlike most of the songs that had been playing here, was a familiar one.

The opening guitar riffs triggered that odd sensation of knowing something but not identifying exactly where it was from. The best way I can describe it is like when you're leaning back in a chair and just about to fall over, but you don't.

Except, as the song continued on, my proverbial chair fell right over and crashed to the floor.

Because I knew the song quite well. And hearing it sent a shiver up the back of my spine.

It was a top forty hit from a few years back.

But that's not why the song was so familiar.

Because I knew the musician.

I'd fought with him.

And I'd watched him die.

It was Knell. A shock-rock heavy-metal pop star who could have been the love child of Eminem and Ozzy Osbourne. He looked like a mash-up of Billy Idol and Justin Bieber, and his voice sounded like a clowder of cats that had fallen into a blender. I thought his lyrics were inane drivel but his backup band were solid musicians.

The catchy music beat continued, and I noticed plenty of the patrons bopping to it as the song's opening lyrics kicked in.

I got this fire in my bone
It won't leave me alone
I got this fire in my bone
Makes me harder than a stone

I shook my head as a group of people at the table to my right who looked like they could have walked off the set of *Sons of Anarchy* sang along to the chorus.

Motoring through this half-baked life
Got a slut by my side, ten times hotter than my wife
Got a Porsche in my drive, got some smack, got some blow
Got a date with destiny, so on with the show
On with the show
I'm solid don't you know
On with the show—on with the show

I sat there biting my bottom lip hard as I watched them, thinking about the first, and last time, I'd watched Knell performing that song. It was on stage on *Late Show with David Letterman* where we were both guests. The other thing we had in common, of course, was that we were both also werewolves.

Apart from the wolf that had attacked me and inflicted

me with lycanthropy, Knell was the only other werewolf I had encountered.

I didn't get the chance to learn about his affliction, because he died that same night. And, while the biographies and documentaries about his life included his penchant for the occult, there was nothing particularly insightful related to the fact he could turn into a wolf. One difference, for him, was that he seemed in control of the change; and his human consciousness remained when he was in wolf form. But for me, when the wolf takes over, it's lights out. I sometimes pick up fleeting memories of my time as a wolf, but that's about it. I have no control of myself when in wolf form, and I have no control over when the change happens.

Gail, who'd come with me to the studio, was a huge fan of Knell's music, and was thrilled at the possibility of meeting him. We weren't together at that point, but Knell knew how deeply I still cared for her; and when she did meet him, he took her hostage in order to get to me.

That was, to me, another reminder that it wasn't good for me to get involved with someone. Maybe it was better that things didn't work out with Lex. I seemed to attract the sort of trouble that required a vigilante response. It could lead to someone I love being the target of attack should the wrong people learn my secret, the way Knell had.

When the song finished, the bartender was standing at this end of the bar, talking to another patron a few stools down who had been bopping and singing along to the Knell song.

"Love that guy." He said. "He used to come in here all the time when this place first opened. Before he released his first album. Before he became a star."

"Before he became a splat, more like," I muttered, thinking about how Knell had come to his end. "Talk about returning to Skull Crusher."

Oh no.

I realized I had said that aloud.

I glanced at the surrounding patrons, simultaneously taking in their scents to see if I could detect any sign they had heard my completely inappropriate comment.

Fortunately, nobody seemed to have had heard what I'd just said.

What the heck was wrong with me? My inhibitions had gone out the door. I was drunk. Again. I needed to stop drinking and get out of here.

If I did see Lex, I would likely say or do something stupid because of all the alcohol in me.

Besides, the thought of that night with Knell, and what had happened, with Knell, and Gail, reminded me the potential circumference of risk that anybody I was close to might come within.

I motioned at the bartender that I was ready to close out, making that signing motion, like signing for a check that seems to have become a universal gesture despite the fact that most times a person pays for their tab it's with a handheld electronic device that you either tap or key a pin code into.

As out-dated, perhaps, as the charades gesture for "Movie Title" where you peek through an "o" shape formed with one hand while pretending to crank an old-fashioned movie camera with the other.

And yet, we still understand what it means.

How is it we can easily pick up on silly things like that, and yet constantly misinterpret one another?

Maybe it was a good thing I'd messed things up with Lex. It could save her from getting close to me, potentially save her from getting hurt.

What if she had been walking with me when I encountered those PFA thugs in the parking lot the other night? She could have been hurt, or even killed.

"For the best," I muttered, as I finished paying up my tab.

No more drinking. No more pursuing Lex.

Let the poor girl escape this curse I had no choice but to live with.

Now that it was half-past 9 PM, it was dark outside. The "Rock" wannabe doorman smirked, and I smelled the condescension he felt for me as I walked out. Perhaps the term *walk* was a bit of a stretch. Shamble, shuffle, stumble might make more sense; not to mention I was, admittedly unable to maneuver in anything even closely resembling a straight line.

I was about a dozen stumbling steps past him when I heard him murmur "As usual, wise guys can't hold their liquor."

I was tempted to turn and fire back at him the fact that liquor refers to alcohol with a concentration of 30% or more, and that I'd been drinking beer, but quickly came to my senses.

Given how much I'd had to drink, I wasn't looking for a repeat of my most apt performance as a human punching bag from a few nights earlier.

Not to mention that, despite the refreshing blast of the cool night air, I was feeling a little dizzy and a quick turn on the spot like that might have quickly dropped me right on my ass.

It was enough for me to concentrate on the act of placing one foot in front of the other and finding my way to the street and hailing a cab.

The alley seemed to be much longer that it had been when I was heading in the opposite direction earlier. That or some joker was stretching it out ahead of me as I walked.

I was almost positive of the latter.

I shook my head and took in a deep breath.

This recent habit of too much drinking needed to stop.

The fresh breath brought me a startlingly familiar scent.

Lex.

It was recent. Fresher than the previous notes I'd picked up on her earlier.

She'd come back while I'd been at the bar?

But I hadn't seen her, hadn't picked up her fresh scent when I was inside.

I stopped.

Should I go back inside? Look for her?

No. It was better for her if I just kept my distance.

I kept walking forward, and realized, as I did, that I was inadvertently following her scent. She'd been here but had left. She was somewhere ahead of me.

It's possible that she came to the door, spotted me at the bar, and then turned and left.

And I wouldn't blame her.

As I reached the end of the alley, I hoped she'd be far away, already into a cab and off.

But that wasn't the case.

She was there, about a dozen feet to my left.

But she wasn't alone.

There were two other people near her. She was helping a woman up off the ground as this tall guy dressed in a brown jumpsuit and a hockey mask was taking a swing at her head.

Chapter Eighteen: A Zelda-like Quest to Fight an Unbeatable Foe

I was too far away to get there in time as the tall, masked man who looked like Jason from *Friday the 13th* threw a punch directly at Lex's head.

She swerved and shifted enough to one side for his punch to connect with her left shoulder.

The blow rocked her back a step. She stumbled and fell onto one knee.

I was moving towards them and was still a few feet away when, I saw Jason then do something unexpected. Instead of either kicking her or punching her again, he took a wide stance, planting both feet firmly at shoulder width, bent his knees slightly, and brought his flat hands palms together in an odd praying position in front of his chest.

Odd choice.

By then I was close enough to tackle him.

"You'd better pray!" I yelled as I dove at him. "Because if you've hurt her—"

He was almost seven feet tall, but because he'd had his

knees bent, my shoulder connected with his upper chest. He looked like a waif in terms of his body shape, but I connected with something pretty solid, as if he were more like my bouncer friend The Rock.

Because my tackle from the side had taken him by surprise—a surprise that I could detect in the scent he gave off—he fell, hitting the ground hard on his back.

I heard the wind come right out of him and immediately rolled off him, scrambled to my feet, and shook the dizziness of the alcohol out of my head as best I could.

Despite being winded, Jason was also back on his feet quickly, his burning anger directed right at me. Which was good, because his attention was no longer on Lex and the other woman.

As Jason stepped closer, he threw a punch at me, but I was able to anticipate the strike because of the sudden changing in his breathing and his scent. He missed, but came close, because the fist flew at me quicker than I had expected.

In response, I threw a right hook at his face.

The solid strike sent his hockey mask flying, but his head barely recoiled from the blow. His face remained almost as still and stoic as the bristly brush cut blond hair on the top of his head.

A punch like this would typically be all it took to drop the average man.

This wasn't good.

He drove a fist straight at me, striking me in the chest and knocking me back right off of my feet.

What the hell?

Sure, I was drunk, and thus a bit unsteady on my feet. But it wasn't just that.

This guy was a lot stronger than he looked. And far more powerful than those thugs the other night in the parking lot. I suspected I was dealing with somebody who, like me, had some sort of supernatural strength.

I was on my butt on the ground, my hands behind me propping me into a sitting position, when he sent a side-swipe kick that struck my left shoulder and the side of my head, throwing me to the side face down onto the pavement.

Fully expecting Jason to jump onto my back, I braced myself, but nothing came.

I whirled my head to see him in profile a few feet away, facing Lex, and standing in that sumo-style pose, his hands pressed together in front of his chest in a praying position.

His face looked like he was constipated or trying desperately to pass a kidney stone, when a loud crackling accompanied a glowing yellow light originating from between his palms.

As he pulled his hands apart, his fingers and thumbs still touching, the light morphed into a bright yellow ball. He then thrust his arms away from his chest and the yellow ball hurled at Lex.

"No!" I yelled.

But the light fizzled in the air in front of her, as being absorbed by some invisible shield.

Jason let off an air of incredulousness, and I heard his heart skip a beat.

"No," he said. Then he repeated the word.

He hadn't been expecting that.

Lex wasn't giving off the same confusion.

She took a single step toward him, and he bolted down the street.

By then I was back on my feet. Lex wasn't looking at either me or the fleeing man. She was focused on the terrified woman she'd been helping up who was still on one knee. The woman gave off a scent of both extreme fear and pain.

Jason's long legs had moved him quickly down the street.

I took off after him.

Half a block ahead, he turned left into an alley.

A second later there was another bright yellow flash of light coming from the alley followed by a louder crackle of energy than before.

I rushed around the corner into the alley, but he had simply vanished.

Seemingly into thin air.

Not just visibly. His scent trail stopped there too.

His scent had stopped just a few feet into the alley.

What the hell?

I stood there a moment, taking a long whiff, just to be sure. I picked up a subtle—even to my enhanced senses—metallic odor in the air.

Based on this magic exit, his super strength, and the yellow ball of light he fired at Lex, there was no doubting I was dealing with another supernatural human.

The voice of Lex and a female voice drifted to my consciousness from a block away. The woman was thanking Lex for helping her.

I rushed out of the alley and back down the street to the two women.

As I got within a few feet, I picked up a sense of confusion from Lex. "Are you two okay?" I said as I approached.

"Yeah," Lex said.

"Yes, thank you," the woman standing beside her said. She turned back to Lex. "And thank *you* again."

"It's the least I could do," Lex said to her. Then she addressed me. "What are *you* doing here?"

"Never mind me. What just went down here? Who was that guy who looked like he stepped off the set of *Friday the 13th*?"

"He was definitely PFA."

"What about that ball of light he threw like some sort of reject from *The Legend of Zelda*?"

"No, idea," she said, and I thought I caught an odorous hint she was hiding something. "I was walking by and heard a commotion and saw three of those PFA dicks with masks yelling nasty and angry things at..."

"Renuka," the woman offered.

"At Renuka, here. Most PFA gang members are spineless bullies. They're good when ganging up on one or two helpless people when nobody else is around. They're mostly talk and threats. They'll destroy property, hurt people, but only when they can slip away.

"Only a few them are bold enough to stand and fight.

So I called out to them to stop what they were doing. Two of the three of them took off. The third guy, the tall one, shoved Renuka before following them.

"I approached Renuka and was helping her to her feet when I saw he had returned. I realized he wasn't running away, just trying to catch me off guard."

She put her hands on her hips. "There. I've answered all of your questions. Now, what were you doing here, Michael? Following me? Don't you have a girlfriend to get back to?"

"I think the phrase you're looking for is: *Thank you.*"

"Thank you for what? Temporarily distracting him? I'm perfectly capable of handling myself, thank you very much."

"I saw that. The ball of light he shot at you died in mid-air right in front of you. What the heck *was* all of that?"

"No idea," she said, just like before. And, like the last time she'd said that I picked up on the fact she was lying. She again changed the subject. "You still haven't told me what you're doing here."

"I came to Skull Crusher looking for you, Lex. My phone died right in the middle of trying to explain about the other night."

I turned slightly, shaking my head as I was trying to plead my case, and suddenly Lex's face looked shocked. It came with the mingled scent of shock, curiosity, and concern.

"Oh my God, Kal. Your face. It's all bruised. That's not from just now. He only hit you once. What happened to you?"

"That's what I've been trying to tell you. It's why I never texted you back, Lex. I got jumped by a bunch of PFA thugs the other night on the way back to my hotel. I was unconscious and recovering."

Lex brought a hand to her mouth.

"Okay, I see that there's a lot for us to talk about."

"I lot that both of us need to explain," I added.

"Yes. Of course. But first things first. Let's get a cab, first make sure Renuka is brought safely home, then you and I can play twenty questions.

"Sound good?"

"Yes, thank you," Renuka said.

I nodded. "Yeah, I'm game for that."

Chapter Nineteen: A Romantic Fool on Venice Beach, Far Away in Time

Most of the cab ride was spent in a combination of silence and small talk as we escorted Renuka back to her home. I sat in the front seat while the two women sat in the back.

Lex and I learned that Renuka worked as a dishwasher at a nearby eatery and was walking to the bus stop that would take her home when she was accosted by the PFA thugs.

After Renuka was dropped off, it got more awkward as Lex and I were trying to figure out where to have the conversation we needed to have.

"Have you ever been to Venice Beach?" she asked.

"This is my first time in LA."

"It's settled then." She told the cab driver the name of some restaurant and we were off, again, mostly silent, with me sitting in the passenger seat beside the cab driver, and Lex in the back seat.

The driver dropped us off in front of our restaurant. I had no idea where we were, other than being able to see that, just down the street the road ended on the water-front, based on the way that a couple of blocks ahead everything ended in a large dark expanse. It surprised me I wasn't able to smell the salt water of the ocean.

Lex paid the cab driver, and we got out.

"C'mon," she said, leading the way into the front of the restaurant. "I'm famished. They not only have the best pizza, but their jalapeno topped pretzels are to die for."

She seemed playful and energetic, but I couldn't tell what was going on underneath. I suspected she was still either angry with me, or at least still questioning me. But what I'd just seen suggested things were already okay. My ability to scent her emotions seemed to be muted, again.

I silently cursed at myself for drinking too much at *Skull Crusher Brewery*.

I realized how useless I was at navigating relationships without my heightened senses. Oh, who am I kidding? Even with my senses at full wolf strength I'm about as adept at personal intimate relationships as a cat doing macrame.

Again, it was all small talk as we got to a table, and then Lex took over, ordering the appetizers, those pretzels she had been talking about, and a couple of the house special margaritas.

She paused in the middle of the order to ask me. "You don't have any food allergies, do you?"

"No allergies to speak of. But I do have a pretty nasty reaction to arsenic."

She shook her head and laughed, like we were old friends and she'd heard me share this chestnut a dozen times already. I realized I'd used that same joke at Gulp the other night, and she must have been paying attention. Then she ordered a salmon-topped pizza, assuring me it was among their best house specialties.

When the waiter left to fetch us our drinks, Lex's face turned serious.

"Sorry that I took over there. I'm just starving. And I know what's best on the menu here. Now that that's taken care of, let's get down to the business at hand, shall we?

"I was at Skull Crusher for a number of reasons. One, because it was far away from Gulp and my other regular hangouts, and I was trying to avoid you; I didn't need you to embarrass me again in front of the regulars and bartenders there. Two, because I love their brisket. And, three, I was pissed at you. I thought we'd had a real connection the other night, and then you ghosted me. Then you nagged me until I took your call and then hung up on me. I needed to cool off somewhere else."

I opened my mouth and leaned forward about to explain, but she raised a hand palm out.

"Hush your yap. It's my turn to talk. You'll get yours."

I closed my mouth and leaned back in my chair again as she continued.

"When I got to the brewery, I realized I didn't have any cash on me. So I popped out to go to a bank machine. But when I got back, I saw you sitting at the bar. I took off, pissed that you'd somehow tracked me down. But I really wanted their brisket, and I'm too stubborn to let some jackass who'd rejected me stop me from that simple pleasure, so I went for a really long walk. I love walks. And this one helped me to blow off some steam. I returned a few hours later, figuring you'd be gone. But you were still there.

"I decided to hail a cab and get out of there. And that's when I spotted Renuka being hassled by those jerks."

"Yeah, the PFA," I said. "What the heck was that all about? That yellow ball of light he shot."

"Not yet, mister," she said. "We're not going there yet. I explained what I was doing there. Now you've got until the time they bring the appetizer to explain this girlfriend business. If I don't buy it, you're out of here, and I'm enjoying both drinks, the appetizer, and the entire pizza myself. Got it?"

I paused, looking at her silently as the waiter arrived with the margaritas. We nodded our thanks to him and he said he'd be back shortly with the appetizer.

"Got it."

We both picked up our drinks and took a sip. There was no toast or clinking of glasses.

"I don't have a girlfriend," I said. "I haven't had a girlfriend for years. Nobody."

"Then what the heck was this 'mostly single' business?"

"I had been with someone many years ago. Her name was Gail. But it ended. I took it hard. Gail returned as a friend a couple of years ago, and until very recently, I'd been having trouble with that, always thinking that maybe if I waited long enough, things could work out again.

"But only in the past week did I finally accept things; did I realize it was time I moved on.

"At Gulp the other night I was crushing on you big time, Lex. Really enjoying our conversation. You're an amazing person. Bright, beautiful, funny, charming.

"This was the first time since Gail that I really felt something for someone. Something beyond a basic physical attraction. But I'd spent so many years stuck on that previous relationship, focused on Gail, that I stumbled; I was so used to thinking of myself as taken for so long, as committed to someone, that I forgot myself. Forgot that I had only been Gail's guy in my mind.

"And the mind is a frighteningly powerful thing."

I paused and took another sip.

"So, I messed up. I mis-spoke. And I'm so sorry. I think maybe I was afraid because I was crushing on you in a major way. Maybe it was some sort of self-conscious sabotage. I don't know. Lex, I've never been good at this."

I couldn't read her scent, so couldn't tell if she was accepting what I was sharing or not. Her poker face was so solid she could have likely been the person Kenny Rogers was sitting across from that warm summer's evening on a train bound for nowhere.

Just then the waiter appeared with the pretzels. They looked amazing.

Lex thanked him and then looked back at me, that *The Gambler* stone cold look on her face still.

"So, what's the verdict? Am I digging into this pretzel,

or am I hitting the bricks?"

Her face contorted into a wry grin. "Okay, I'm buying what you're selling. For now. You can stay for the appetizer. But now I want to hear about what happened afterward, that night. Those bruises on your face. About you not returning my texts the next day."

Even though I couldn't read her, it seemed like her disposition softened toward me. Maybe I wasn't so bad at navigating personal relationship things. Heck, even a cat might accidentally form an accidental interesting pattern when fumbling around with a string of yarn.

As we both picked away at the appetizer, which was as delicious as Lex had described, I relayed the details about the encounter on my walk back to the hotel, getting beat up, and my pal Buddy showing up in the nick of time. I shared how he'd taken me back to his hotel room and kept watch on me while I recovered. I didn't, of course, share the details about my normally heightened wolf senses and strength that had seemed to disappear.

I was getting to the part about my suddenly dead cell phone battery during our phone call when the pizza arrived.

"So?" I said. "Does this earn me a chance to stay for the rest of the meal?"

She grinned across the table at me. "Why don't you serve yourself the first slice. I want to see the look on your face when you take your first bite."

I smiled and reached for the pizza. Even without my enhanced senses it smelled amazing.

"But don't get too comfortable, Buster. I still haven't

yet decided on desert."

I slid a slice onto the plate in front of me and then served one onto Lex's plate. I paused, waiting for her to start eating.

"You're starving," I said. "Go ahead."

"No way. I said I wanted to see your reaction."

I obliged. It was exquisite.

"Wow," I said around a mouthful. "That is amazing."

She grinned, those gorgeous cool blue eyes and high rosy cheeks smiting me in a similar way that the pizza had impressed my taste buds.

Lex dug into her pizza. I waited until she had swallowed her first mouthful before asking.

"So are you some sort of black belt? What makes you think you could take on three PFA thugs on a dark street?"

A wry smile crossed her face. "Really? You're asking *me* that? I should ask you the same thing about your own encounter in a dark parking lot. And apparently I fared a bit better than you did."

"Touché."

"I have a bit of history with some members of the PFA. So, when I spotted those goons hassling Renuka, I knew they'd split the minute they'd been challenged.

"Most of the members of this gang are all talk and immediately turn tail and run the minute they are challenged. Which is exactly what they did.

"Of course, as you saw, the tall guy turned back around and attacked. And that's when you showed up."

"But he wasn't just a regular thug."

"No," she admitted. "He was definitely something else."

"This guy was strong, Lex. Not in any normal way. I haven't been in many fights, but I've never seen someone, especially such a scrawny guy like that, take a punch without a reaction."

"For a guy who says he hasn't been in many fights, you certainly have a knack for rushing into things head-first."

"What can I say? I'm a bit of a boy scout.

"But on top of that unnatural strength, he does this yellow ball of light thing. What the heck was that?"

"Seriously!"

"Have you ever seen anything like it?"

"No. That was something else."

When we'd briefly discussed it before, I'd been able to detect some sort of deception on her part. She seemed to know something more than she was revealing. But now, thanks to the alcohol in my system, I was getting nothing. And her poker face was on task.

"How about you?" she asked. "Have you ever seen anything like it?"

I thought about the fact I was a werewolf. About my encounter with Knell, the only other supernatural creature I'd ever fought. I knew that there were, as Hamlet said, more things in heaven and earth than are dreamt of in our philosophies, but this was the first time I'd seen that sort of magic.

It made sense, of course. If what I experienced was

possible, why wouldn't there be other paranormal or supernatural things?

"No," I said. "Nothing like *that* at all." Which was, technically true, despite experiencing other supernatural phenomenon.

"And then, when I chased him to the alley, he vanished. Into thin air. Poof. Gone. Like that. I know I've been drinking. But I'm not that far gone.

"You mentioned being mixed up with these PFA guys before. What do you know about them?"

She took a long drink of her margarita before responding.

"It was a bit of a dark period in my life.

"I had this girlfriend. Sacha. She was this kick-ass bad-ass metal-head type. I really admired her take-no-bull attitude and her strength.

"We were pretty tight. She was actually my roommate for a few years.

"Anyway, about two years ago, she hooks up with this guy, Marco. She'd been with plenty of guys I didn't care for. But there's something off about him I don't like. Something beyond just being a jerk, you know?

"So Sacha and Marco start to get really close. And Sacha behaves differently, drawing away from me. They took turns staying at the place Sacha and I shared and Marco's place. I started seeing less and less of Sacha.

"This one time, when my bedroom door was opened, I saw Marko walk between the bathroom and Sacha's room with just a towel on. I'd never seen him without a shirt on before, and I spotted a tattoo just below his left shoulder on his back. It's one of these."

She took a case of lipstick out of her purse and drew a figure on the napkin.

"I don't get it." I said. "What is it?"

"It's the PFA symbol.

"Marko was a member of the PFA. Once I spotted that, I did as much research into the group as I could. They're a hate group that hides behind their devotion to the United States of America. They claim to be patriots, but only for a specific type of American."

"Yeah, I'd read a few things about these guys before that parking lot encounter. They seem to be pretty active here on the west coast. A neo-Nazi type of extremist group."

"They started here. But what I learned is that they're different than any neo-Nazi's I'd previously read about. And their methodology stands apart from the alt-right movement.

"Unlike those other groups, they're still mostly local, so they're not nearly as widespread; and they've remained far less vocal, quite a bit more underground than those other groups, at least until recently. They originated here, and much of their core operation has remained here.

"And one of the other things I learned about them that the media hasn't really picked up on, but what seems to set them apart is that they're like a cult. There's a deeply religious core to them that's not a part of the more typical fundamental alt-right, that skews towards being skeptical of organized religion, many members identifying as secular or atheists.

"No, the PFA definitely believe in God, or at least a god-like deity. As best I could determine, they follow something that feels like a home-grown offshoot of Luciferianism. And they worship an entity they call Balakaii. It's a name that I couldn't find in any source. But it might be derived from the demon Balam or Balaam, because he is seen as three-headed. He possesses the heads of a man, a bull, and a serpent."

"How do you know so much about this group?"

"I've done a lot of digging, a lot of research. But," she turned her eyes away from me to stare at her drink for a moment and then took a slow, deliberate sip. "I've also done a lot more to get to learn about them.

"Once I noticed the dramatic change in Sacha's behavior, I became concerned. She had stopped having long conversations with me or wanting to go hang out and party like we used to do. The more she was seeing Marco, the more she pulled into herself, and away from me and our long-term friendship.

"We'd been best friends since college. She was practically like a sister to me. But when I tried speaking with her, to share my concerns about what she seemed to be getting into, she would have nothing of it. She wouldn't hear a single negative thing about Marco or about his spiritual ways."

She paused and took another drink of her margarita, finishing it. She signaled for the waiter to bring us another round. I looked at my half-finished drink.

"Drink up," she said. "You're going to need this once I explain a little more."

I obliged and finished my drink. I was already feeling the effect of the previous drinks, so why the hell not? At this point it was like throwing a thimble of water onto a waterlogged bullfrog.

Lex stared at the table in silence while we waited for the waiter to return with our drinks.

Once the waiter departed, she sipped at her fresh drink and stared at the table as she continued.

"I figured the only way for me to get to Sacha was to stop questioning her, and to embrace the path she was on. It was rare for me to ever have time with Sacha without Marco around. But the next time the two of them were at our place, I started to chill and give off an air of acceptance, and mild interest.

"It took almost a month, but eventually, Marco seemed to pick up on the change in me. The two of them included me in on more of the things they did together.

"As I got closer, spent more time with them, I eventually learned something about their way. The men in their cult take on multiple mistresses.

"Marco, or perhaps, even, the two of them as a tag

team, were courting me. Embracing me into their relationship. We were...we were becoming a throuple."

She picked up her drink and downed half of it in a single gulp. The whole time she kept avoiding looking at me.

"Shit," she said, staring at a point in the center of the table. "I've never shared any of this with anyone before. Why am I telling *you* this? I actually like you, Kal. I feel like such a whore telling you this about me."

I didn't need to the ability to scent her emotions to understand how distraught and frightened and vulnerable she was. I reached across the table and placed my hand on top of hers.

"Listen, Lex, you don't need to tell me any of this. But I understand. It's okay. I get it. And I'm not going to judge."

She closed her eyes, took a deep breath, and then opened them, and looked up directly into my eyes.

"No, Kal, I do have to tell you. And I know you won't judge me. I can tell just by how you look at me, the way you listen to me, that you're sincere, that you really care. I felt that the other night. There was something more than a superficial mutual attraction going on. Which was why I was so disappointed when I thought you had a girlfriend. Because I thought we had connected in a deep and meaningful way."

"I felt that too. I feel that, Lex."

"I've never had this with anyone. Especially not someone that I've just met."

I thought about Gail, about the way we had hit it off

on the first night we had met for dinner. My instant connection with Lex was on par with that in the unique mutual click instantaneously happening between us that couldn't have been more obvious if it were audible.

I'd never experienced that before Gail, and I didn't think it would ever happen again.

"It's a rare thing," I said. "But I'm glad to know that we both feel just how beautifully you and I have connected."

"I'm so glad you sat on that stool beside me, Kal."

She turned her hand around inside the hand I had laid atop of hers and squeezed.

I squeezed back.

"It disgusted me, being with Sacha and Marco, but I had to do it. I loved Sacha like a sister, and I would do anything to get her back, save her from these monsters she had been brainwashed by.

"But I got close enough to be welcomed into the fold. Into the cult, more like.

"I know I said it was disgusting to be involved in threesomes with Sacha and Marco, but to be honest with you, I think what's worse is the fact I'd been present listening to the things these people say about Blacks, about Hispanics, about Asians, about immigrants. And just sitting there and saying nothing. With a big stupid smile on my face as if it's not some of the most twisted and deeply disturbing bullshit I've ever heard in my life.

"I can forgive myself for whoring my body out in order to try saving my dearest friend. That's just something done to my body. But I don't think I'll ever be able to forgive myself for being a silent enabler of any part of that. That betrays who I am at the core of my soul. And not just because it's wrong and against what I believe. But because I betrayed my own blood."

Her eyes were welling up and turning red.

"I know it may not show in my skin color and hair," she said. "But I'm half-black, from my father's side.

"Kal, I betrayed who I am. I betrayed my own people. I betrayed my father."

I squeezed her hand tighter as a pair of thick teardrops, one from the middle of each eye, tracked in almost perfect synchronicity down her face.

I tried to tell her I was so sorry, but wasn't able to get out a single word, because I was choking up myself, seeing her in so much pain; seeing her beat herself up.

All I could do was squeeze a little harder and bring my other hand overtop of our clasped hands and pat hers gently.

She looked up at the tears running down my face.

She smiled and shook her head.

"You're really something else, you know," she said, placing her other hand into the digit ménage in the middle of the table. "Have I mentioned how glad I am you took that stool beside mine?"

I nodded, and in the pathetic squeaky voice I sometimes adopt when I'm truly emotional, I said. "You did." I sounded like Mickey Mouse on helium.

She laughed, snorting through her nose.

There we sat, half crying, half-laughing, with runny noses, neither of us wanting to remove our connected hands, and looking at one another.

I realized I was falling for this magnificent woman big time.

"I've got more to share," she said. "But I've lost my appetite. Why don't we go for a walk?"

Chapter Twenty: Night Winds Whisper on a Walk After Midnight

After settling the bill and using the restroom, Lex and I left the restaurant. She'd been right, the food there had been amazing. It's too bad we hadn't finished it; but we'd at least had a decent fill.

Not that the food seemed to help the alcohol in my system. My senses were still muted. Well, muted as compared to regular. I suppose it's a little privileged for me to be complaining that my sense of smell and hearing, for example, are like that of a normal human.

But I suppose one can get used to whatever becomes that core baseline for their experience.

Lex led me out the restaurant, heading left and we turned left again at the first street, or I suppose that would have been south, since the Pacific Ocean was straight ahead.

We didn't do more than small talk at first as she pointed out a few of the more interesting local establishments and sights along the way, even if they were not visible.

"Down there, just another block, and on the water-front is the outdoor gym known as Muscle Beach. Arnold Schwarzenegger used to be a regular there, back in the day."

In the same way that the fresh and cool night air was a welcome pause from sitting inside, this more sight-seeing tour-guide talk was like taking a deep and cleansing breath.

It wasn't until we got to the Venice Canals, an Italian-inspired neighborhood that comprised a series of man-made canals and adjacent pedestrian walkways and bridges that spanned multiple blocks, that she got back into the more serious conversation.

"You've heard the stories of Nazis attempting to man-ufacture super-soldiers in their desperation to win World War II, right?" Lex asked.

"Yeah, something like that."

"There were several reports indicating that soldiers were being injected with methamphetamine and other performance-enhancing super-drugs.

"I just read a book that just came out this month called *Hitler's Monsters*. It's about how the Nazis drew upon a number of different pagan, paranormal, witchcraft, oc-cult practices and experimental sciences in an attempt to gain power, keep power, shape propaganda, and pursue their vision of racial utopia and a dominating empire.

"The PFA has adopted a similar approach. Yes, on the surface they are NRA-card-carrying advocates. But be-neath the surface they're working to weaponize their very bodies."

"Why would such a *master race*," I said, "need to take drug enhancing injections."

"It's not just drugs. It's a combination of drugs and pagan potions and ritualized spells. There's this weird dog's breakfast of magic and science. It's different every time. They call it the Ritual of Ascension. Or they sometimes call it *To Rise* or *Getting Risen* or *Going to Rise*.

"Their belief is that, as the master race, they are endowed with the ability to accept the graces of Balakaii, the deity they worship, who has enabled them with the ability to accept the Ritual of Ascension."

"The result of this ritual, these drugs and chemicals and potions, is *that* what we witnessed outside the brewery with that ball of light?"

"I think so, yes."

"Had you seen anything like that before?"

"Something like it. Nothing *that* powerful, though. I have witnessed people with enhanced strength and seemingly impossible powers. But the side-effects of these experimental treatments aren't consistent. They're random. And rare.

"Plenty of members had undergone the treatment, but no powers emerged.

"Marco gained extraordinary strength in his left arm, the arm he'd taken an injection into, but nowhere else. They even tried giving him the same injection into all three of his other limbs, but there was no effect.

"The same injection into different people, or into different areas of the body, can have a diverse range of effects; including, most commonly, no effect at all."

"What about negative side-effects?"

"Well, I'd say maybe psychosis, but they're already psychotic." She laughed. "Sorry, just trying for some comic relief."

I warmed up to her even more. A woman who laughs in the face of stress and awkward uncomfortable situations is a woman after my own heart.

"In all seriousness though," she said, "there's a risk with every injection, every ritual and incantation, every potion. They seem to have learned that too many can kill.

"But, also, sometimes a single attempt kills a person." She paused, closed her eyes and took a deep breath before continuing.

"Apparently our body chemistries are all so different. They react differently to the enhancements. I suppose that maybe our minds, too, are wired so differently, that perhaps that too can be a factor."

"How do you mean?"

"You know how some people claim to be psychic or Mediums? That they are in tune with the paranormal, with departed spirits? That they can perceive things that other people can't?"

"Sure."

"I've often thought about those people the way I look at a sommelier."

"A sleepwalker?"

She snorted out a laugh. "No, sorry. Wasn't laughing at you. But that's funny. A sommelier is a wine expert. Someone who can taste and pick up on all kinds of specific nuances, ingredients, flavors, and essences in a wine.

Heck, I drink a wine like a chardonnay and might describe it as dry and full-bodied, but a sommelier would describe it as buttery with lemon-zest and baked apple undertones and an essence of vanilla from the oak barrels. They might also describe the region it is likely from, or the conditions the grapes were grown under.

"The whole point is their taste buds are finely attuned to such things. Whereas the average person never notices or attends to such things."

"Okay, sure."

"I think that Mediums, or others who are sensitives, perhaps have a similar ability to detect, feel, hear, smell, and see things that the average person can't. It's not all that different. It's just extra-sensory perception that eludes most people. Like natural born wine enthusiasts or fancy chefs.

"So maybe there's also something about a person's natural born disposition to the supernatural that's at play."

She paused as we were about halfway across what looked like the last pedestrian bridge in the canal neighborhood.

"I don't know," she said, picking at a fleck of chipped paint on the bridge banister until it pulled free and then flicking it into the darkness of the water. "I've done a lot of reading and a lot of thinking about this. I'm still trying to figure it out, but at least that's the theory I've landed on."

I stood beside her and had to fight the natural desire of wanting to put my left arm around her. It just felt *that* comfortable. Like we'd known each other for the longest time and it was the most natural thing to do. Instead, I pressed both hands against the rail. I was never that forward, would never dare do something like that.

"So, the theory you're working on is that these rituals and potions and chemicals, they react with different people's natural body chemistry, or DNA, or whatever, and that unique reaction is what causes the powers to either manifest, or not."

"Something like that."

"It's like a spin on the *Wheel of Fortune* or something."

"Yeah. Except there's more than one of those *Bankrupt* slices in this wheel's pie.

"I mentioned that sometimes the enhancement ritual injections or consumptions can kill a person, or, if not, then incapacitate them in a way that they might as well be dead. I saw it happen a half-dozen times in the almost full year I spent with this group.

"Three of them died within forty-eight hours of what ended up being a lethal injection. One died within an hour of consuming a potion. One woman lost any connection with the brain's consciousness. She couldn't speak, didn't seem to understand any communication to her at all. She just sat there like some sort of living and breathing human doll, drooling, and with no control over her bladder or bowels. This other guy lost complete control over his body. Full paralysis. Which continued to expand over times. After another day he couldn't even blink. He didn't live more than a few days, because as the paralysis spread eventually it reached his heart.

"Marco explained to me that the failures resulted from the fact that those people weren't pure of blood, and obviously not meant to be part of this new evolution of the master race.

"And for those who didn't ascend, some might never *Rise* but they were at least worthy enough to serve the cause and could remain soldiers in the Balakaiin army.

"All members whose bodies don't develop some sort of super-enhancement are given a DNA test. If it is determined that they possess what they call an infection from the less than desirable races, they are expelled from the group. Some of them disappear. And that was either because of their shame in not being a pure blood member of the master race, or, in a couple of cases, they were disappeared in secret by the PFA itself, if you know what I mean."

"So how big is this group? How many members?"

"I never elevated high enough to learn that much. There is a hierarchy. I remained at one of the lower-level ranks. This particular branch I was a member of, where Marco was one of the right-hand men of the local leader, had maybe fifty or more members."

"And how many of them displayed enhanced or supernatural abilities?"

"About half the group. Maybe twenty or so of them. Of course, only five or six of them have enhancements that might be considered powerful.

"Like Marco's super-strength in his one arm. Or this woman who could run really fast. There's another guy who can cause an intense migraine-like pain in other people just by staring them in the eyes. And one who can communicate with cats.

"There was a woman whose skin developed an armor-like thickness that protected her from plenty of physical harm. I watched them testing her by striking her with baseball bats. She barely flinched. Someone even shot her with a .45 caliber handgun, and it lodged in her skin, but only broke the skin by maybe an eighth of an inch. She was able to pluck it out."

I thought about the tall Jason dude who threw that ball of light at Lex but then also disappeared into thin air.

"But they can also have multiple powers, too, right?"

"I'd heard of such things but hadn't seen any firsthand. At least not until earlier tonight."

"That guy shot a bolt of light energy at you, or something like that," I said. "And then he disappeared into thin air. That's two. But another thing was that when I hit him, he barely felt it. That potentially means he has three unique powers."

"They might not all be as useful or powerful. Remember, that ball of light he shot at me seemed to dissipate before it reached me. So maybe it's only a short-range thing."

"Good thing he wasn't closer to you."

"That's for sure."

"Had you ever seen that guy before?"

"He looks familiar, but I didn't know him. I remember a tall blond guy like him coming into the group as a new recruit, just before I ended up leaving."

"Do you think he recognized you?"

"No, I doubt it. He didn't act like he recognized me. I was just a bystander daring to help what he saw as a lesser human."

"So," I said. "You mentioned you were with the group for almost a full year."

"Yeah,"

"How did you manage to get out?"

She looked up at me quietly and then turned and started walking in the direction we had been going. "C'mon. Let's keep walking."

We left the bridge and were back into what looked like a regular neighborhood of streets and houses. Lex was quiet for the first couple of blocks, and I said nothing, figuring she needed a bit of space to sort out what she was sharing.

She started speaking again once we turned left out of the neighborhood and walked past a large marina to our right.

"As I mentioned, I was part of this throuple with Sacha and Marco.

"We did things together. Things I'm not proud of. But I never got the chance to be alone with Sacha. Not once in the nine months we were there together. Marco, as one of the super-powered soldiers, was often out on missions. We were never privy to any of the details of those missions, and he never spoke about them, except to call one a success and another a failure. But we were never left alone when he was out. There was always a pair of these lower-level non-ascended soldiers, usually a male and female pair, assigned to be with us.

"So I never had a chance to speak with her one on one. But I also got no sign that she was there against her will. She was normal in many aspects, had memories of our past together, but didn't enjoy talking about it. But I had never, before, heard her say or do such vulgar and racist things. Sure, like anyone, she wasn't perfect, and had prejudices about some things. But this was different. It was like she was brainwashed into believing things that I knew went against who she was as a person.

"I tried, in as many subtle ways as I could, to get through to her. But I couldn't. We were never alone. And the few times I tried, I failed. It's like Marco and the others were on to me, or at least, they were always suspicious. Not just of me, but of Sacha. Even when I had seen no evidence she was anything but compliant in their ways.

"Even I had to play the role. I had to say and do things I'll never forgive myself for. Calling people, to their face, names I would never, ever call them. Because I wanted them to think I was one of them; needed to keep trying to find a way to save Sacha from them."

She paused and started to say something and then her voice broke and she stopped, took a deep breath.

"Kal, I called this woman who was walking with her two pre-school children, past us a bunch of *sand niggers*. I yelled it at them. They were just walking past. The PFA group I was with started harassing them and yelling at them, and I needed to show I was one of them, believed the things they believed, so I repeated the slurs and threats they were yelling.

"I'll never forget the look on that one little girl's face when I yelled out at them. I said: *Why don't you fuck off back to your desert home, sand niggers!*

"Her sweet and innocent eyes, as she looked up at me, completely confused and filled with fear; that will always haunt me. And her words, Kal. Her words to her mother that I overheard.

"She said, 'Why did she say that Mama? This *is* our home.'

"I've done plenty of things I'm ashamed of, plenty of things I regret. But that's one of the things I would take back in a heartbeat if I could."

Her breathing hitched, and she gasped.

"You didn't mean it."

"Yeah, but that little girl didn't know that. And she's going to live with that threat and insult the rest of her life."

Her hitching turned to open weeping, and this time I put my arm around her as we continued to walk. I've never been that forward in advancing a relationship with a woman. But that's not what this was. This was someone I cared about who needed comforting. Funny how my ability to connect and reach out changes so dramatically with the intent.

She cried for a bit with her head resting on my shoulder as we continued to walk, a little slower than before, around the eastern side of the marina. I had my left arm across her back with my hand on her side and she'd put her own right arm around my waist.

It felt completely natural walking with her like that.

We kept moving forward in silence, well after her tears stopped. Apart from the occasional interjection of a direction she indicated, which was just a single word or two, or, sometimes, pointing in a particular direction, we navigated through the other side of the marina and along a bike and walking path with water on both sides of it that lead back toward the ocean. It was dark. There were no streetlights here, and it almost felt like we were walking off into a void.

"There's a pedestrian bridge a little ways down we can cross," she said, seeming to sense my discomfort.

I laughed. "Funny that you're the one assuring me. I'm supposed to be the big tough strong protective man, aren't I?"

"We can take turns being the big strong man in our relationship."

Then we were both quiet.

I thought about those words.

Our relationship.

What did it mean? Well, apart from the fact it meant she obviously had forgiven me for my screw-up the other night.

And it had just been a few hours earlier that I had resolved to let this go; thinking it might be the best thing for Lex. After all, being close to me could lead to danger.

But hearing about the PFA and trying to figure out how she was mixed up with them made me realize she'd already been in proximity to danger. My special abilities and powers might come in handy to help her.

I thought about my special abilities. And the abilities that some Proud Fighters of America who had *risen* had achieved. I wanted to learn more, understand the source of it all. Could there be any relation to where my powers originated?

The thought of that sent a shiver down my spine.

No. I wasn't like them. Yes, I had enhanced supernatural abilities. But mine had been passed on by another werewolf. Not by some devil-worship meets a Doctor Moreau and Doctor Jekyll and Mister Hyde type of ritual. And sure, I wasn't perfect; I know I carry some prejudices. But I wasn't a neo-Nazi ass wipe. I wasn't like them at all.

I didn't ask for these powers. Heck, I didn't really want them. But I had purposely tried to use my powers to help others, to assist where I could.

These PFA monsters were using their powers to stomp on and harm others.

I had no idea what the hell I was getting myself into, but there might be some value in my enhanced supernatural abilities here.

Maybe Lex and I had come into one another's lives at just the right moment. Because I needed someone like her, and she needed someone like me.

We were quiet a bit longer, still walking with our arms around one another, when she finally spoke. At that point, she also slipped out of my embrace but then reached out for my left hand with her right.

"That was nice," she said. "But we can walk a little

faster this way."

She led us over a bridge that led into a beach-front neighborhood.

"I had started to tell you how I got out of the group. But then I got side-tracked.

"I think I side-tracked myself on purpose, because this next part is even more difficult to talk about."

Considering all that she had already shared. About the white supremist catcalling, the threesome relationship, all of that, I wondered what could be more difficult to share. I said nothing, just listened.

"As I was saying, I had to play along, pretend to be like them, as I was trying to stay connected with Sacha in the hopes I could reach her, and get her out of it.

"One of the things I had to do, once I'd been with the group long enough, was undergo the Ritual of Ascension. You rarely got that honor until you'd been with the group a minimum of six months. And if you had proven yourself; usually by completing a specific mission, striking out in a planned attack. For Sacha it had been ten months; and for me, it had been almost nine. Because we were the property of Marco and he was one of the higher-ranking soldiers, we didn't need to prove ourselves in that way.

"Also, it was a bit of sexism. No man would ever be accepted without going through that same initiation. But women were more the property of men, and even the ones in the group with special powers were still considered lesser. So, the two of us being mere chattel, or playthings of Marco, meant that step wasn't necessary.

"Sacha and I were slated to undergo the ritual as part

of the same ceremony. It was the two of us, another woman, and a couple of men we didn't know very well.

"Four of us. All given the same injection, all drinking from the same chalice, all blessed with the same incantation, as we sat in a pentagram shape, naked, our backs to one another, each facing a different point of the pentagram where red candles burned.

"One man died within minutes, falling to his side and frothing at the mouth. Sacha and the other woman collapsed into unconsciousness. I felt dizzy, and there was a strong buzzing in my head, but I remained awake. The other man screamed out in agony and we all watched, in horror, as his left hand started to mutate. Black curved talons slowly grew from his hand.

"Nothing happened to me. Sacha was still unconscious, so they rushed her off to an infirmary. The other woman who had passed out came to and nothing seemed to have happened to her. Just like me. They pulled us away and locked us into separate cells.

"We stayed there a few days. They were waiting to see if anything happened to us. I'd asked the guards who kept bringing us our food what had happened with Sacha, but nobody would talk to me.

"After a couple of days, with neither me, nor the woman in the cell on the other side of the brick wall from me showing any signs of ascending, they administered DNA tests.

"She was fine. Hers returned pureblood, and she was accepted into the group as a lower-level servant or minion, still beholden to the man who had recruited her into his harem.

"Mine, of course, revealed the likeliness of my African descent. I was cast out of the group.

"Marco wanted nothing to do with me. I was slapped around and degraded by some of the lower-level minions. I was sure they were going to kill me.

"But they did something worse. A soldier I'd never seen before, brought me photos and printouts. They were of my family, my brother, and my mother. My father had already passed on. But these were recent pics of my little brother Davy, and his wife and children. And of my Mom in the nursing home where she lives. The printouts were details of where they lived, where my brother and his wife worked. Where the children went to school.

"They made it clear that, if I were to breathe a single word to anyone, they'd go after my loved ones."

She was quiet for a moment as we continued to walk.

"That's not the worst of it, though.

"The person who brought those threatening pictures and documents to me also let it slip that Sacha hadn't made it. The Ritual of Ascension had put her into a coma, and they were declaring her brain-dead and would pull her life-support at the end of the day.

"I begged to be able to go see her, to say goodbye. They laughed, slapped me around some more.

"The next thing I knew I was waking up in a trash dumpster behind a mall. They must have either beaten me to unconsciousness or drugged me or something. All I had were the clothes on my back.

"When I returned to the apartment Sacha and I shared,

it had been ransacked. And when I called into work where I had taken a leave of absence, I was told I was being let go and was given a package.

"The PFA had let me know, in no uncertain terms, the power they held over me. And if I dared breathe a word of anything to anyone, they had the means to get at me, and at my family.

"That was over a year ago. I moved to a new apartment. I got a different job, eventually. And I stayed away from anything related to the PFA. I pretty much had to start over all again. Rebuild a new life. I suppose, with the way I'd grown up, having to move from town to town and rebuild a new life every time our family moved away, I'd become used to that as the norm for me. Things returned to a degree of normalcy. There were no other break-ins at my place. No other job incidents. It appeared that the PFA was no longer meddling in my life. If I let well enough alone, they left me alone."

Lex was quiet again.

After a few beats of silence, I spoke.

"Lex, I'm so sorry. So sorry."

"I've never spoken a single word about any of this anyone, Kal. You're the only person I've ever shared this with.

"And we just met. I don't get it. But there's something about you, something about the way I feel connected to you. I don't know. I don't understand this. I was never good at sharing. I'd always kept a wall up. Sacha was the only one who I ever let that wall down for.

"Until now. Jeez, Kal. I don't get it. I've known you for

just a few days and yet here I go spilling everything. Sharing everything. Sharing secrets I vowed to myself I would never share.

"You haven't judged me. You haven't made me feel less of a person for the things I've admitted that I've done. You've listened. You've comforted me.

"And I know, deep down inside, that I can trust you, Kal. That there's something about you that won't let you betray that trust. How weird is that?"

"Not weird at all," I replied. "I feel that connection too, Lex. I think it's why I was so awkward the other night. I've never been good at relationships. Never been smooth with women. But I felt something with you that's quite rare. And I think it scared me.

"But you are a remarkable woman. I'm in awe of you. And I want to get to know you more, Lex. Tell me more about you."

We walked a few blocks, along winding roads. I hadn't the fainted clue where we were, but Lex seemed to know the path. She shared that she loved to take long walks. At night. Often by herself, and through these neighborhoods. She loved sunsets and especially loved being awake when the sun rose. She occasionally suffered from insomnia and when that happened, she would just walk, alone with her thoughts.

She said that she was so thankful to share the experience of just walking, and talking, with me.

We eventually found a bench in a small patch of green space along the side of a street that overlooked the black expanse of beach and ocean over top of some houses.

"This is a bench where I normally like to sit and watch the sunset. It's the perfect spot. Come on, let's sit here. Let's wait for the sun to rise so I can experience that with you.

"And you can tell me a bit more about yourself."

We sat on that bench, cuddled together for hours, looking out at the darkness over the ocean, and we shared. We chatted. We talked. We exchanged stories about little things, experiences, moments in our adult and teen lives. Things we enjoyed. Things that moved us. Some of our hopes, dreams, and fears.

It was amazing.

At one point, when it was quiet, decided to share my most intimate secrets with Lex. She had, after all, opened up about so much. And, having witnessed supernatural phenomenon, knowing it was real, she would likely understand.

"I admire just how much you opened up to me and shared things with me that I know were extremely difficult to talk about," I told her. "And that has inspired me to share something with you I have never voluntarily told anybody else about. Ever. Only two other people know this about me. One of them figured it out. The other, I had no choice but to tell.

"You mentioned how meaningful sunsets are for you. Funny you should talk about that, because sunsets have taken on a pretty significant meaning for me," I said. "Because for about ten days during each month, they truly have a most life-altering meaning to me in a way that most people wouldn't believe.

"But I'm pretty sure, considering what you've experienced, Lex, that you'll believe what I have to share."

I paused to see if she was going to interject anything before I continued.

But all I heard from her was a cute subtle snore-like sound.

She had fallen asleep, with her head on my shoulder.

I turned my face, gently kissed the top of her head, left my face pressed into her hair, breathing her scent in, and closed my own eyes.

There would be plenty of time to share that secret with this beautiful and remarkable woman I was most definitely falling in love with.

Sunday, June 18, 2017

Chapter Twenty-One: Wine Bottles in Sight, Afternoon Delight

L ex slept for several hours. I was too wired to sleep, so I held her and marveled at the slow and subtle change in the sky as the darkness slowly morphed into the light of dawn was in sync with my enhanced senses returning to normal.

I realized that, over the years, I had become far too dependent upon my supernatural senses, relying on them to help me navigate the world, and my interactions with other people.

But the alcohol, and, likely, the painkillers I had been taking, had muted those senses, so I'd been engaging with Lex with a mostly normal sense of smell, taste, touch, and sound.

It felt normal.

Perhaps the first normal relationship I'd had in my adult life.

I compared this to what I'd had with Gail.

Yes, I was finally at a place where I could consider myself being over Gail, but I would never forget that very special thing we had. And she had become the landmark relationship in my adult life that I would likely forever compare every other relationship to.

But falling for Gail had been with my supernatural powers at the forefront.

Falling for Lex was done without those senses.

It was rather brilliant not knowing, through anything but normal human perception, how the person I was interacting with was feeling. I couldn't sense her emotions, hear her heartbeat.

My interactions with Lex felt more honest, more pure.

And I felt more *me* than I had in a long time.

As I listened to the occasionally rasping sounds of Lex snoring softly beside me, I was in awe of just how endearing I could find the subtle nature of such an acoustic phenomenon.

She had mentioned that she suffered from insomnia, so I could only imagine how precious and restorative this sleep was for her.

I was honored to be a protective force looking over her while she slumbered so innocently and peacefully. She had been through such pain and sacrifice all for a dear friend that she loved; and after all she'd given up, had lost that friend anyway; and then had to rebuild.

She exuded a strength and conviction that inspired me.

Her breathing eventually changed as she was coming out of the deep slumber along with the subtle shift in her heartbeat.

As she slowly drifted back to consciousness, she stirred. I rubbed my left hand along her arm and shoulder.

"Good morning, Beautiful," I said to her.

She opened her eyes and looked up at me, her heart racing at hearing me call her that. I felt myself melting into those gorgeous light blue eyes as she replied, without pause, "Good morning, Handsome."

My own heart did backflips at hearing those words.

She slipped an arm around my waist and squeezed.

"It feels so natural waking up in your arms. I haven't slept that well in ages."

My heart, which had previously done a backflip launched into a pattern more akin to a Mary Lou Retton floor routine.

"How long was I asleep?"

"A few hours."

"You just sat here the whole time?"

"Yeah. You were right. It was an amazing experience seeing the sun come up from this spot."

"Aw, I wanted to experience that with you."

"I'm down for it if you want to do this again."

I heard Lex's heart do its own version of an Olympic style floor routine. I felt like I was betraying and intruding upon her privacy.

"Then you're on. Except, I want us to watch the sunset together. Oh, Kal, it's magnificent. We'll watch the sunset and the sunrise."

"Sounds like a plan to me," I said. "I don't have to be back on the set until tomorrow."

"We get the whole day together?" she asked. And her heart went right back out onto the gymnast floor mats. My heart raced right alongside hers.

"If you like," I said. "I don't want to be presumptuous, Lex, but I really enjoy my time with you."

"Me, too."

We sat quietly, holding one another. Our hearts, both still rapidly beating, actually began to beat in sync. I didn't want to move, to change a single thing.

"Oh, okay," she said, after about a minute. "I'm famished. And I really need to pee. I live just a few blocks from here. Why don't we head over to my place and I can whip us up a hearty breakfast? I make a killer omelet. Does that sound good?"

"Will there be coffee?"

"Definitely."

We walked the several blocks to Lex's, hand in hand the entire time. We talked more about little things, this time about our favorite foods. Variations that started with breakfast foods we liked, then brunch and lunch items, then dinner and snacks.

It was obvious that we were both quite hungry.

Or maybe, and perhaps this was because I was also in tune with her emotive scents and heartbeat, we were both hungry for something else.

As we walked to the house, I was both excited and nervous as hell.

I wanted, desperately to kiss her, to taste her lips, to hold her against me, to experience what it would be like to make love to her. The idea both thrilled and terrified me. It had been years since I had been with a woman. And I had only been with a single woman in the past twenty years. I was definitely no Romeo, or Casanova.

Heck, when the movie *The 40-Year-Old-Virgin* came out, I felt personally attacked, like Steve Carell might have been basing it somewhat on my own situation or even mocking my extremely limited sexual experience.

Because I felt like I was intruding upon Lex's privacy with my enhanced senses, when she put on the coffee and asked how I took it, I asked if she had any Irish cream.

When she wasn't looking, I topped my mug up with more of the thick rich and sweet liquid.

It was easy for me to continue topping up my coffee with the sweet alcohol because Lex refused to let me help with breakfast. She told me to sit back and enjoy the coffee while she prepared it.

I couldn't help remarking to her that sitting and watching her do anything was a wonderful visual treat.

The Buzz returned to me by the time the omelet was ready. And, in conjunction with the buzz, my senses were again muted. I could no longer intrusively pick up on Lex's emotions.

I preferred this state. Interacting with Lex felt more authentic. And given my normal anxiety about relationships, it helped reduce my inhibitions.

Breakfast took over two hours to eat because we were so engaged in conversation, in the ongoing back-and-forth sharing that can happen so easily with the right person. And it's not as if the things we talked about had to consistently be all that deep and meaningful.

The conversation meandered all over the place, and ranged between tales of past loves, fond childhood vacation memories, favorite movies and old television shows, to causes we strongly believed in.

It was delightful.

We worked side by side at the sink. I washed the breakfast dishes while she dried, and we talked and laughed with the enthusiasm of newly acquainted friends, but the comfort of an old couple.

It felt right.

By the time we had finished breakfast and the cleanup, it was already noon. Lex mentioned she was feeling hungry and wanted to show me a cool spot from her neighborhood that looked out onto the ocean. She suggested we prepare to pack for a charcuterie style picnic lunch.

When she wasn't able to decide which of two wines to take, because the red went with the meat and cheese, but the white wine would go better with the dandelion salad and the homemade shortbread cookies she had baked the other day.

"Why don't we just drink both," I said, worried about losing that buzz.

It was a magnificent afternoon.

More conversation, more casual flirting.

My stomach, and my heart, were doing flip flops the entire time. And the great thing was that, apart from the look on her face, the way she looked at me, occasionally touched or held my hand, I had no insights into her own heartbeat or emotive scent.

Maybe this was why things didn't work out with Gail.

Gail knew what enhanced powers I had, understood that I could read her emotions off her scent, her heartbeat.

I could tell she loved me, because I could sense it. But I never considered how uncomfortable that might make her feel. How exposed.

It's not like I was a threat to her. Being exposed and vulnerable is part of the intimacy of a relationship, but it's not like the person you are with has the ability to probe your inner thoughts and feelings.

Considering Gail's past, the betrayal, the violation, of so many of the men who'd taken advantage of her trust in them, it was surprising the two of us could ever even connect in the beautiful way that we had at the beginning of our relationship.

Of course, it didn't last long. My deception, lying to her about my lycanthropic nature, led to our ultimate downfall.

Because she knew that being with me meant that, even if it were unintentional, I was constantly violating her most intimate feelings, thoughts, and emotions. There would be no privacy when it came to being with me.

That was too much like the violations of her past. And she couldn't go there.

It was funny how this revelation finally came to me in the midst of the throes of falling head-over-heals for another woman. It's interesting where and when the clarity can come.

But as I sat there on the blanket, my arm around Lex, holding her and looking out over the ocean, I finally properly understood how and why Gail couldn't be with me.

So how would I navigate my relationship with Lex in

a way to avoid that?

Earlier this morning, before she'd fallen asleep, I had intended on telling her I was a werewolf, and about my enhanced senses.

I didn't want to start a relationship with rejection.

But that would just be a first step.

How could we possibly get over that inadvertent personal violation?

I couldn't possibly stay drunk all the time.

Could I?

"Are you okay?" Lex said. She nestled up cozily against me while we sat looking out over the water, most of both bottles of wine depleted. "I just felt you tense up. Is everything all right?"

"Yeah," I lied. And then I paused, thinking about how my relationship with Gail had started off with deception. So, I started with a partial truth. "I was just thinking about whether you might think I have a drinking problem. Pretty much the whole time we've been together I'm always drunk."

"Oh Kal," she said. "I don't think that. But I have picked up on the fact you're extremely nervous. You did mention, more than once, that you've never been all that confident around women."

"I suppose I have, haven't I?"

"More often than you've repeated the same dumb dad jokes."

She pulled away from me so she could look me in the eyes. "I get the feeling that you like me. You do like me, don't you, Kal?"

"Yes, of course. You are a remarkable, beautiful woman, Lex. I really like you. A lot."

"Good. Because I like you, too. A lot."

We smiled at one another and she was close enough to kiss. I wanted desperately to kiss her. It felt like the right time to kiss her. But I had never been good at that.

"This is normally that beautiful romantic moment where, in a movie, the couple would kiss and seal the deal."

"Yeah," I said. "This would be the ideal spot, wouldn't it?"

"Then why haven't you kissed me yet, Kal? What is it that–?"

She couldn't finish the sentence because my lips were already pressed into hers. Gently, slowly, but firmly.

Her lips responded in the way I had hoped, welcoming mine in a magnificent embrace. I pulled back and looked at her, looked into those beautiful blue eyes, lifted a hand to brush a stray hair from the side of her face back then letting that hand linger on her cheek and caressing it. She nestled her face against my hand.

"That was nice," she said. "Well worth waiting for."

I leaned in and kissed her again, this time harder and more urgently.

This time she opened her mouth slightly and her tongue prodded against my top lip; at first tentatively and inquisitively, and then, as my own lips parted, she pushed inside.

I let her tongue do its exploring before lifting my tongue to meet hers.

It was a kiss that lasted hours. We held each other tight as we fused together, lips and tongues dancing and twisting together while our hands explored one another's bodies.

The kiss went on and on.

At one point she pulled back, laughing, and said: "Wow, you'd been holding that in for a while, haven't you? You were waiting for an implicit invite, weren't you?"

"Maybe. I didn't want to assume."

We then kissed again. Longer, this time.

As we continued kissing, she laid back on the blanket, and I slid on top of her.

She broke the kiss and laughed again.

"Okay, so you're a man who moves slow, but I can feel that little soldier down there standing at attention and ready to move on rather quickly."

I laughed, feeling my face turn red. I was sporting a full erection.

"You're so hot. Your kisses are so sensual. Sorry, Lex, I can't help it, I--"

"Shush," she said, placing a finger on my lips. "Kal, just so you know and that I'm one hundred percent clear about this, I want you."

I stared down at her, saying nothing. It had been so long since I'd been with anyone. My "little solder" as she called it responded on its own by throbbing against the side of her leg.

Even through my jeans and her dress, she felt it.

She giggled again.

"You haven't said anything, but I think he just spoke for you."

"Oh, I'm capable of speaking on this. Lex, I want very much to make love to you," I said, leaning in closer and pressing my lips against hers.

We kissed again for a while before Lex pulled back and suggested that we take this back to her place.

Hastily, we packed up the remains of the picnic lunch and then walked, hand-in-hand, back to her apartment, stopping almost every block to kiss once more. When we got back, we deposited the picnic wares in the kitchen and she led me by the hand to her bedroom.

As we sat on the edge of her bed, I placed my right hand on her cheek like I had done in the park. She nestled her face against my hand, then she lifted her own hand to mine, turned in to kiss my palm, then guided my hand overtop of her left breast.

Beneath the cloth of her dress, her nipple hardened against my palm.

As we kissed again, she lifted a leg overtop of me and straddled me with us both still in an upright sitting position. With the dress lifted and out of the way, she pressed herself against me, moaning as she felt my returning stiffness meet her.

We kissed like that for a moment before she gently pulled away and smiled at me. The intensity in her eyes was incredible, and I felt myself throbbing against her. She giggled. She leaned back, a little more, still smiling into my eyes, a delightful twinkle in them as the movement pressed her even harder against me, and then slowly lifted her dress over her head. There she was, so beautiful, so sexy, so desirable, in a purple bra, her stiff nipples raising the fabric in a way that turned me on even more.

I looked from her magnificent breasts and back into her eyes. She reached around behind her back and undid the straps of her bra, her eyes never leaving mine as she let the fabric of the bra fall.

I leaned back to take in as much of her as I could. I realized she hadn't been wearing panties underneath her dress. This exquisitely beautiful and sensual woman was naked in front of me. I realized I could spend the entire day just admiring her and be completely satisfied.

"You are so beautiful. So sexy."

"And you," she giggled. "Are still fully clothed. I want to feel your bare skin against mine, Kal," she said, unbuttoning my shirt then slipping her hands against my bare skin and chest. She ran her fingers against my nipples and they stiffened under her touch. I let out a moan.

She pulled my shirt off my shoulders and once I was clear of it, I reached up and placed both hands on the sides of her breasts, cupping them gently.

I kissed her on the lips, gently, like that first kiss, then leaned down and placed a similar single gentle kiss on each breast, with my lower lip grazing against the nipple.

She moaned as I did this.

I then tilted my head back up and kissed her.

Our tongues pressed urgently against one another and I felt my passion, my desire for her grow quickly to a maddening height.

A height that was too quick, too intense, I realized, with a sudden moment of panic.

She felt my body stiffen.

"What?" she said, her words muffled because her lips were still pressed against mine.

My entire body spasmed and shuddered as I orgasmed right there, inside my underwear and jeans.

Lex's eyes were wide as she looked at me.

I groaned and sighed.

"Did...you...just...?"

I nodded.

"I'm sorry, Lex. I don't know what happened. I mean, I know what happened. You're do damn hot. I just lost control. I'm so sorry."

"Oh, Kal," she leaned in and kissed me, then pulled back again. "Don't be sorry."

"Talk about a disappointment."

"No, it's no disappointment. That's one of the biggest compliments you could give a girl."

"Really? Seems to me like it's a sign of a lack of male virility."

"Are you kidding me? It's a sign of how turned on I make you. If anything, it makes me want you that much more, if that's even possible."

"Well," I said. "Let me just, uh, go clean up."

Still embarrassed, I moved into the bathroom, closing the door behind me, and thinking about what an idiot I was.

A moment later, after I'd gotten my jeans and underwear off, the bathroom door opened, and Lex was standing there in her beautiful naked glory.

"Let me help," she said. She grabbed a face cloth, wet it under warm tap water, and then sank to her knees and cleaned me off.

"Lex, you don't have to do this."

"Shush," she said. "It'll allow me the chance to appreciate this part of you up close."

She commented on the bruises on my legs and to my stomach while she wiped me with the warm cloth, occasionally placing a soft kiss on a few of the bruises. As she gently wiped up the mess and cleaned me up, I couldn't help but feel myself begin to stiffen again.

"There we go," she said. She stood, her left hand holding my slowly growing excitement as she kissed me.

"C'mon, let's slip under the covers."

She took me by the hand and led me to the bed.

We kissed and the feel of her naked body against mine was incredible. We rolled around together on the bed. After a few minutes, she whispered. "Take me now, Kal. I want you inside of me."

I moved between her legs and tried to oblige. But, despite my rising excitement, I wasn't getting back to my full previous glory.

"Uh," I muttered. "Well, this is embarrassing."

"Oh, Kal. It's fine. You were just...I mean, it's rather soon after. Give it some time."

I smiled at her. She was so compassionate; so understanding.

"In the meantime," I said, "lay back and enjoy." I kissed her on the lips, then her earlobe and neck, then traced a line of kisses down to her breasts, then her stomach, then further.

I'd hadn't been able to pleasure her in the more traditional sense, but she commented several times as she writhed and moaned beneath me that she had no idea what I was doing, but please don't stop.

She alternated from pressing my face harder against her, squeezing my head between her thighs and laying back. At one point, as her excitement rose to extreme heights, she called out. "Take me, Kal. Take me. I want to feel you inside me now!"

I moved up, and, though I was turned on internally, it wasn't quite so evident with what she had earlier called my little soldier. Instead of standing at attention, he was more half-slouching.

"Dammit, Lex, I'm sorry."

She took my face between her hands.

"No, don't be. This happens."

I kissed her again, then slid back down and made love to her with my lips and tongue.

When it was over, we held each other.

"Lex, I'm so sorry that I—"

She cut me off. "No, don't apologize. It happens. You're going on almost no sleep, and you've been drinking. It's fine. It happens from time to time. Besides, I've never been able to reach orgasm that way before. Ever. That was incredible."

"Good. I'm glad. I just want to make you feel as amazing as you make me feel, Lex."

"Oh, you achieved that, all right. You might have been

a bit tongue tied and awkward when it comes to relation-ships or making moves, but once I get you speaking, you're quite the cunning linguist."

We both giggled.

"Pleased to be at your cervix ma'am."

We laughed again. It felt good to be lying in her arms and laughing. I didn't know it could ever be like this, that I could have something like this with anyone again.

"Again, I'm sorry about not being—"

"Shush," she placed a finger on my lips, which I kissed. "Would you please stop apologizing? It's so damn Canadian of you. Give it a rest, would ya? Besides, you're not going anywhere for, what, two weeks at least, right? We've got plenty of time for lovemaking."

"Yeah, you're right."

"C'mon," she said. "You haven't slept at all, and you're still healing from that beating you took the other day. You need some sleep. Roll over, let me hold you."

I did as she requested. She snuggled up against me and held me tight.

I thought about what she'd said. We had a couple of weeks together. *Then what?* I go back to New York? She stays here? I started to worry about that.

But that worry didn't last long. It felt so natural, so wonderful, being in her arms. That comfort, and the lack of sleep finally took over, and I drifted off into a warm and sensual darkness.

It was dark when I woke. I realized we must have slept

for a good several hours.

Despite how I was slowly drifting back to consciousness, there were two things I was aware of. I could smell Lex in that deeper wolf-natured way. The way I'd been able to smell her before getting drunk the other night. She was still holding me, still pressed up tight against me.

There was an additional smell. It was the smell of her sex, of the lingering residue of her from before, both on her and on my lips and tongue.

Which led to the other thing I was startlingly aware of. I was hard, rock solid. Painfully so.

Lex was sleeping deeply. I could hear it in her breathing, hear it in her heartbeat. I marveled at it.

I slowly shifted in the bed and looked at her. She stirred a little and her heartbeat shifted as she drifted back to consciousness.

She opened her eyes and looked at me.

"Hello, handsome," she said.

"Hello, beautiful," I said.

"So you're not just a wonderful dream I had. You're real."

I leaned in and kissed her.

This time, as we were kissing, I could truly taste her like never before. I could taste the essence of her the way I had previously only smelled the essence of her. And she tasted so familiar, as if this was a taste, a flavor I had longed for and needed my entire life.

"Oh," she said, her eyes flitting down to where my erection was throbbing against her thigh. "Speaking of real. I can feel that you're real ready." She took my left hand and guided it to between her legs. She was moist. "So am I."

This time there was nothing halfway about it.

As I slid into her, I could read the pleasure in her eyes, and hear it in her breath and the beat of her heart. I almost came in the exquisite intimacy and pleasure of that moment. But I held myself back from the brink this time.

We made love. Tenderly, passionately, intensely, our heartbeats in continuous sync throughout the experience. We came together, then collapsed and fell asleep before waking up about a half hour later. Instantly aroused with the moistness of our touching skin and sweat mingling together, we started again, exploring, touching, caressing, kissing, then making love, as if it was the first time each time we did.

It wasn't just making love. It was giving and receiving love. It was a connection that I felt through every single sense of my being. I didn't know that I could ever have this again.

We repeated this cycle of sleep, wake, then lovemaking over and over until the wee hours of the morning, when we finally collapsed, sweaty and exhausted and slept for a full two hours. Then, waking, we made love again, one more time before we both had to get up, shower, and get ready for work.

Monday, June 19, 2017

Chapter Twenty-Two: Why Is It That Aves And Traffic Lights Emerge Without Warning?

I know that look in your eyes," Craig beamed at me from the other side of the giant metal coffee urn where he was filling up cups for both of us. "You're in love."

I shook my head and smiled, trying to deflect the probing as I was selecting sandwiches for our two plates.

"What are you feeling today? Egg salad, tuna, or cucumber and tomato?"

"I'm all about the egg," he said. But I could scent he wasn't done with his line of playful interrogation. There was only a slight pause before he continued.

"The real question is, what are *you* feeling today, big guy? What are *you* all about?"

I shook my head again. "Carrots or potato chips?"

"I know that look. That stunned and far-away look in your eyes. You're not here. Not even close. You're re-living whatever it was you were up to with her last night, aren't you?"

"Do we have to talk about this?"

"Chips."

"What?"

"I'll have the chips. And yeah, we have to talk about this. Listen dude, when we first met you weren't exactly moping around, but there was a particular vibe about you every time you mentioned your ex-girlfriend back in New York. You talked about her a lot, and every time you did, a sad darkness came about you. You might have been a bit better the last time I saw you, the night after you said you'd gone to watch Alicia Witt performing live, but it was still there. Now, though, it's gone. You're like a new man. So, you're damn straight I'm going to keep asking you about it.

"C'mon, tell me about her. Who is she? Where did you meet?"

I reflected on Craig's intuitive nature as we took our plates and coffee cups to a nearby picnic table. I had the benefit of being able to smell people's emotions and the telltale beat of their hearts, but there were others, like Craig, who, with no paranormal sensory ability, picked up on things. They were in tune with the world and the people around them.

Lex had spoken about that. Sommeliers and mediums. Different ways people seemed to be instinctively in tune with vibes or essences in people or in consumables that others weren't.

Craig was like that.

I shared how I had met Lex at Gulp and then bumped into her again at the brewery. I left out details about our encounter with Jason outside Skull Crusher or anything having to do with the PFA. I just stuck with high level details about the fact Lex and I had seemed to have a spontaneous connection.

Craig relayed how it had been exactly like that when he and his wife first met. And that the two of them had been together for a little more than a dozen years and neither of them had looked back. Only forward. And only toward one another.

It was a foreign, but wonderful feeling just being able to share. I think the uniqueness came because Lex and I were at the very start of something; and beginnings can be so refreshing and energizing. Every new moment of discovery was heightened—perhaps in the same way that my heightened senses took things in in a fuller, richer way.

That day in the studio was closer to my original expectations of what it was going to be like working on a movie set. Of course, there wasn't really much work for me to do. I was merely there for either the director or perhaps some producers to check in with. Not that they did all that often.

And it reminded me of the reality of what happens when a movie gets made from a book. It's no longer the author's story. Sure, the movie's premise and overall plot arc is based on or inspired by the book. But it's someone else's baby—someone else's creative project. It's their interpretation and version of the same story.

But I felt lucky that I got to be there.

And on the handful of occasions when the director himself interacted with me, JP Heartschwinger actually treated me with respect. Craig had been right when he said the beating I'd taken a few nights back had put him in a good mood. I know it had to do with the pre-movie publicity it leant; but another part of me wondered if there wasn't also some personal satisfaction he took knowing that had happened to me. I could, after all, scent an underlying subtle odor of the disdain he still held for me, the way you might detect the scent of stale farts lingering in the fabric of an old pair of jeans.

It had been a while since I had been in this state of mind, and I was reminded of the way the perspective of the world took on an entirely new hue. Everything seemed brighter, fresher, more vivid.

I had to check myself before I started singing The Carpenters song about birds suddenly appearing. That led me to remembering one of my favorite lines from *The Naked Gun* where Leslie Nielsen, as Frank Drebin tells Jane Spencer how, since he met her, he noticed things he never knew were never there before: 'birds singing, dew glistening on a newly formed leaf, stoplights.'

Thinking about that movie made me want to ask Lex if she'd seen and enjoyed them. I was a big fan of most of the films Leslie Nielsen had been in. I looked forward to those moments of sharing those little things, of introducing one another to the the various cultural things we'd each enjoyed.

The entire day on the set was a positive one. But I spent most of the day, when I wasn't thinking about Lex, looking forward to seeing her again at the end of it.

Just as I was walking up to my hotel room door, I could hear my cell phone inside the room vibrating on the desk where I had plugged it in that morning.

It was the short dual tap vibration pattern that usually accompanied an incoming text message.

Earlier that morning when I'd got back to my hotel to grab a change of clothes before heading to the movie set, I plugged in my phone and had left it there. It had been dead for almost two full days—Lex didn't have the right charging cable for it at her place—so there was no point in plugging it in for the five minutes I was there changing clothes. I'd just left it.

When I got in, I picked it up and noticed a text from Gail.

Hey Stranger. Haven't heard back from you. Everything okay?

I hadn't spoken to Gail since the beating I'd taken. Heck, I hadn't talked to her since getting to LA. And that had seemed like several weeks ago, despite it only really being about five days.

But it was funny. The old Michael would have missed her, wanted her to be there. Needed to share everything he had experienced with her.

That wasn't the way I was feeling right now.

I scrolled back to see that there were a few previous texts from Gail. The next one had come in yesterday, at about the time Lex and I were having our first kiss.

Did you get swallowed by the San Andreas fault, Andrews?

Nope, I mused, considering when she'd sent it and how I had been swallowed by something even larger, more powerful.

The first message had been from two days ago. Saturday afternoon. When I'd been on my way to Skull Crusher Brewery.

How is LA treating you?

"It's treating me so much better than I ever imagined," I said, staring at that message. Then the Randy Newman song "I Love L.A." started going through my head. In particular the chorus, and the opening, where he sings about hating the cold and damp of New York.

There was one other text, that one from Craig, just checking in to see how I was doing. I also had a few messages. One from Anne, Mack's assistant, also checking in on how I was feeling, and another from Gail. I played back Gail's message three times.

"Hey Andrews. Just checking in. I saw a trailer for *Spider-Man: Homecoming*. It's coming out July 7th. Assuming you'll be back before then, because July 3rd would likely be the very last safe day for you to travel. Looking forward to catching it with you."

Gail knew my deep love for the wall crawler. I had been a huge fan my entire life. Part of the reason I'd wanted to move to New York was to live in the city Peter Parker lived in.

It had been a fantasy of mine to enjoy the Spider-Man movie franchise with a woman I loved. But the Tobey Maguire films had come out prior to Gail and I meeting. And the second batch of films, the ones with Andrew Garfield in the lead role, came out after Gail and I had broken up. Gail's message reminded me I would be back in New York when the new Spider-Man movie was released. The movie opened on July 7th and my flight back was for the morning of the 3rd. Gail mentioned that day, having looked at the lunar calendar to check my cycle. Since I typically turned into a werewolf when the moon phase was 80% or more. The lunar phase for July 3rd for New York City was expected to be 74.7%. And in Los Angeles that number was 75.7%.

So, she was right. July 3rd was the last full day it was safe for me to make the flight back.

It was sweet that Gail knew and attended to my cycle. I forgot what it was like to have someone I knew and trusted I could talk to about my affliction.

It reminded me why it was important to discuss and share this with Lex. So we could have that too.

But I also wanted to share my love of Spider-Man with Lex. And there was the thought that, when this movie came out, I would be back in New York, and Lex would be in LA.

Unless I was able to change my flight. Stay here to see the movie with Lex. To spend more time with her. The few weeks we had already seemed like too little time.

I considered how I might plan out where to run and roam safely as a wolf. I needed to scout out the green space of the Hollywood hills that were north of my hotel. Determine a place to stash some clothes. Or, if things worked out with Lex, we could plan on having her meet me with a change of clothes, in a designated spot.

So many things to plan and do.

But working those things out with Lex would be worth it.

I deleted Gail's message.

I considered calling her but didn't want to get into anything. I didn't want to talk about getting beat up. And I wasn't comfortable sharing this budding new relationship.

Instead, I texted her:

Hey Sommers. LA is great. I love it!

(Of course, while I was typing it, inside my head I was shouting the lyrics from that Randy Newman song I'd just been thinking about)

Movie set is awesome. Sorry I didn't message back. Film production schedule has been crazy. Left my charging cable back home, so phone was dead for several days.

After hitting send I reflected on how, just a handful of days ago, I would have wanted to tell her everything. Meeting my driver Argyle and the cool connections to *Die*

Hard, discovering the awesomeness of seeing Alicia Witt performing live at The Hotel Café, hanging out with the regulars at Gulp, learning that Knell used to be a regular at Skull Crusher Brewery. I would have shared my encounter with those PFA thugs and laughed at how Buddy always seemed to show up at some random but just right time. Not sure I would have relayed the crying I did while watching Alicia Witt perform, or later that night, nor the thrill of meeting Lex.

But now, I didn't really want to talk to Gail. She represented the old Michael. I was done with the old Michael. I wanted to explore the new me, the one that Lex brought out in me.

I wanted to be the new Michael.

No, not the new Michael.

Kal.

Lex's Kal.

Tuesday, June 20 through Wednesday, June 28, 2017

Interlude: A Cunning Wolf Left Turn Yada-Yada

I hate when I'm watching a movie or reading a book and I get to this part where I'm riveted and on the edge of my seat, thrilled about the possibilities of what's about to happen, eagerly anticipating the next move.

But then the author, or director, takes a sharp and unexpected left turn.

You're following along, enjoying the ride, and suddenly, out of nowhere, the style, the pace, the forward momentum shifts. You get a summary, an overview, an interlude style sequence of events that gloss over the details.

An old Seinfeld episode called it "The Yada-Yada." When someone is telling a story and then, instead of offering details, they "yada yada yada" over the best part.

Except, what is the best part? I suppose that's in the beholder's eye.

But a yada-yada that is relayed from a storyteller can partially be evidence that the person relaying the story doesn't want to bog the listener down in what they feel are unnecessary details.

It's a technique to keep the action moving forward.

Sometimes there are moments in stories where years

pass, even with important details, such as in *The Princess Bride* where, after declaring their love for one another, Wesley goes off to seek his fortune and is reported to have been murdered by the Dread Pirate Roberts, and Buttercup is broken up about it and vows never to love again.

All that is told in a quick episodic summary—and despite it being a devastating and life-altering moment for Buttercup, it's more of an interlude than a detailed account. Because the good stuff, the heart of the story, comes after all that.

Other times, an interlude can be, in one story, a brief mention, but come back elsewhere in that universe to be explored in detail.

George Lucas, for example, did that in the first *Star Wars* movie. Obi Wan talks about having fought alongside Luke's father in the Clone Wars. It was an undefined number of years in their youth, and a period that was mostly skipped over in the original series of nine movies. But it was explored and expanded upon in an animated movie and television series.

That's because there are moments and details and stories that aren't necessary to expand upon within certain contexts. Most people understand what a "happily ever after" is after all.

And such is the case with the relationship between me and Lex. Well, except, it wasn't one of those endings, it was more of a "happily in between" moment.

After my first day back on the movie set, I returned to Lex's apartment. We drank together, ate together, watched the sunset together and then made passionate love repeatedly.

We spent nearly every moment of the next ten days together. I had been drinking in getting to know her; but I was also drinking a considerable amount of alcohol too. While being able to smell and hear those more intimate aspects of her, I still felt it was a violation. I didn't want to have those insights. I wanted to experience her like I would be as a normal human, without enhanced or gifted senses.

I felt that would be a more real and authentic way to get to know her.

And along the way I kept coming up with excuses for not telling her about my affliction. Things were going so well; I would be moving back to New York all too soon and knowing about that part of me might be a moot point.

I was falling in love with her, but also terrified about what would happen when I left. So, we didn't talk about that. We spent our time together reveling in the moment, in the passion, in the shared experience.

I was in regular contact with New York during that time. Mack and his assistant Anne checked in on me. Mack made some crude comments about being glad I'd been getting my rocks off and threw in at least a half-dozen *I told you so*'s making sure he got credit for this new action I was receiving. He also made an inappropriate comment about where his fifteen percent on all of that might be. On the flip side, Anne was compassionate and understanding, was pleased that I sounded so happy, and, of course, worried over me like the motherly person she was, despite me being at least ten years older than her.

Gail had found some sort of reason to text and call several more times during that week. It seemed like she was aware I had moved on, and I did look forward to being able to hang out with her without that strange compulsion and relentless attraction I had for her getting in the way. But I didn't yet feel ready to talk with her about Lex, so I'd let most of her calls go to voice mail.

My days were spent on the movie set, hanging out with Craig, and enjoying that bond. I hadn't had a close male friend in years. While Mack and I were in constant contact, I'd never consider him a friend, and couldn't even imagine doing anything with him for fun. Buddy, my traveling salesman friend, was perhaps the closest male friend in my life. And I saw him maybe four or five times a year.

Craig wanted me to keep him apprised of the budding relationship with Lex. In return he had shared that his brother-in-law was a police detective who was assigned to work in collaboration with a special division of the CIA responsible for domestic terrorism. He'd mentioned it because he wondered if, considering how I wrote mysteries, having a connection like that might come in handy.

In LA I was a new person, a different person.

A normal person.

Ironically, because of the constant flow of alcohol into my system, my senses remained muted.

I relished that normalcy.

I wondered at how it might be possible to live a normal life. Like a normal human. Without enhanced powers, without the need to have to use my abilities to save the day.

The days and nights seemed to last forever.

In fact, I reminded Lex of that Bryan Adams song that had come on the radio at Gulp the afternoon we'd first met. Lex and her friends commented that the artist was Canadian, and so was I, their new friend.

In that song, "Summer of '69" Adams sings about a summer that seemed to last forever.

It was like that in many ways.

But it many other ways, it was also over before we knew it. Because as filled and as rich as those days were, as little sleep as Lex and I got as we were exploring one another's bodies and hearts, those days also seemed to pass so quickly.

Like an interlude or yada-yada moment in an epic love story.

Those were good times. Pure times.

As Kid Rock sang about, we were drinking whiskey straight from the bottle and we weren't thinking about tomorrow.

But that purity and those good moments most definitely didn't last.

It was good. I was normal. Lex and I were together. I should have known. You could almost set your watch to the way it would roll out.

Of course, in retrospect, one has to acknowledge that reality would eventually set in.

A reality announced by a single gunshot and a blood-curdling scream.

Thursday, June 29, 2017

Chapter Twenty-Three: A New Chapter in the Origin Story of Lex and Kal, The Dynamic Duo

A gunshot echoed over the valley. Followed by a high-pitched scream of unabashed terror.

Lex and I looked at one another from where we sat on the bench—that same bench where we'd sat to wait for the sunrise that first night. The bench we had returned to multiple times to watch many sunsets in the previous week. We'd been there to watch the sunset, and as the night sky darkened, we had remained there, just talking, as we were in the habit of doing. It was after ten when that first gunshot interrupted the conversational flow.

As we were looking at one another a second gunshot echoed in the night, followed by another scream.

Then a third gunshot.

But no accompanying scream.

It all happened in less than five seconds.

We were both on our feet and rushing toward where the gunshots and the screams had come from.

We might be too late.

But we both ran.

Towards the danger.

I reflected on how I had seen her rushing to a woman's defense that night outside the brewery. We hadn't talked about that at all. After she'd shared her experiences with the PFA, we didn't talk about that at all. We'd avoided any discussion of that. Just like I had avoided discussing my lycanthropic curse.

But as we ran towards trouble, I realized we were more alike in yet another way.

Neither of us thought to pick up our phones and call the police. Our first reaction was to rush in to help.

Despite having had my fill of drink to keep my powers muted, my legs were longer than hers and I could thus run faster than Lex.

Within seconds I was half a block ahead of her, not bothering to hold back. The rush of the night air in my face was refreshing, and seemed to clear my head, and open up my senses, and my strength.

I pushed harder, ran faster. Within a few more seconds I was already a couple of blocks ahead of Lex. The sound of her footfalls on the sidewalk behind me were receding as I picked up strength and speed.

The road I was running on turned right and up the hill. If I looked back, I knew I wouldn't even be able to see Lex anymore.

But I wasn't worried about her. She was a tough cookie. She could take care of herself. I needed to push harder to get to whatever was going down and hoped that I wasn't too late.

As I ran, I picked up on a familiar scent.

It was faint, but I recognized the lingering smell I suddenly picked up. It was that Jason guy from the night outside the brewery.

I homed in on that scent and used it as a beacon. He was obviously the source of the trouble. I followed the scent left, down a walking path along a hilly green park area between houses that led to the next street. Judging by his scent, Jason was somewhere up on that next street ahead of me.

I could hear Lex, still really far back. She was breathing hard, her heart was racing, and I could sense confusion in her scent. She hadn't seen me turn off the road I'd been running down and onto the path.

Admittedly, I was a bit relieved.

I knew she could take care of herself, but this Jason guy possessed supernatural powers. She might be a solid match for the average mugger, but not someone with enhanced strength and powers. If the danger was ahead, at least she was far enough back, and nowhere near where the melee was about to go down.

Up ahead I heard a pair of male voices arguing that came to me as the wind shifted.

"Why did you have to shoot?" a voice hissed. Even though I'd only heard him utter a few words the other night, I pegged it as Jason's voice. "I had it under control!"

"The little spic deserved it." A nasal-sounding second male voice responded.

"He did, but I was going to take care of him. That gunshot is going to bring people."

The voices were coming from the next street. And that's where the scent led, too.

But off to the right, I picked up the scent of a woman who was giving off the mixed scents of terror and grief. I could smell blood and the lingering scents of a young male and freshly discharged gun powder as I came to a kick scooter laying on its side on the curb.

The smell of blood was coming from the kick scooter and the grass beside it. The blood scent trail led to the side of the house where the woman was.

I picked up two distinct blood scents. One from the male child, and the other from the same angst and fear-filled woman.

Based on the current input I was processing, Jason and the other male scents had headed straight down the road I was on, but their voices had come from the next street down the hill. The fearful female and male and blood trail scents led around the side of the house.

I moved around the house and saw a woman lying on the grass, cradling a young boy who looked perhaps five years old in her left hand. She was crawling, on her side, using her right hand to pull her forward, further away from the street.

The frantic heartbeat of the woman came to me, but the boy's heart was not beating.

"Ma'am," I called out. "I'm here to help. Have you been shot?"

Her heart jumped at the sound of my voice.

"No," she replied, stopping from the frantic pseudo-crawl. "I mean, yes. In the leg. I'm fine. It's my son. Please, call for help. He needs an ambulance."

His pulse was racing and his heartbeat was still strong, but he was in pain and shock.

I pulled my cell phone out and dialed 911 and handed her the phone.

"Here," I said. "I don't know this area. Tell them where we are. I'm going after the ones who did this to you."

She took the phone, and I listened for the racing footsteps of the three men I'd been tracking. Their scent would lead me down the street, but the voices I'd picked up and the footfalls I was hearing told me they were ahead on the next block. If I cut through this yard we were in, hopped the fence and went straight to the next street, I'd likely intercept their path.

As I raced through the yard, vaulted the six-foot fence, and rushed through the yard and past its house to the street I could hear the operator on the line pick up. "911," the female voice said. "what is your emergency?"

"We've been shot!" the woman gasped.

"Kal!" Lex's voice briefly came to me from the other street up the hill. "Where are you?"

She was still far away. Hopefully safely out of range of the lunatics I was tracking.

As I moved along the side of the one house, I picked up on the sound of heartbeats from people in the neighborhood houses. Curtains cracked open as folks were cautiously peeking out to see what was going down. I picked up on the sounds of at least two other people calling 911 from inside their houses.

I pushed forward, picking up the scent of Jason and his two male colleagues. They were off to the left, down the street, perhaps a block away but heading in my direction. I overheard Jason's voice again.

"I ought to leave you two losers behind, but I want Marco to punish you for your insubordination."

"You might have powers," the nasal voiced male responded. Unlike Jason, his voice revealed he was a bit out of breath from running, and his voice came off like Peter Lorre playing a nefarious bad guy in one of those classic black and white films. "But you're weak when it comes to purifying our city."

The third male grunted in agreement. He, too, sounded out of breath.

That's because Jason has super enhanced powers, I reminded myself.

I cleared the house and snuck past a set of hedges that lined the driveway. Then I crouched in the shadows between the bushes and the limo parked there, waiting for them to get closer.

As I lurked beside the car, a familiar scent came to me. A male I knew, but not Jason. The tall man's scent was still drifting in from the south. This other familiar scent was from a male who'd been standing here much earlier. But I couldn't place it.

I didn't have time to figure it out, because Jason and the other two were getting closer.

"You didn't follow my orders." Jason said.

"That's one less little wetback that's going to grow up to be a drain on the system." Peter Lorre replied.

The third man laughed in response to this, just as they were about to pass the car where I was hiding. Judging by the sounds and scent, the nasal guy was closest to me.

I flung myself out sideways and tackled Peter Lorre, my body taking him down as my right foot kicked Jason square in the head. Lorre hit the pavement hard, the wind completely knocked out of him, while Jason stumbled back from the kick.

I wasn't sure if it was the surprise or the fact I wasn't as drunk as the other night that caused Jason to reel so dramatically from the blow; but either way, I was pleased with the result.

All three of them were wearing masks. Jason was sporting a goalie mask, like he had been the other night, while Peter Lorre was wearing a rubber old man mask, and the non-vocal one was wearing an Einstein mask.

The third guy, Einstein, was unscathed from my attack and just stood there, shock reeking off of him.

I sprung up, grabbed Jason by the front of his sweater with my left hand and flung him back against the back of the limo in the driveway. He hit it, hard, his head snapping back and connecting with the back window, cracking the glass. The car alarm started going off.

Einstein rushed at me and I grabbed him by the rubber mask, pulling him down and forward, and stepping to the side as I let his forward momentum send him face-first into the back of the car.

His head shattered the taillight of the car and he fell to

the ground. I suspected he wouldn't be getting up any time soon.

From where he laid on the pavement, Peter Lorre was leveling a gun in my direction. I shot a foot at it, forcing his arm, and the gun to my right just as he pulled the trigger.

The next second or so seemed to be slowed down, like some dramatic nightmare sequence.

Immediately after the gun discharged, I felt the bullet just missing the side of my head and I heard two things. A man's grunt of pain followed by a voice from behind me.

"Michael?"

I recognized the voice instantly and connected it to the scent I'd detected only moments earlier.

It was Argyle.

That's why the male scent of the car was so familiar. The limo in the driveway was Argyle's. This must be where he lived.

I turned, saw that Argyle, who had been approaching from up the driveway, had been shot. He was holding both hands against his chest and blood was pouring from between his fingers.

The bullet had missed me, but hit Argyle.

I looked back at Peter Lorre to see him bringing his arm, and the gun back to center to fire again.

"No!" I yelled, launching myself at him.

I drove a fist into the center of his face with my left hand, smashing his nose, while simultaneously grabbing his left hand with my right fist in an upward motion.

The gun went off again, this time firing up into the air and I squeezed as hard as I could, crushing the bones of his fingers.

The gun fell to the pavement as he squealed in pain.

Jason ran into my back and had me in a choke hold with his right arm wrapped around my throat and crushing into my windpipe. With his left arm he maneuvered my own up and against the middle of my back.

I struggled to get out of his grip, but his strength was a solid match for my own.

As Jason held me, Einstein was up again and approaching, ready to pummel me in the stomach. I had a panicked flashback to that night in the parking lot and getting the snot kicked out of me again.

But no. Not this time. I hadn't had nearly as much to drink. Either that or my body had become accustomed to the volume of alcohol I had consumed earlier that evening.

I got my right leg up to deflect the first punch from Einstein. But his second punch hit me in the ribs on my left side.

I extended my right foot out, which pushed him back, and with my right hand, tried pulling Jason's arm away from my throat. I couldn't pull it off but was able to reduce the chokehold he had on me.

Einstein moved in again, getting in another blow before I let go of Jason's arm long enough to grab his mask again and twist the rubber mask sideways, blinding him. I followed that with a sideways fist hitting him hard in the side of the face.

I heard the crack as I connected with his cheek bone and nose, and he stumbled down onto one knee. A fresh smell of blood filled the air, and he let out a shriek of pain, tearing at his mask. I kicked him square in the chest, winding him and sending him onto his back on the pavement.

"For one of the members of the Master Race, seems like buddy there isn't all that tough."

Though he didn't say anything, I could sense that my jibe had annoyed Jason from the odor he gave off.

Jason ceased the chokehold as he spun me around and threw me hard against the limo.

I turned, pulling in a solid breath as I spotted him standing a few feet away from me with his hands in that middle of chest praying position.

He had a look of deep concentration on his face as his fingers came apart, revealing a yellow crackling ball of light. This one was smaller than the one he'd attempted to throw at Lex.

He flung both hands out in my direction, and the ball of light struck me in the center of my chest.

It was like he had hit me with an invisible wallop of Thor's hammer. The force was powerful enough to pitch me back in the air. My lower back hit the back of the car roof and I did a backwards somersault onto the hood of the car.

I shook my head as I lifted myself to my hands and knees.

Jason had taken a few steps around the side of the car and was a couple feet away as he pressed his hands together to prepare for a second energy ball strike.

I groggily looked at him and helplessly waited for the next powerful blast.

Chapter Twenty-Four: Hide and Seek, Marco Polo, and Whose Lie is it Anyway?

In the split second I was deciding between flattening myself against the car or ducking behind it, something flashed into view from Jason's right, striking him from the side.

It was Lex.

I had been so pre-occupied with Jason that I hadn't smelled or heard her.

She struck him in the stomach, and, because he'd been in his sum-wrestler/buddha-style pose, she had caught him completely off guard.

He stumbled backwards as Lex took several shots at the side of his face with her right hand. I heard the connection of her blows and he gasped in pain with each strike. How was it possible that her punches could have that kind of effect on him?

Did Lex actually possess enhanced strength?

Why hadn't I noticed that with all of the modified between-the-sheets wrestling we'd done?

I mean, sure, she was indeed strong. A finely-toned

woman with a sleek athletic body and taut muscles. How was it possible she could have hidden that strength from me the whole time we were together?

I was utterly confused.

But of course, I was also extremely thankful.

Jason stumbled back, and Lex got in another three quick shots.

"Woah," I said to Lex, scrambling off the hood of the car. "Nice. Remind me to never piss you off."

Jason struck at Lex with his left hand, hitting her in the shoulder, as I was now close enough to throw a punch at his face.

My fist connected, but not nearly with the amount of super force I'd intended to deliver. Despite it being a somewhat normal and feeble punch, it still rocked his head back.

I looked at my fist, confused. My sense of smell and hearing had muted. What the hell was happening with my enhanced powers?

Jason kicked at me and caught me square in the stom-ach. With his right hand he managed to fling Lex off of him. As Lex and I both stumbled back, Jason brought his hands together in that preying pose.

That constipated look came over his face as Lex and I glanced quickly at one another.

I was debating whether I should I rush Jason, or step in between him and Lex.

Apparently, Lex had been thinking the same thing. Be-cause as Jason's hands came apart, we both leapt in the direction that would block the other person from the energy ball blast.

We crashed into one another, both of us completely shocked.

Oh no.

It meant the energy blast was going to hit us both.

I looked over to see that his hands had come apart but there was no yellow energy ball floating there like before.

"What the fuck?" Jason muttered.

The three of us stood there looking dumbfounded at one another when a brilliant flash of yellow light lit up the driveway completely backlighting Jason.

A thin black sliver in the middle of the yellow ball opened up in a way that reminded me of the Eye of Sauron. From it stepped a tall and handsome blonde man with a broad face and square jaw. His cold blue eyes immediately fixed on Lex.

"You!" the Aryan featured man yelled, glaring at her.

He then placed a hand on Jason's shoulder, pulled the tall man back into the dark sliver in the center of the rounded pillars of yellow light. The ball of light expanded to fill that black space and then faded away.

The two had disappeared.

And I at least had an idea of how Jason had pulled off that magic trick the other night. Okay, maybe no idea how, but maybe a little bit of the what.

It had been some sort of magic temporary portal that opened up then closed immediately.

That must have been the residue of what I'd heard and

smelled in the alley the other night when Jason had disappeared.

They were gone.

It was just Lex and I.

And Argyle.

"Argyle!" I yelled out, leaping over the back of the car to the side where my friend had fallen. He was unconscious, but still seemed to be breathing. My ability to hear his heartbeat or breathing was gone. Again.

"Hang in there, Argyle. Help is on the way." Even with my hearing back to normal, I heard the sounds of an ambulance.

I lifted Argyle up so his back was resting on my leg and his head was in the crook of my right arm. With my left hand I tried to staunch the flow of blood from the bullet wound.

"Come on, Argyle, hang in there. The ambulance is on its way."

A few feet away, Einstein was coming to, but Lex was kneeling on his chest and had his arms pinned to the pavement.

"You know him?" Lex asked.

"Yeah. Remember that awesome limo driver I'd told you about? The one who suggested I visit Gulp? This is him."

To Argyle I whispered. "C'mon, stay with me, my friend. Stay with me."

"The ambulance is almost here," Lex called.

"C'mon, c'mon, c'mon," I muttered.

Then I looked back over at Lex.

"What the heck was that yellow ball of light they stepped through?" I asked.

"I don't know," she said. "I've never seen anything like it."

"What about that Hans guy?"

"Hans?"

"The guy with the square jaw who stepped out of the portal. Seemed like he recognized you."

Even from a few feet away I could see her face go pale.

"That was Marco."

"Oh."

I didn't know what to say. I couldn't read her scent or hear her heartbeat. I had no way of knowing what she was thinking or feeling.

Something odd had been happening, with my enhanced senses and strength coming and going. It had started happening ever since I got to LA.

No. I remembered that night before I flew here, when I'd walked to Central Park, expecting to change into a wolf. But it never happened. Despite it being a night with an 84% full moon my lycanthropic change hadn't happened.

Did this mean that my werewolf blood was altering?

That I was no longer half man/half wolf?

That maybe I was slowly changing to normal again?

I didn't have time to process that, or what it meant that Marco had spotted Lex, because, in my arms, Argyle let out a huge final sputter and blood gushed out from the sides of his mouth.

I looked down at his eyes, staring vacantly up at me,

through me. Remembering the mirth, the intellect, the playfulness I'd seen in those same eyes, his dead face faded from view, consumed by the blur of tears.

Moments later, many moments too late, the first ambulance and police cruiser arrived.

Lex and I didn't return to her place until about three in the morning. We were questioned, checked over by the emergency responders, and told not to leave town, in case they had any questions.

We relayed the story of what he'd seen and heard, including the masks, that telltale sign that this was the work of the PFA, but skipping any mention of the paranormal. Apparently, none of the nearby onlookers had seen the supernatural feats Jason had performed, nor the mini yellow Eye of Sauron that Marco had stepped out of and back into. The tall hedges on either side of the driveway seemed to cover that from the view of any onlookers.

We learned that the woman and her son, the two who'd been shot, were walking through the neighborhood, returning from a visit to the local corner store, when the thugs approached them, accusing them of befouling a non-ethnic neighborhood with their black presence.

When the two kept moving forward, on their way, ignoring them, the men continued to harass and follow them, calling them names.

Seeing that the name-calling and hounding wasn't getting the expected rise out of them, the one thug had shot the kid. Once in the leg, knocking him off of his scooter. Then, a second later, in the chest.

He then shot the mother and the three of them had fled.

I had arrived less than a minute later.

Too late to do anything useful to help other than the phone allowing her to call for an ambulance. They had both survived.

But I was responsible for that night's second death.

If I hadn't chased after Jason and the two other thugs, there wouldn't have been a fight in Argyle's driveway. Argyle's car alarm wouldn't have gone off. He wouldn't have come out to investigate.

Argyle wouldn't have been shot. He wouldn't be dead.

I was responsible.

The gun was pointed at me; but I had deflected it. Right at Argyle.

They separated Lex and I for questioning, and for a short time, my senses were less muted. I could use that to navigate the interrogation by the police officer who was questioning me.

About a half hour after the parallel interrogations had started, a police detective pulled up in an unmarked car and introduced himself as Hank Reynolds a special detective in charge of a domestic terrorist task force.

When he was introduced to me, he said. "Of course. Michael Andrews. You're the writer working on the set with my brother-in-law. He speaks so highly of you."

"Craig is a great guy and has been a truly welcoming friend since the very first day I arrived," I told him.

I relayed what I'd experienced to Hank, leaving out the paranormal stuff, of course. I not only picked up a really good vibe off of him, but I could tell he was authentic and pure of heart. He truly cared about the injured woman and her son and wanted the men responsible to be brought to justice for Argyle's death. As we spoke, I picked up on the fact, via the emotions I could detect through a combination of the things he said, the things he asked, and the scents he gave off, that it was difficult to pin crimes on the PFA. They weren't just elusive and slippery, but the group itself wasn't officially registered anywhere, and had no discernable home base. They also seemed to have connections everywhere, and in situations like this evening, where a couple of members were captured, they never spoke, never shared anything, and it was typical that any captured PFA soldier would die while in captivity under suspicious circumstances.

I thought about my involvement in the evening's events. How, had I just called 911 and stayed out of it, Argyle would still be alive. I contrasted that to Hank, a trained and compassionate professional who had dedicated his life in the service of others.

I was a charlatan, a fake, a fraud. A guy who had accidentally happened upon some special abilities and might have helped a few people along the way, but who wasn't cut out for this, had no training, and it had resulted in an innocent man dying.

After he finished chatting with me—and I purposely used the term *chatting* rather than *interrogating* because that's exactly how he made it feel the entire time—he moved on to go talk to Lex.

He gave each of us his card and asked us to call him at any time, day or night if there was anything, no matter how small, that we might remember or recall from the events of this night.

My heightened senses, which seemed to be turning on and off all night, were muted and subdued as Lex and I walked home.

She poured us both a shot glass of bourbon that we downed immediately in sync, and then grabbed a couple of tumblers and brought the glasses and the bottle of bourbon into the living room, filling the glasses and setting the bottle down on the middle of the glass coffee table.

She sat in the armchair.

I sat on the couch across from her.

"So, we have a few things to discuss," Lex said. "Because I have to be entirely frank with you, Kal. The truth is, I'm falling in love with you. Big time. In a really bad way. I've never felt this way about anyone else before. And I've never felt so loved, so purely and genuinely loved, by anyone. Ever. But I feel it when you look at me. I feel it in the way you talk to me. The way you touch me. Everything about you screams that love to me, Kal.

"I know you haven't said those words to me, Kal, but you never need to. Because I know it. I feel it. It's just there. Ever present. All the time. I think I felt it, or at least the respect and adoration that led to that love, that first day we met. When I was talking, you actually looked at me; attended to the things I was saying. You were interested, listening, engaging.

"Even when you messed things up with that 'mostly single' line I knew I would give you another chance. But I wanted to make sure you worked for it. To prove to me that you would work hard at correcting the mistake. Which you did.

"And while we've shared so much with one another, I know that we've both been holding onto things we haven't yet been willing to talk about. Perhaps for fear that the other person won't believe it, or it might be too much for the other person to handle.

"But seriously, look at what we witnessed tonight? Look at what we saw happen the other night at the brewery. We can't pretend that these supernatural things don't exist. Enough playing games, here.

"So, whose lie do we want to lay on the table first? Yours or mine?"

I was going to ask her what she meant. It was a default position for me to hide my lycanthropic nature. But I knew what she was talking about.

We'd both rushed right into danger without a second's pause. And we both fought a bunch of pretty scary bad guys. Again, without hesitation. We'd both done that back at the brewery. And we'd done it again tonight.

"Let me go first, Kal."

She finished her bourbon and poured herself another.

"When I was telling you about the way I got kicked

out of the PFA, I wasn't telling the whole truth.

"The part about where my *Getting Risen* process failed. That part was true. At least as far as the PFA were concerned. The treatment had no apparent effect on me. And the DNA testing they'd done showed my heredity to them. They wanted me out of the group.

"But you never really leave. Not alive anyway. They forced me out of the group, but I was one of their sleeper cell informants. Kept at a distance and not welcomed to any of the inner circle PFA gatherings or activities. But if they reached out and needed a favor, I would be there to give it to them.

"The PFA has tentacles that reach into almost any sector. My experience working at tech companies, meant they would occasionally reach out and request access to internal documents or files.

"I had to obey, follow their orders, do as they said, or they would go after my family. That part, which I shared is true. They held that over me.

"They had only reached out once in the time since I'd left the group, so mostly, I was at least free from them; well, free from the day to day. Other than being on call, I at least had my other freedoms."

"Okay," I said. "That's not much of a lie. It's pretty close to what you had already shared and what we already talked about."

"That's not all."

"No."

"The treatment seemed to do nothing from all appearances. But I always suspected there was something more underlying. Something not visible, not evident. But there just the same.

"I wasn't sure, because it wasn't obvious. But ever since the treatment, I haven't had a single serious accident. And I'm normally quite accident prone," she laughed.

"The first time I wondered about it was this time I was walking downtown and attending to my phone instead of paying attention. I stepped out into the street without noticing that a car had blown through the red light. The car was coming right toward me; I was directly in its path. But suddenly, the storm drain cover collapsed beneath the car's driver side wheel, and the car spun to the left out into traffic.

"The storm cover made of rungs of iron, suddenly collapsed at exactly that moment. It was simply beyond normal.

"The following week I was out with friends and this waitress was walking toward our table with a tray full of food and drinks. She tripped on something on the floor and launched the tray right at us.

"Several glasses and plates and the tray hit the friends I was sitting with. And a couple of them were drenched. I remained mostly unscathed, with barely a drop of liquor spilled onto me.

"I noticed little things like that happening all the time. This one time I was cutting big thick carrots, and the phone rang and I looked over as I was slicing. Only I twitched the hand holding the carrot as I looked away, and I was pressing down with enough force that it should have sliced the tip of my fingertip right off. But somehow the knife struck the ring on my second finger. On my second finger, far from where the blade had been aimed. It was like the knife somehow rerouted in mid flight.

"The other night, when that tall guy in the hockey mask tried to hit me, I dodged out of the way. Considering how fast he was moving, and the fact we know he has some sort of super strength and speed, I never should have been able to dodge him."

"But he still hit you," I said.

"Yeah, but he barely hit me. He knocked me over a bit. The punch he'd been lining up should have smashed my nose in. But he missed.

"And then, a minute later, when he sent that yellow ball of energy at me—"

"It dissolved in the air in front of you," I said.

"Exactly. Almost as if it had—"

"Been absorbed by an invisible barrier."

"You're getting really good at finishing my—"

"Sentences," I quickly slipped in.

We laughed.

Lex took another drink of her bourbon.

"Michael, I think that I must be some sort of walking good luck charm. That's the only way to explain why he wasn't able to deliver a direct hit to me. How that energy blast didn't hit me. Why I've been able to dodge, without any apparent skill or even seriously trying to, so many things that were trying to harm me.

"It's like I've been inflicted with some sort of curse. Or at least, the opposite of a curse. Some sort of charm spell that prevents me from being injured by physical attacks."

"That could explain how you were able to surprise him earlier tonight and actually struggle with him. Because I've never fought anyone who possessed that type of strength."

"Yeah. About that. I suspect that, despite what you've told me, you've been in more than your fair share of fights. Because my lucky charm nature doesn't explain how you could fight with him."

"Well," I said. "I suppose it's my turn to share my tale, or my curse, which is more the case. I actually started to tell you about it that night after our encounter at the brewery. When we were sitting on the bench waiting for the sun to rise. I started to share what a sunrise and sunset can come to mean to me, but you had fallen asleep. And I put it off; trying to figure out the right time.

"But to be honest, Lex, I was enjoying just being normal with you, and not having to think or worry about my own curse."

"Your own curse? Do you have some sort of past with the PFA too? Is that why you were attacked in that parking lot that first night I'd met you?"

"No. Nothing like that." I said. "My curse is more related to the cycles of the moon."

And I relayed the full story of how I'd gained my wolfish affliction and the resulting side effects. My enhanced abilities when I was human and how I'd had to live and plan things out according to the cycle of the moon.

I then explained how, ever since I'd arrived in LA my enhanced powers seemed to fade in and out, seemingly at random. But that I noticed when I'd been drinking, because I didn't drink that much normally, it helped keep the sense muted.

And that I preferred not having those enhanced senses. Because it meant that, with a few exceptions at moments where my extraordinary senses of smell and hearing had kicked in, Lex and I were connecting authentically. I couldn't read her feelings or emotions and preferred it that way over the more intrusive nature that my senses had forced onto me.

I also expressed how I had always thought my enhanced abilities, my senses, my strength, could be useful, helpful for others. But that they'd done no good tonight. How, if anything, me using those powers caused Argyle's death.

As I expected, Lex believed me. And she understood.

It made sense that she didn't find it unbelievable. She had seen supernatural things already. Not to mention the fact she seemed to be a walking lucky charm.

We sat there for a moment, each of us taking turns staring into our bourbons, then looking at each other.

"We laid it all out on the table," she said. "The lies we'd been holding in. I shared mine. You shared yours."

"Yeah, we've said it all. Except for one thing. We both talked about how we're falling for one another, but I haven't properly expressed it to you directly."

"I told you, Kal, you don't need to. I can see it in your eyes."

"Be that as it may," I said. "I still want to tell you. I love you, Alexandria."

She stared at me, and a teardrop rolled down her left cheek.

"I know," she said. "But say it again. Don't call me that. Please, just call me Lex."

"I love you, Lex."

"I love you too, Kal."

She stood up, taking me by the hand, and leading me to the bedroom.

Friday, June 30, 2017

Chapter Twenty-Five: The North and South of a Magnet for Trouble

I'd been so looking forward to introducing you to my brother-in-law Hank before you left town, but I suppose there's no need now, is there?"

Craig beamed a huge grin at me from across the lunch table and then shook his head, still smiling. "I planned on inviting him to swing by tonight at the little going-away send off we're having for you. But, no need for that. You have his contact info."

"You were right," I said. "Hank and I hit it off. He's a good guy. Are you sure you two are brothers-in-law and not actual brothers?"

Craig laughed and the smell of pride and love he had for his brother-in-law was palpable. "That's exactly how I felt when I met him. I grew up with sisters and always wanted a brother. And ever since marrying his sister, that's exactly what he's been for me.

"I knew you'd like him. You can trust him, too."

"That was clear from the moment he introduced himself," I said.

"Wow. Two run-ins with PFA since you've been to town. It's like you're a magnet for trouble."

I considered that for a moment.

Prior to getting scratched by that other werewolf, I had only been in two fights in my life. Well, if you could call them fights.

One time, in grade six I was punched in the face in the school yard when we were standing around, and this husky fellow named Ronnie who was a bit of a show-off was bragging about how strong he was. I smirked, muttered "Yeah, you are strong," and made a show of sniffing my armpits then making a foul face. Despite my initial perception of his lesser cognitive abilities, he caught the meaning of what I was suggesting and threw a right hook at me, knocking me right off my feet and leaving a solid swollen bruise.

The other time, when I was a junior in high school, I was walking into a local arcade when I spotted Ronnie and a bunch of his cronies standing in a circle around this much younger kid and giving him a hard time, shoving him back and forth and calling him names. I told them to leave him alone, and they obliged by turning their attention on to me. The kid got away as I found myself in the middle of their group, getting pushed and shoved, and then, when I stumbled to the ground, getting kicked while they laughed. They eventually tired of kicking me as I laid there sobbing on the sidewalk.

But that was it. It wasn't until I had developed the extra strength and enhanced senses that I seemed to find trouble and insert myself into the melee.

Blame it on an upbringing of reading Spider-Man comics. And my love of the meek and nerdy Peter Parker who develops super strength, speed, and agility and then uses his superpowers to fight crime and help others.

Yes, I had certainly helped a decent number of people over the years, and I was proud of pretty much every single one of them.

But those powers came with a cost, because of the werewolf curse.

Initially, they'd been why I had lied to Gail, lost her trust and lost that relationship. But then, over the years, because my enhanced senses kept cluing me into the fact that Gail had strong romantic and passionate feelings for me, despite her consistently telling me otherwise, I'd stupidly maintained hope that we'd get back together.

Being able to sense beyond the surface level had been useful in business negotiations and in hand-to-hand combat, but it led to an insight into romantic relationships that nobody should have.

Part of the reason why things with Lex felt so good was that, with my senses flagging so much since I got to Los Angeles, I had the chance to get to know her in a more natural and authentic way.

And it felt perfect.

It was strange how my enhanced senses came and went. This morning, for example, when I woke up and saw her lying naked beside me, my hearing and smell were at full volume. I could tell she was in a deep sleep from the sound of her breathing and her heartbeat.

She was lying on her side, facing away from me, and I spent maybe thirty minutes staring at her, marveling at how beautiful she was.

Then, unable to control myself, I gently stroked her shoulder and rubbed her back, relishing in how good it felt to touch her.

I looked at the butterfly tattoo on the small of her back with its beautiful wings and ornamental decorative lines. I remember gently kissing it the first time I'd seen it and asking Lex when she'd gotten it.

She had shared it was to cover up the red PFA symbol that she'd had to tattoo on her back when she'd become a member in her attempt to save her friend Sacha.

After escaping from the group, instead of having it removed, she'd had a tattoo artist adapt it. The red combination overlapping P, F, and A symbol had been modified into the body of the butterfly. She'd told me that the butterfly symbolized the surface freedom, but that, like the experience of becoming one of them, and of losing her dearest friend, there would be no escape from the indelible impact that had had on her.

My heart ached for the trauma and suffering she'd been through, and I marveled at how strong this woman was, both emotionally, and physically, as I caressed the taut muscles along her back and left shoulder.

As I continued this gentle massage, I could hear her heartbeat and breathing change, scented a slow conscious awareness come to her. She slowly turned, looked me in the eye, smiled and said: "Good morning, Handsome," and then we'd made love, slowly, gently, beautifully.

When I first slid inside her, I could feel and sense her passion and emotion, and it was a truly mind-shattering experience, feeling my love for her and her love for me mingling together like that. But as we progressed, my hearing and smell became more and more muted. But the passion I held for her became stronger.

I woke with my senses completely intact.

Then they slowly faded, almost in harmony with the time she first woke.

I considered the moments of when my senses seemed to be muted. I had assumed it was because of the alcohol, and I think the alcohol did have an effect. But something I hadn't really noticed, was that there was another correlation.

My senses were muted when I was near Lex.

It was as if her charm or curse, or whatever it was that was protecting her, was protecting her from my enhanced sensory abilities.

And that explained why I had been experiencing the constant muting of those senses.

It meant that, with Lex, I couldn't probe her inner feelings, couldn't intrude upon a place I never belonged.

I could be normal when with Lex.

And we could love one another through active and willing sharing, not through reading her emotive scents and the sound of her heartbeat.

"Hello," Craig's voice came to me. "Earth to Michael. Where've you been, my friend? You seemed to blank out there for a moment."

"Oh. Sorry about that. I suppose I have just been thinking about what you said about me being a magnet for trouble. Then I started thinking about Lex, and how she is like that opposite pole to the magnetic charge I bring.

She's like the South to my North."

Craig shook his head.

"Oh man, you're in deep. But I love it. She seems perfect for you."

"She is," I grinned. "She really is."

"I can't wait to meet her tonight."

The gathering, that evening, took place at a bar close to the studio lot. It was just a handful of the crew and some of the cast members from the film. The director, JP Heartschwinger, didn't join us. The bar we were at was far too low brow for people of his magnitude. But he did offer to pick up the tab, a nod to the fact that he had finally accepted the fact I wasn't a threat to his film, but a member of the team.

JP had sent Velma, his assistant, to the gathering, along with his credit card. Considering that he was willing to give up having her at his beck and call, even for a few hours, was one of the most generous things I'd seen him do since arriving on the set.

And I really liked Velma. She reminded me, in many ways, of Anne, Mack's assistant. She was kind, patient, steadfast, and reliable. And though Heartschwinger treated most everyone like peons there merely to do his bidding, Velma was never unkind or disrespectful to anyone. Like Anne did with Mack, she made up for his crassness.

Craig was behind organizing the event. This was a role

he took on amongst the entire crew. He was the one who tracked birthdays and special moments, wanting to ensure that everyone was respected and acknowledged.

We drank and snacked on the pub fare hors d'oeuvres and laughed and shared fun times together. This crew was an interesting extended family. And it was clear that Craig relished being a central social force at bringing them together.

It was as if he was the master carpenter for relationships.

Lex arrived about an hour after we had arrived. And I knew she was there the moment she'd walked through the front door, despite us being in the back. I had smelled her, heard her distinctive heartbeat amongst the music and loud chatter of the post-work-day bar.

There was an odd scent coming off of Lex when she first arrived that I couldn't put my finger on. A mingled sadness, disappointment, anger, and fear. Something had happened to her that had really gotten to her.

As I kissed her on the cheek and embraced her, I whispered in her ear.

"What's wrong? What happened?"

"I'll tell you after," she said. "Right now, we're celebrating your last day on the set."

"You sure? We can leave now."

"No," she insisted, smiling. Even as my enhanced sense of smell was fading, I picked up an authentic desire to just have fun and enjoy the moment in her. "It's fine. Besides, I've been looking forward to finally meeting Craig."

It was wonderful getting to introduce her to Craig, these two people who were so dear to me. The two of them hit it off immediately. I shouldn't have been surprised. Both Lex and Craig were gregarious and warm people; and, over the past couple of weeks they'd each heard me say nothing but glowing and positive things about one another.

In several ways, the new man I had become since arriving in Los Angeles made me much like the child of these two very fine people who had taken me in, welcomed me, and given me hope that my life could be something more, something bigger, than just a lone wolf wandering around a large metropolis.

And of course, as expected, and true to the theory I'd worked out earlier that day, after Lex had arrived my senses returned to normal human perception.

At one point, when I went to the restroom, I noticed how, once I was removed from proximity to Lex, my enhanced senses returned to their full form.

I looked forward to sharing this revelation with her.

Chapter Twenty-Six: Normal and Lost Together

I should have seen this coming," Lex said as we stood in the doorway to her apartment and surveyed what could have been a cross between a temporary college party hangout thrashed by a group of rowdy college kids and a hoarder's paradise, with a bit of a war-torn feel to the place.

There were holes in the drywall, broken windows, furniture was destroyed and spread in pieces. Glassware, dishes and clothes were scattered all over. The cupboard doors in the kitchen were ripped completely off their hinges, as were interior doors. There were burn marks on the pieces of furniture and walls. And it looked as if someone had gone into one of the trash dumpsters outside and emptied their contents on top of the mess like some sort of rotten cherry topping to it all.

The PFA symbol…

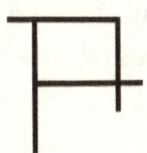

...was spray painted in various sizes in blood red paint on the ceiling walls, and the few spots of non-littered floor.

When we had arrived at Lex's apartment, the door had been slightly ajar. We looked at one another before she opened it up, thinking that someone might have broken in.

But when we opened the door and saw the devastation, the wild destruction, and, in particular that blatant symbol of hatred, we knew.

"I should have seen this coming," she repeated.

On our Uber ride back to her apartment from my party she had shared the thing that I'd sensed had been bothering her.

She had been let go from her role as project manager at the software company where she had worked. The director she reported to explained that it was cutbacks and related to a downturn in the economy. "But I know for a fact," she said, "that the tech sector has been seeing unprecedented growth in the last nine months.

"It was the PFA. Their tentacles have a nefarious reach. I should have known. I should have suspected this. Should have seen this coming."

"We need to call the police."

"No," she said. "Not yet. First, I need to get ahold of Davy." She was talking about her brother.

She called her brother, learned that he and his family were fine and then, without sharing her background with the PFA, explained that she had crossed paths with them and they were now attacking her and threatened to attack her family. She told Davy to get their mother out of the nursing home and immediately flee to a hotel, ideally paying cash. That they were in danger.

She told him not to hesitate, not to take more than the immediate things they needed. Davy, his family, and her mother, lived in Vegas. It was at least a four-hour drive. But the PFA could have sent members there at the same time they had broken into her apartment.

And she'd been home since early afternoon, since being let go from her job. She'd only been gone for about two-and-a-half hours, going to meet Michael and his movie set colleagues at the bar.

Which meant they must have only just been there.

While Lex was on the phone with her brother, I got on a call with Hank, Craig's brother-in-law. I explained that Lex's apartment had been thrashed, and we were worried that they'd gotten the address of her family when wrecking the apartment. And was there anything Hank could do via his CIA connections, to assign protection to Lex's family.

Hank was a good guy. He shared that the PFA were definitely a local group, and didn't have operatives, at least according to the intel he had, that existed beyond the Greater Los Angeles Area. But he asked me if there was anyone I should be concerned about in New York, in case they looked me up and tried to exact their revenge on me. I gave him the address of The Algonquin Hotel where I lived, of Gail's business, and my literary agent, saying those would be the only potential places they might show up. He said he'd have someone local look into that. And he assured me that Lex's family would be watched and protected.

Hank said we didn't have to wait there for the officers to arrive and declare it a crime scene, and he suggested we get out of the apartment, in case the PFA came back, or were watching the place. I told him we would head over to my hotel. He said there'd be an undercover officer assigned to monitor the place.

The entire apartment looked the same as the living room and kitchen. Lex and I picked through the wreckage, but virtually everything she owned was destroyed, including her suitcases. All of her clothes were torn or shredded. Not a single article was left untouched or undamaged.

There wasn't really anything to pack. She basically had the clothes on her back, her purse, and the light jacket she'd been wearing when she left for the bar.

We called an Uber and took it back to my hotel. Just as we were walking in, Hank called my cell phone to let me know that his contact had arrived at Lex's brother's home just as they were leaving and had followed them to the nursing home where their mother had been picked up. He was going to continue watching out for them and would report back every few hours.

That was a huge relief to Lex.

It was also a huge relief to me.

Sure, I had taken out some muggers, some thieves, some bad guys; even had a hand in helping foil a bit of an underground gang a couple of years earlier. But I was just an amateur vigilante. I wasn't trained in dealing with domestic terrorists and wouldn't have the first clue to know where and how to "take down" these types of cult-based bad guys.

Hank, his team, the police, and the CIA were the professionals assigned to deal with such things.

It took coming to Los Angeles, getting to the lowest of the lows I had experienced, and finding myself re-born, with a new love, a new outlook on life, to come to terms with the fact that a single man with a few extra-sensory powers and superhuman strength were definitely going to be no match for the likes of the PFA.

Sure, maybe I was good at stopping a petty thief or pulling a cat out of a tree. But this was well beyond my limited abilities and know-how.

Hank showed up to talk to us in person, keep us abreast of what was going on, and texted me three more times to let me know that Lex's family were in a hotel together and the operative assigned to protect them was reporting every hour.

His visits, and his calls, and texts, were enough to remind me that this was his vocation, this was where he thrived. I was a writer, not a crime-fighter, and definitely not at all equipped to deal with this type of domestic terror threat.

This wasn't a comic book. This wasn't a movie. This was cold hard reality.

Leave crime-fighting to the trained professionals and the multitude of resources.

Lex and I stayed up the entire night, talking, again.

Only, this time we weren't sharing and getting to know one another like before. This time, we were exploring what this personal attack from the PFA meant. She wanted to head to Vegas to be with her brother and mother, but also didn't want to face them, knowing how it had been her personal involvement with the PFA that had put them in this danger. She couldn't face them, and hadn't spent time with any of them in person since first getting involved in the PFA, because she couldn't face them.

Not with what she'd done. Not with who she'd had to pretend to be when infiltrating the PFA.

She was satisfied, based on Hank's assurances that they were far enough away, and protected, especially with Hank's special forces looking out for them.

We discussed the idea of her returning to New York with me so we could figure this out together. Where she could rebuild her life, far away from the PFA. Where we could explore building our own lives together.

I shared the theory of how her charm against bad luck seemed to work when I was with her—how it reduced my intrusive enhanced sensory ability—and how that allowed me to be a normal human when I was a human.

The discussion turned to how she would be there for me, meet me in the mornings during that time of month for me with a fresh change of clothes; instead of me having to rely on hidden stashes of clothes. That we could properly be a team.

We even discussed the idea of the two of us returning to Los Angeles once things with the PFA settled down. I didn't, after all, need to live in New York. I could write novels anywhere. And there were far richer and more extensive green spaces in the rolling hills and mountains that surrounded LA. Perhaps living with the fact that I turned into a wolf during the moon's full cycle would be easier to bear in such a different landscape.

I told her that living with being a werewolf would be easier to bear because I had her to share that burden with. Not to mention that, when I was a human, I could be a normal human again, and that she was the balance I needed in order to be a me I hadn't been for well over a decade.

We spent much of that night holding and comforting one another while talking, then falling asleep, and then waking and talking more, in the same cyclical manner we had previously woken and made love before falling asleep again.

It wasn't until the early morning, with the sunlight streaming into the hotel room that we made slow and deliberate love to one another, while solidifying the fact that, despite the things we had each lost, we were both richer and better off, for having one another.

Tuesday, July 4, 2017

Chapter Twenty-Seven: Looks Like We're in For Turbulence, I Know the End is Coming Soon

The flight attendant's voice on the overhead speaker sent the most terrifying chill down my spine.

"Please be advised that we will be delayed for another hour while we wait for ATC clearance on our revised schedule, and where we can fit into the takeoff queue. This is a reminder to remain in your seats with your seatbelts fastened. We also remind you that all of your larger electronic personal devices should be stored in the overhead bins or under the seat in front of you. Your smaller devices, which you can store in the seat pockets in front of you, should be set to airplane mode."

I shifted uncomfortably, feeling the hot beads of sweat pouring down my forehead. My shirt had already soaked up the clamminess of my back.

No, this wasn't possible. It couldn't be happening.

We should have gotten off the plane earlier, during that first flight delay, when the plane was still parked at the gate and they hadn't closed the doors.

But that first delay was only fifteen minutes, waiting

for a crew member who was late via a delayed connecting flight. The second delay, while we were still at the gate waiting for Air Traffic Control clearance, was only another half hour. The third delay, which they didn't specify a reason for, was another forty minutes. But this latest delay, an additional hour, this was pushing it too far.

I glanced out the window at the sun as it was making its way slowly towards the mountains in the western sky. It was still hours away from touching down here in the Los Angeles hills.

But we were heading to New York where it was three hours ahead. The original schedule for this flight would have gotten us back with several hours to spare between landing and nightfall.

The nightfall of a full moon. Okay, not the full moon, yet, but one that would be more than three quarters full. I normally didn't turn into a werewolf until it was closer to an 80% full moon, but I remembered my cycle had been off prior to leaving New York. And who knew how Lex's proximity might further alter my condition.

I was worried and glad to be getting back early.

At this rate, with the additional hour-long delay in our flight, we would likely land just as the lycanthropic change came over me.

Damn, we should have tried to get on a flight yesterday.

I turned away from the window to look at Lex, stare deep into her light blue eyes. She stared back at me, placed her hand comfortingly on top of my own. Despite not being able to sense her emotions, I felt her love for me quite clearly and plainly.

"This isn't good," I whispered.

Lex suggested that maybe she could feign having a heart attack or some other medical emergency that could get us off the plane.

As she was relaying this idea to me, the flight attendant came back on and announced that they had been granted clearance and we would take off within the next fifteen minutes.

Lex looked at her watch and I saw her mind whirling. She was doing the very same calculations I had been doing in my own head.

"Okay, this means," she said, "based on an 8:30 PM sunset in New York, that we'll have at least a half an hour leeway before the change happens. It's not like we have checked bags. Heck, even if we had checked bags, we could still get off the plane and split the airport. Obviously, we wouldn't be able to get to Manhattan. But maybe there's some green space close by."

"Weequahic Park," I said, remembering the research I'd done about Newark and the surrounding area. "It's a huge green space with a large lake. And it's next to Newark Airport. It's huge. It would be perfect."

She smiled at me, which had the immediate effect of calming me, like a balm on my very soul.

I loved being able to problem solve with someone who knew my most intimate secrets.

"I love you, Lex." I said.

"I love you, Kal."

We kissed.

I was so thankful that Anne had arranged to get Lex a seat right beside me in business class on my return trip to New York even if it meant bumping the flight by a day. We'd been inseparable for the past few weeks, and now that I'd experienced what we had together, I wasn't sure if I could bear to be apart from her.

We were about four hours into our five-hour flight when the pilot announced we were heading into a bit of turbulence because of the heat waves being experienced across the United States.

It got extremely rough. Lex and I held one another's hand throughout the experience.

After the turbulence settled, the pilot thanked us for bearing with him.

I had been so on the edge of my seat during the turbulence, and prior to takeoff, that I felt winded. Lex wiped a bit of sweat off my forehead for me.

"Hey there champ, why are you so nervous? The turbulence is over."

I laughed. "I'm just really tired. Exhausted."

She giggled and pressed her head against mine. "Me too. We're almost there. Close your eyes."

I closed my eyes as I snuggled my head against hers. It felt good to be with her. I thought about how much better it would be when we weren't strapped into the seats of a plane and I could hold her in my arms.

The next thing I knew, I had fallen asleep.

Because I'd awoke to the sound of the pilot speaking. It wasn't on the intercom. I was hearing him talking to the co-pilot. My super enhanced abilities were picking it up. He was talking about the heat wave in New Jersey and how the thinner air would make it more dangerous to land. Flight take-offs and landings were being delayed, and they were going to circle over the greater New York area waiting for the sun to set and the air to cool down enough when they'd likely get the go-ahead it was safe to land.

I opened my eyes, just as he was coming on the PA system to announce this update.

Lex was sleeping beside me. Of course she was. That's how my enhanced senses had returned. When she was asleep, my paranormal abilities were no longer muted.

Lex woke as the pilot made his announcement.

"What do I do now?" I asked Lex, when he finished sharing the delay that would mean landing after nightfall. "Lock myself in the restroom?"

"I don't know," she said.

"Oh," I said, feeling the tingling and ringing sensation in my head, the aura that I knew meant the change was about to happen, coming over me. "It's happening now. It's happening early."

"The altitude must be causing an altered reaction," she whispered.

I looked down at my hand, the one Lex was clasping, and watched incredulously as tufts of fur started to grow out of the back of my hand. Simultaneously, I felt the tautness of my arm muscles stiffen and jerk.

I had never been conscious of the change to wolf before; I had always blacked out. I'd never experienced it happening. This was different. Lex and I stared at my hands as my fingers retracted and the bones of my hands compressed. It was excruciating and I let out a squeal of pain.

What the hell was happening? Why was I experiencing the change consciously? With the pain I was feeling this early in the process was it even possible for me to maintain sanity while it was happening? I remembered that theory I'd had about why Knell was a raging psychopath.

There is no way a person could remain of sound mind experiencing this intensity of anguish.

I looked into Lex's eyes, tried to tell her I loved her, but my lips were no longer working. I realized my face had been distorting and my jaw was elongating.

She didn't look horrified about the creature I was turning into; she appeared completely empathetic.

"It's okay, Kal. I'm here. I've got you. We've got this."

Her words were soothing, and I focused on them as the pain in my body and my entire head intensified.

I closed my eyes, started to pray that Lex would be okay in dealing with the bizarre repercussions of her travel companion morphing into a wolf in the middle of a flight.

And then, the pain started to retract, to retreat.

The aura, the tingling, the crushing pain in my bones, it all went away. I looked back down at my one hand that had been morphing into a paw and saw it was reforming back to its normal size and shape. The tufts of fur had returned to regular dark human hair on the back of my hand.

I moved my jaw as I tried to speak.

"It's...not happening," I said. "I'm not changing."

"Thank God," she said.

"No," I said, realizing what was happening. "Thank you, Lex."

"What do you mean?"

I thought back to how that magic energy ball had dissolved in front of Lex. How she'd been able to fight with that tall Jason guy as if he didn't have any super strength at all. How, when she was conscious, my paranormal senses didn't work around her.

She didn't just possess a good luck charm aura that protected her from harm. She also could completely neutralize magic and the supernatural.

Lex herself was the charm to the curse that I had been living with for years.

When I was with her, I could be one hundred percent human and normal.

All the time.

Talk about an amazing new chapter in my life.

"It's you," I said. "Your charm, it isn't just reducing the side effects of my enhanced wolf powers. It's working to allow me to maintain my full humanity.

"It's you, Lex. You're giving me a new lease on life."

I paused and grinned at her as the horrible pun came to me.

"Or maybe I should say a new *Lex* on life."

She groaned.

"Why don't you just stick to writing mystery thrillers and leave the comedy to the professionals?"

"Lex my love," I said. "I'm going to do more than that.

I'm going to leave the comedy, and the heroics, to the professionals."

She squeezed my hand and I lost myself in her beautiful eyes as the Rush song I'd been thinking about on my flight to LA came back to me.

Fly by Night.

"Change my life again, indeed." I whispered.

Author's Notes & Acknowledgements

I initially started writing *Fear and Longing in Los Angeles* in November 2017 as part of NaNoWriMo. I should have known that was a bad omen, because the first book in this series, *A Canadian Werewolf in New York*, was initially undertaken as a 2006 NaNoWriMo Project. I didn't finish that book until 2015, and it wasn't published until 2016.

At least the time between starting to write and publication had been significantly cut down this second time. I cut the timeline down from 10 years to a little over 3 years. But stick around, dear reader, to see when I plan on releasing the next one, which, as of the writing of this note, I haven't yet begun.

Can you tell I thrive on the tension of a deadline?

I wrote about 51,000 words of *FALILA* in November 2017. Then I put it aside. I knew there would be at least another 30,000 words to write, but I ended up working on numerous other projects, while *FALILA* sat on the back burner.

I didn't start working on this novel again until the summer of 2020 when I released *Stowe Away*, a novella that takes place between *ACWWINY* and *FALILA*. That one was given the numeric value of 1.5 since it wasn't a full-length book and it takes place in the timeline between those two novels.

But a most interesting parallel between *Stowe Away* and *Fear and Longing in Los Angeles* happened. In the same way that the character of Bridge grew on me the more I wrote her, so, too, did the character of Lex in this novel. Lex was originally imagined as a nod to a friend I'd made in LA and was initially a plot device to play two roles. One, to distract Michael from his fixation on Gail, and two, to introduce him to the underbelly of the white supremacy group.

But Lex had her own plans. Both Michael and I fell in love with her and realized that we wanted to explore her character in more depth. So, her role grew significantly.

I was inspired to write *ACWWINY* or, at least the short story *This Time Around* that eventually morphed into *ACWWINY* after my first trip to New York. And, similarly, I drew upon two trips to Los Angeles for *FALILA*.

Julie and Joe Strauss, the couple I dedicated this book to, kindly met up with me on my summer 2017 LA visit and took me to a few local beer places they recommended; it was my first visit to Venice Beach (and Muscle Beach), and that's where we enjoyed the amazing salmon pizza and jalapeno pretzels that Michael and Lex have. I knew Julie from previous writer conferences I'd attended, but this had been my first time meeting her husband Joe. Joe and I bonded over our love of craft beer and the Canadian rock band *Rush*.

Some of the characters, including Lex, Kortney, and Max, were inspired by friends I made at Gulp on that same visit. My experience there, getting to chat with the bartenders and a group of regulars who welcomed me with open arms, really did give me a friendly "Cheers-like" vibe. In particular, the friendly and welcoming regular Andrea, who partially inspired the character of Lex and played the Norm Peterson to my own version of Cliff Clavin on a very fun afternoon and evening spent at Gulp. Andrea, also known to friends as Dre, allowed me to play on the multiple names from a single name motif. The originally planned cover for this book used a beautiful sunset photo she had taken and shared on social media. She graciously allowed me the use of it. It would have matched the original cover motif for *ACWWINY* too, but in the summer of 2020, I had Juan Padron, a cover designer I started working with, re-do the entire series for me.

The Loews Hollywood Hotel was where I'd stayed when I was in LA in 2014 to do a keynote talk about the future of publishing at the 30th annual *Writers and Illustrators of the Future* gala event. That week I had explored much of the neighborhood and enjoyed morning runs through adjacent neighborhoods and up into a few trails through the Hollywood Hills. I had intended on having Michael explore those hills when turning into a wolf; but he and Lex had other plans, returning to New York rather than sticking around LA. So, I never got to explore that area in the fiction. At least not yet anyway. The two might have to return to LA in a future adventure and I may get that chance.

That spring 2014 trip to LA was also at a time in my life where, like Michael, I had been feeling an overwhelming sense of longing with a strange grief and sadness that I couldn't explain. Apparently, my subconscious had been trying to tell me something that my conscious mind was oblivious to. Shortly after my return from that significant keynote talk, my wife of 17 years told me our marriage was over. She had been waiting to talk to me about it until after my trip, because she didn't want to ruin the "high" I was experiencing, getting to be flown into LA to speak in front of a massive audience at a prestigious gala event.

Even when our relationship was failing, she was always respectful. And I admire her for that and many other things. We have maintained a solid friendship throughout the split and the divorce. I had been, at the time, too thick to be able to see that our romantic relationship had ended long before that fateful discussion. (Even though, as I can now see in retrospect, I'd been feeling lonely for a long time prior to that. I just didn't realize where it had been coming from).

Be that as it may, though I appreciate the time we had together, as well as our son, if it weren't for the ending of our relationship early in 2014 I would never have been open to meeting and falling in love with my partner, Liz.

There's a special story related to Skull Crusher Brewery that ties back to me and Liz as well as to my friend Julie (of the Julie and Joe team I mentioned earlier). Because I am researching haunted bars and breweries for another book (*Spirits Untapped* is a book Liz and I have been planning on writing together), I'd discovered a brewery not far from where Julie and Joe live that is allegedly haunted. It's called Phantom Carriage Brewery. I asked Julie if she could check the place out for me and send me pictures. She's not into dark creepy horror stuff, but she went, very hesitantly, and was disturbed by the macabre theme of the place (which is somewhat similar to what's described in the novel). Julie is a writer of contemporary women's fiction and romance and ended up adapting a fictional version of Phantom Canyon Brewing into her 2018 novel *Prosecco Heart,* where she has her main character, Tabitha, meet up with good friends Mark and Liz at Skull Crusher Brewery. (That inclusion was, of course, a nod to us). Julie's version somewhat exaggerated the horror elements of Phantom Carriage (she took a significant amount of creative liberty), but I loved the scene so much, I wanted to ensure Michael Andrews got to visit that same location.

So, I incorporated part of that same scene in this novel. When Michael first gets to the brewery, hears a woman yell out about seeing a penis projected onto her friend's forehead and then there's a commotion as she'd pulled over to a table, that's Tabitha from Julie's novel, interacting with Liz and Mark. I couldn't resist a nod to that hilarious moment in *Prosecco Heart* and thought it would be fun to imagine Michael at the other end of the bar and overhearing part of that moment.

And if you're looking for a fantastic romantic comedy read, check out that novel by Julie. It opens up in a uniquely humorous and outrageous way (How is "Tabitha Lawson Hamilton never intended to greet her mailman in the nude" for a memorable opening line?) and is filled with plenty of laughs, and romantic twists and turns.

Speaking of romantic comedy, Alicia Witt, who has starred in numerous Hallmark Christmas romantic comedies is a brilliant indie musician I admire. And she's every bit the sweetheart I portrayed in the chapter where she appears. As a Kickstarter supporter of hers for her

15,000 Days EP release, I had her write a custom song for me which I wanted to use to propose to my partner Liz. Alicia not only wrote the song but generously conspired with me to perform it live on a 2019 visit to Toronto. She performed the song, which Liz and I danced to, and at the end of the song I proposed, right on the floor of the historic Horseshoe Tavern that *The Tragically Hip* sang about in their song "Bobcaygeon."

While I never got to see Alicia at The Hotel Café on my LA visits, I knew she had played there semi-regularly when she lived in the city. Having experienced a couple of in person performances by Alicia, as well as numerous virtual "pandemic-times" streaming concerts from her personal living room, I tried to write an authentic perspective of what attending one of Alicia's concerts would be like.

Alicia graciously allowed me to fictionalize her in this novel, and also gave me permission to use lyrics from two of her beautiful songs. If you haven't heard Alicia's music, you are truly missing out on a delightful treat. She is as talented as she is compassionate and kind.

Joshua Essoe, editor extraordinaire, was instrumental in helping me plan out and plot the nefarious nature of the PFA. His insight, council, and advice remain priceless, and he prevented me from heading down a few different paths I had almost accidentally taken. I also owe thanks to Jamie Ferguson and DeAnna Knippling for their editorial insights, and support. When working on this book, I returned to some of the great suggestions and tips they shared with me on writing *Stowe Away*.

Similarly, Scott Overton, friend, fellow writer, and the narrator who gives Michael Andrew voice in the audiobook versions of the "Canadian Werewolf" novels also helped me tweak a few moon-phase corners I had backed myself into.

And, as always, a huge thank you to Liz Anderson, my partner, and the person who regularly listens to me share tales of these imaginary friends of mine. Liz doesn't only patiently listen, but she also shares advice, both in the plotting and planning as well as in her role providing feedback as a first reader.

While researching for this novel, I found Eric Kurlander's 2017 Yale University Press book *Hitler's Monsters* intriguing. Many of the items researched for that book helped establish the occult background of the Proud Fighters of America, and many more helpful insights from that book will appear in the next novel in this series.

Speaking of the next book in this series, I was about three quarters through *FALILA* when I realized I wasn't done exploring the battle Michael and Lex have with Marco and the PFA. I had two choices—make this novel twice as long or split it off to explore in a longer story arc.

That action will carry forward in the novel *Fright Nights, Big City*.

In the meantime, since I really should be working on the next book rather than these notes, I'll leave you with a peek at it on the following pages.

Thanks for being a reader.

Mark Leslie
February 2021

Next Book: FRIGHT NIGHTS, BIG CITY

STOP SPREADING THE NEWS
THERE'S NO LEAVING TODAY

Not when the Big Apple comes under attack from an infectious worm threatening to rot it, and the entire nation, to the core.

Michael Andrews thought he'd found the perfect woman for him. A companion whose own powers neutralize his werewolf curse. But his plans on settling down and giving up the vigilante lifestyle are fleeting.

The hatred, the fear, and the monstrous attacks on innocent civilians are growing and spreading as supernatural monsters roam the city streets at night. The neo-Nazi *Proud Fighters for America*, aware of the special abilities that Lex possesses, track her down and plan on leveraging her powers for their own nefarious purposes.

With Michael's powers nullified in Lex's presence, the couple is forced to divide in their attempt to conquer, and Michael turns to his ex-girlfriend and her knowledge of the occult world in order to understand how to fight this rising evil.

But will two supernatural forces of good operating separately and one paranormal scholar be enough to vanquish a growing legion of evil?

Fright Nights, Big City takes place immediately following the
events in *Fear and Longing in Los Angeles.*

About the Author

Mark Leslie is a writer, editor and bookseller who was born and grew up in Sudbury, Ontario, spent many years in Ottawa and Hamilton, Ontario and currently lives in Waterloo, Ontario.

When he's not writing, Mark attaches "Lefebvre" back onto his name and works as a writing and publishing coach and consultant. As Director of Self-Publishing and Author Relations for Rakuten Kobo between 2011 and 2017, Mark established Kobo Writing Life which represents between 10 and 18% of Kobo's weekly unit sales, larger than any of the major publishers.

A bookselling veteran for more than twenty years, Mark has worked at virtually every type of bookstore, has sat on the Board of Directors for BookNet Canada and also been President of the Canadian Booksellers Association. He has given talks across Canada and the United States, in London, Paris and Frankfurt on the bookselling, writing and publishing industry.

Mark can be found online at **www.markleslie.ca**.

Selected Works

Non-fiction paranormal:

- *Haunted Hamilton: The Ghosts of Dundurn Castle and Other Steeltown Shivers* (2012)
- *Spooky Sudbury: True Tales of the Eerie & Supernatural* (2013) – Co-written with Jenny Jelen
- *Tomes of Terror: Haunted Bookstores and Libraries* (2014)
- *Creepy Capital: Ghost Stories of Ottawa and the National Capital Region* (2016)
- *Haunted Hospitals: Eerie Tales about Hospitals, Sanatoriums and Other Institutions* (2017) – Co-written with Rhonda Parrish
- *Macabre Montreal: Ghostly Tales, Ghastly Events, and Gruesome True Stories* (2018) – Co-written with Shayna Krishnasamy

Fiction:

- *One Hand Screaming* (2004)
- *Evasion* (2014)
- *I, Death* (2016)
- *A Canadian Werewolf in New York* (2016)
- *Nocturnal Screams* (Short Fiction Series) (2017/2018)
- *Stowe Away* (2020)
- *Fear and Longing in Los Angeles* (2021)

Editor:

- *North of Infinity II* (2006)
- *Campus Chills* (2009)
- *Tesseracts Sixteen: Parnassus Unbound* (2012)
- *Fiction River 23: Editors' Choice* (2017)
- *Fiction River 25: Feel the Fear* (2017)
- *Fiction River 31: Feel the Love* (2019)
- *Fiction River 32: Superstitious* (2019)
- *Obsessions* (2020)

* 9 7 8 1 9 8 9 3 5 1 2 3 9 *